Fate OF AMBER

KERRI ANN

Cover art by Bound to Be Book Covers
Edit by Rebel Edit & Designs
Formatting by Shannoff Formats

Kerri Ann. Fate of Amber

Table of CONTENTS

Dedicating a book is like writing a blurb for the back; bloody difficult! But I'll do my best. If I forget anyone, please know I love you tons.

To my family who let me wander off into the stories, thank you for giving me a moment or more to live in those lives. I avoid you, I close off and I spend too much time at Starbucks; but you get it.

To the lovely and talented Book Haven Promotions, Amanda, Erika, and Nicole. You ladies are amazing and I'm so glad I was introduced to all of you. I have those days where I'm wishing on that last rabbit's foot that you never leave me.

My DLHB's and the Dirtiest bunch. You are the best group of women (and Levi) I could ask for. Thank you for the dirty pictures, the silly memes and the interaction that shows me you care. When I need you, you're always there with the laughs, the constant contact with me to keep me writing and trying to put me back on track for the next project. And yes, Jan you are the woman with the pictures that just keep on giving.

What to say about the special women -- Christina, Belinda, and Nicole. You have my back, you keep me thinking of 'what next' and remind me not to take life too serious. I look forward to finding you online to chat with everyday even though you're miles away. Vegas will be epic, and the police will have their hands full.

As always Geri Glenn you are the shit, woman. Dana Hook, the mastermind behind the story, you keep me looking like a princess with your edits. Shannon for the formats that are spectacular, thank you for handling the rush when I need you most. Most of all Leanne at B2B, your fucking epic covers make everything amazing!

I'm so happy that you read me, I'm amazed everyday that you like my stories and that I'm someone you want to interact with. Thank you to those that are unnamed, or those that are just meeting me for the first time. I hope to keep you happy for years to come.

Chapter ONE

This Filly needs a Stallion

Thiea

Once upon a time there was a small princess. She was cared for and tended to like a spoiled, blessed, and loved little angel. With shoes, dresses, and every type of toy imaginable. She had it all. She was happy. Everyone gave into her whims, coddling and cooing at her adorable, sickly sweet charm.

Argh! Who am I bullshitting?

After being dumped on the steps of an orphanage in the Bronx as a swaddled baby, I endured years and years of revolving foster sisters and brothers. All until I ended up gaining a fantastic family for ten solid, awesome years.

Then they died. The end.

Wow, what a Disney movie waiting to be told. Fuck that. What a lovely bedtime story for my children, I suppose.

Children?

That requires an instrument only a man can provide, and without one of those, such a thing won't take shape. My life is what it is and I might as well accept it; an unending travesty of unlucky happenstance where no man is in my bed. At least not a worthy one. I have high standards, and with my lacking, I find it hard to locate one. I know, bitch much?

Staring at the mirror, like I'm expecting the vision to change me into the beauty from the Ugly Duckling story, I wish and I wait. The plainness of my features is horribly apparent to me. The see-through sea green eyes with flecks of red seem dangerous to most; frightening to the rest. My freckles lack pattern, streaming across the bridge of my slight, almost hawk-like nose. The imperfect circles are haphazard and in no way pretty. Still. If that isn't enough of a deterrent for my Prince Charming, there's the mental, dark red hair. I can never get a handle on the fire red frizz that curls in all the wrong spots, sticking out like the snakes of Medusa.

But really, why stop there?

Then there's my gangly, pin-thin boyish body without proper womanly hips, the tiniest A-cup bee sting tits, and long fingers that just accent the total package.

Which often makes me wonder, what were my real parents like?

Do I look like my mother or my father? Who gave me this awesome red hair and transparent, non-tanning skin? Were they natural reds, or did I just happen to get the odd gene? The questions always swim in my mind like sharks waiting for the chum.

They had to have cared for me somewhat though, right? After all, I wasn't left in a dumpster for just anyone to find. No. I was left at an orphanage on Fifth, wrapped in a chenille blanket wearing a monogrammed peach onesie. And thank fucking God the name they gave me was cute, and not something like Henrietta or Mildred.

Nothing that would scar me for life like Gertrude either, so I'm blessed they gave me something pretty. *Athena* was written in tiny script across my outfit with an amber necklace laying lightly across my chest.

The necklace consists of pea-sized amber beads perfectly spaced on a thin foxtail twenty-four karat white gold chain. It came with me and I've never had the heart to take it off. Creepiest part is that it always seems to fit. Whether I was a tiny baby or a cranky teenager, it was perfect. I've inspected it over and over, looking for flaws and an opening, but nada. No clasp to open, but it's the perfect shape so it doesn't strangle, tangle, or ever needs to be removed.

I stopped thinking about it being weird somewhere around the age of ten, but it still sits in the middle of that chummy water of *why* I was left in the first place.

Understanding that things can't be changed, I crank the tunes on my Mac to make the figurines on my desk dance like bobbleheads. I shake off the nobody-loves-me-abandoned-Cinderella mood and return to my reason for dancing; it's my goddamn birthday. I ready for the end of another uneventful day at my tiny, yet fabulous shoe boutique on Bloor Street, tucked into a building just down from the Bata Museum. Where else would you put a fashionable shoe store but beside the museum dedicated to feet, right?

It's only a few hundred feet of space, but it's enough to keep myself and three employees hopping daily. My parents, God bless them, left me this shop and I love it. Work—if that's what it can be called, as I love what I do—admittedly sometimes goes your way and sometimes it just falls to shit. Today the shelves in my tiny store had to be restacked after a section fell. An older gentleman had left a 'present' for us in the bathroom, and the kicker to the 'Oh shit' day was a lockdown for an apparent stabbing just outside our doors.

Ambulances, police, reporters, and rows upon rows of rubberneckers paused near the scene of the crime, making it difficult for me to get out for my usual coffee in the afternoon.

Closing time was a godsend as tonight is ONLY about me.

My birthday. My party. ME!

I'm turning twenty-nine, and as it's the last vestiges of recklessness before the serious age attack of thirty, I'm going to enjoy it fully.

Once you're there, there's no turning back. You are a full-fledged member of society. A locked down loser. No more fun and games, and you have to act the role of *Daisy Jane* adult.

Fuck that.

I'm going out on a high note before I leave the roaring twenties. Fables and urban legends will be created by my exploits.

As I start to consider closing and running out the door for higher ground, I'm approached by Jason. He's like watching skin peel off a snake. In so many ways it's just wrong, creepy, and yet Animal Planet addictive. He is *so* not my type. With his five-foot-five frame—which puts him a few inches shorter than me, even with his curly, ginger, pubic fro hair—I think he feels it makes us connected in some odd way. His scrawny, pipe cleaner arms lack any dimension of strength. Ever heard of a bench-pressing loser? And the button-down, perfectly pressed dress shirt—of which is buttoned to the top—totally shows the grandness of his geek status. His slouched jeans just accentuate the fact that he has no ass. And not to be outdone by such attributes, his green, fluorescent braces express the standard high school math club, pushed into a locker geek that I avoid at all costs.

"Are you sure I can't take you out for sushi and sake? I think your birthday should be special. I could make your birthday *really* special," Jason says as he restacks the same boxes for the third time, still out of order.

"Thanks, Jason. Really, I appreciate it, but I'm going out with Cassie and I'd hate to ditch her. She's been planning this for weeks. But good on you for trying," I say for the fourth time today as I walk away.

It's been ages since I've had a man above or below me, but even if he was the last—wait…no. Even if he *was* the last known male specimen alive, I would hold out for toys and watch the human race dwindle and die out. After all, I have standards, and Glee geek is not in my *A* list.

Anyhoo.

So Cassie and I are going out tonight. I'm getting tanked and getting laid if possible; the dirtiest kind I can find. I want it in the back of a pickup truck bed, on the side of the freeway with shitloads of onlookers, kind of kinky sex. My bare ass in the air as I smile and wave like a queen.

Cassie decided she was taking me out to the bar tonight after work, and her hubby the cop is picking up our drunk, overtly flirty asses. The other girl at work, Giselle, is pissed she wasn't invited, but when you look like something out of a cosmetic surgery convention, who would? I'm not looking for competition tonight. She's as fake as her double D's with full, pouty lips, thick manicured eyebrows, hair perfectly quaffed, heels from Dolce and Gabbana and outfits from Holt's that I couldn't even dream of ever owning. I may own a shoe store, but even those pretty accoutrements are out of my range. I guess that's why I love being around Cassie. She and her husband are the real deal—gentle, genuine, and oh so sweet.

She met Garron in Ireland where she and her friend, Sharon,

took a trip of a lifetime. Well, it was more a comedy of errors. They broke down on the road to their dream castle, were caught in a rainstorm trying to take a picture of each other practically humping the slimy Blarney Stone, and last, but not least, they stopped at a great looking authentic pub to find they were at a yearly wake for some ass who got caught in a bog and died over a hundred years ago. Really spectacular.

Now, fourteen years together and two children later, they are the happiest couple I've ever met. Not to mention extremely good looking too. Garron could pass as Beckham's older brother, and Cassie looks like Angelina without the lips.

"Hey, Thiea. I'm gonna grab a pizza for the boys and meet you at the house, okay?" Cassie says as she neatly stacks flimsy receipts, one on top of the other.

"Sounds good. I love cold pizza at three in the morning." I finish stacking the racks of shoes back into their pole positions for what seems like the hundredth time today. I want everything ready for Giselle and Jason to care for the store alone tomorrow without issues because my hangover will be epic. I doubt either of us will be in any shape to handle attitude and rude clients.

"You ready to pummel a bottle of Jägermeister?" she asks.

"You ready to keep up, pussy?" I ball up the soft papery contents of an empty box and toss it at her. With a quick look she avoids the projectile, swatting it away with minimal effort as she laughs.

I know this will be an interesting birthday night out. I can feel it in the air. It's electric, and about as exciting as a cat in a hot tub. Someone will have stories for the ages after this.

Chapter TWO

Drunk, Drink, and Headache Material

Thiea

Whoa, what a headache! Cassie just jumped to the top of my 'For a good time call…' list.

This is the last time I drink that much.

Shit. Who am I kidding? There's no sense in lying to myself; I know I'll get drunk again. After all, I just promised myself to go out of my twenties with a gang...I mean bang.

Well, either will do.

Now it's time to answer the important questions, like a game show. If I can't answer, I can't play. As my head feels like a split melon, the first question is what did I drink?

Tequila

Where did we drink it?

Bitsy's Bar and Grill

Why am I wearing a T-shirt that says *I shaved my balls for this?*

I know it's *not* what I left in. Shit, what happened to my clothes?

Now that's a question for the masses. I can't answer that one at all. I'm naked, except for the shirt and what God gave me.

Biggest question Mr. Trebec, is am I at Cassie's house? I reach beside me to see if there's a well-chiseled body.

Nope.

Damn. I'm at Cassie's, all right. Sullivan, Cassie's ten-year-old, is at the end of my bed. Shit, I hope he didn't pee the bed again.

Trying to replay the previous evening's escapades, I find it a bit of a blur. The bartender was nice. There was a burly, thirtysomething-year-old man with arms as large as tree trunks and a chest as wide as a doorway. He'd left us in a side room to wait for Garron after we'd gotten kicked out of the bar over a girl named Sassy. I was kissing her boyfriend. Actually, I think it was while his hands were loosening the fastener on my bra and his tongue was exploring my mouth for cavities that she started on the offensive. Sassy tried unsuccessfully to hit me with a soft right hook. I ducked and landed a great shot to her gut that made her curl up like a baby on the floor. Kicking her a few times for good measure while she was writhing in pain on the floor felt awesome, and as I turned my attention back to the arm candy I'd just won, I felt a wave of victory.

Her guy wasn't the kind you would write home to mom about, but he was certainly the type you'd have sex with and forget it happened kinda guy. A true army boy. With his tight-fitting, black T-shirt showcasing his Special Forces tats that cut across his bulging triceps, I was enamored. Actually, that's what caught my drunkin' ass's attention in the first place. My only objective was to scrape my fingernails down his back and make him scream *Mama*.

As he picked her up off the floor, I swore I saw the sexiest smile creep across his features. For sure, he'd be the face in my mind while

I played with toys. At least until I found a replacement man beneath me.

The last time I saw him was when the bouncer grabbed my shirt and hauled me backwards, toward the front door. My shirt was ripped clean off while I fought to claim my prize. With buttons flying, wearing only a sheer green lace demi cup, I was happily hanging out for all the bar to see.

Like I hadn't already planned that part of the night's festivities? I hope they all got a good look and enjoyed themselves. Judging by the clientele, it was probably the best view they'd had in years.

Nevertheless, it wasn't the way I wanted it to turn out. After that, everything seemed surreal. Luckily, Garron picked us up, brought us back, and we all said our good nights. I tried to sleep, but that lasted all of an hour as the room spun like a merry-go-round at Coney Island. After about three good trips on the Ferris wheel, my unsober ass figured that a glass of water and two aspirins would do the trick, so I headed off to the kitchen.

Sneaking quietly…well, as quietly as I can in slippers and a drunkin' haze, I raid the cupboards and pull out a glass. Stealthily moving around, I slink to the sink and wait for the water to cool before placing the goblet in the flow.

"Couldn't sleep?" Garron asks.

Jumping out of my skin, I almost drop the glass. "Shit! I think I almost peed myself."

Sitting in the nook looking out over the still pond in the backyard, he turns around to face me.

"Pasties and spinning rooms are the worst part of drinking too much," I say, shutting off the water. "Why are you awake?"

With my borrowed bunny slippers and weird, yet appealing tee, I walk over and grab a seat in the plush armchair next to him. Even drunk, I'm curious as to why I'm not the only one sleeping.

"I don't sleep." I've always found Garron's accent charming. I'm a sucker for accents. Like Gerard Butler, any Hemsworth, Sean Connery from any era, or Charlie Hunnam, I melt a little every time. It's something about an accent on a sexy man that swallows me up.

Totally off topic, Thiea.

Garron steals a glance my way, and even though it's only a split-second motion, it's something I will never forget. The way his eyes *glowed* was odd. Not like a snap open glow stick, but more like a cat's eyes in the light at night. The whole iris was shimmering, and it was unsettling.

"How drunk am I still?"

"Don't worry, you're not seeing things. My eyes do things like that sometimes." He says it matter of fact as he keeps his eyes trained on my face. "When the moon is full they react that way to the light. I hope it doesn't scare you?"

Shifting uncomfortably in the chair, I pull my body into the cushions and tug on my necklace, rolling it around in my fingers. I fidget with it incessantly when I'm nervous. I've just seen my friend's gorgeous, drop-dead husband's eyes glow, and I'm freaking the fuck out.

"Why do they glow?"

Watching me, taking my measure, he stills. "I'm sorry if it alarms you. It's natural and I forget sometimes what it can be like." I find myself staring, trying to decipher it like a puzzle. His irises are the color of the sun, a blazing amber with bright flecks of crimson, like brimstone and the stars at night. The flecks are not unlike mine; brilliant and scary.

“You still didn't answer my question. Does it frighten you?” he asks again.

"No." I shake my head, lying. I’m trying horribly to convince us both.

"I’m not human, Thiea." He flashes me his teeth for fuck’s sake, showing me the biggest incisors I have ever seen.

I don’t know how, but I keep my cool. “My, what big teeth you have, Granny.”

Garron laughs and as his eyes twinkle in and out of contrast from black to amber. I try to shake off the fear.

Fuck me. This is weird.

“Sorry. I forget sometimes how they may seem to those who don’t know about our kind.”

“*Our* kind?” I question.

“Yes, Thiea *our* kind. Mine and yours.”

“Ah. No. I’m not a Twihard, and I don’t procure blood in the back streets of hell. Why would you say “our kind?’” I shift back in the chair to skooch further away, becoming one with my cushions.

He smiles and lets out a deep, sexy male giggle. "Thiea, you’re one of us. I noticed it the first time I met you at your shop. And don’t worry, I won’t bite. Well, not anymore. At least since I found my mate in Cassie I don’t.” He gives me an almost quizzical look, like he’s confused as to why I don’t understand. “You’re like us. I know you are. I feel it. I can scent it on you.”

I smell? “Awesome. Just what I needed to know.” Now I *know* why I haven’t found a guy. “Can you tell me how I smell? Is it rose water and heather, or garbage and street bum?”

He laughs loudly, like my idea of smelling good is preposterous. “No, nothing like that. We give off a perfume to others. Just like a married person's ring on their finger tells you they're taken, you give off a specific scent. It's faint, but it's there. You *are* a Dark Worlder."

I must have the most incredulous look on my face as I take all of this in. "How is it you don't know this?"

"I guess I wasn't given the smelly handbook when I was dropped at the orphanage." I pull my feet in closer and turn to smell the skin on my forearm; cigars, rank alcohol, and stale puke. Awesome.

"So…blood drinking, huh? Like Bram Stoker's story?"

"Kind of," he says crassly.

"Am I too drunk to remember any of this, or did you roofie me so I won't remember you stripping me naked while you have your way? 'Cause that, I would like to remember." I pinch myself on the arm to confirm I am indeed awake as I give him the goofiest grin. Garron stares at me like I'm some kind of freak.

Look in the mirror, buddy. You have glowing eyes, big bad wolf teeth, and I somehow smell odd enough for it to be noted. Perfect for my twenty-ninth birthday. If this is the peak of my descent into adulthood, I want to get off this ride.

Calming my overactive mind, I think about his comments, but sitting still seems almost unbearable.

"Look, I was given up by my parents when I was a couple weeks old, and I don't know crap about them. All they did was name me and leave me. No notes, no 'Hey, you're a multi-faceted weirdo and we left you here. Good luck.' There was nada, nothing, and sweet diddly fuck-all. No instruction manual and no teamster card to say I was part of some odd clan. Let's just forget this oddity and say that you've had way too much radiation in the last few weeks. You're having an adverse reaction. That's plausible, right?" I blunder along, nervous as hell about this convo.

Garron's chest rumbles again as he laughs once more.

Not fucking funny, big guy, not one bit.

Rising from his seat, he goes to the kitchen and fills the kettle. "How about I get you a tea? I'll try to explain as much as I can while you're sobering up."

Sighing, I let out a breath I didn't realize I'd been holding and sit back in the chair, trying to get comfortable. "Sure. And while you're at it a cookie would be perfect if you've got one. I think I need some sugar."

This evening's adventure began with tequila, a chick fight for a sexy man that was ripped from my greedy little paws, and the start to a blessedly harsh hangover. Now, here I am. I got up, wanting a drink of water, and ended up with more reasons to drink heavily. Moving around to the far side of the kitchen, Garron grabs two chocolate chip cookies then walks back, handing one to me. As if I'm the one that could bite? With my mind swimming, my stomach churning, and a lack of air in my lungs, there's this deep growing fear it's only going to get worse.

"Thiea, you need to understand the basic fundamentals. There are two parts to this world. There are humans, then there's those like me and you. Dark Worlders are werewolves, all forms of witches, warlocks, demons and shifters; as well as vampires, like me. Some humans are dormant with no outward signs, and there are no tell-tale abilities so they seem totally human. They can live their whole lives that way until they die, not knowing any different."

"Those things aren't real. There are no shiny vampires, no desirable werewolves, and no, 'I will get you, my pretty' waiting to hop up in the middle of the night to scare unsuspecting girls like me who've drank too much, Garron. I'm not a kid. I don't believe in fairy tales." I remove my borrowed slippers and tuck them into a green plush throw blanket that's resting on the back of my chair. Slowly nibbling on the chocolate heaven, I feel like I'm in school again, learning shit that shouldn't matter. History is history. It's where there's dead people, dead stories, and dead deeds.

"Okay. Let's give you something more substantial to believe, how's that for a start?" Pulling the kettle from the stove before it whistles, he pours the steaming hot liquid into our mugs. "I was born August 12, 1230. I was one of three brothers born into my family. I lived a very normal childhood with nothing out of the ordinary. I climbed trees, hunted for dinner, and learned how to cut peat until I hit puberty. That's when the change came. I had headaches if I was out in the daylight too long. I couldn't sleep at night and I was restless, like my soul was being pulled in multiple directions. My mother took me to the nearby lake and explained it all. I didn't believe it either, but eventually I had to accept it. Drinking from others calmed my mind and my soul, and it eased the pain if I went too long between feedings."

Holding his tea to his lips, he takes a long swallow before continuing.

"The day I met Cassie, or the day I fell in love is when I actually started to live as a human. Merrick, my oldest son, will start the change soon, and I'll have to explain it to him. For now, I'm content to just let him be oblivious to the world he doesn't know exists and let him worry about football, girls, and the math class he's failing."

I'm sure I look like I've been zombified as I listen to him. We sit there for at least an hour as he goes into more encyclopedia info than I ever thought I would digest about the supernatural and sci-fi world that he truly believes is normal. I don't do Star Trek or Star Wars, or even the Twilight shit. I'm your basic love stories on a cold day with a warm tea, curled up in a chair with no one but a dream to keep me company.

As the conversation wanders further into the night, we have two more teas, a few cookies, and the excesses of my tequila binge are finally gone. I take a long drag of the tea almost to the dredges and redress Garron about his earlier comments.

"I still think this is all bullshit, but good on you for trying. I'm fine in the sun, I don't have glowing eyes, and no one smells like steak tartar. Plus, I'm pretty sure I've reached and surpassed the whole puberty section of your story. I can't conjure money out of thin air, I don't have a way to bend people to my will, and I don't smell like a wet dog. So what's your next farfetched explanation, smarty pants?"

"Thiea, you are. I know it without a doubt. I don't think you're a vampire, I'm pretty sure you're not a werewolf. Abilities wise, it could be something as simple as being able to feel the history of an object, or you could even be something more complex, but it's hard to tell. I've been alive long enough to be able to sense it, and I've never been wrong."

I think about it, letting it sink in. Abilities? Nope. I can't leap tall buildings, I don't have X-ray vision—though there are times I wish I did—and I don't have super human strength as no strong woman awards sit on my mantle.

"Sorry, Garron, you've got the wrong girl. And it doesn't matter anyway. I'm no one special. I'm just, Thiea." I stand, toss the blanket on the arm of the chair and place my cup on the coaster. "Thanks for this enlightening, yet uncomfortable conversation. I'm going back to bed. The tea was great. Cookies were awesome. But really, I gotta go."

I start off to bed slowly, backing away, creeping back to my room. Locking the door quietly, I crawl back into bed and push Sullivan over to the far side so I can steal a sliver of the covers. Trying to calm myself enough to rest, slowly but surely, I drift back to sleep.

My dreams are fitful though. They're of Cinderella and Rapunzel eating cookies under a bright moonlit night, which in itself feels strangely calming. With glowing crystal blue eyes and thin daggers for nails, I watch the vision transform. Rapunzel dissipates in a wisp as Cinderella's form morphs until I see my face instead of hers. The profile of my face is different than I've ever seen, but I still recognize the basic shape of it. It shifts; hardening along the edges until my cheekbones become tight and sharp. The normally dull red tresses are alight where flames lick the tips of my hair in a blaze of garnet and blood. My eyes sparkle and twinkle like burning amber orbs with crimson flecks, making me look dangerous and otherworldly. I look beautiful—in a dark and sinister way.

In the dream, I'm speaking to Garron as he cowers on the ground, tears streaming down his dirt encrusted face. He's pleading and begging for his life, as if I'm the instrument of his death. I stand stoic and sullen, almost detached as I speak to him.

As the dream shifts to show the brightness of day, I find I'm standing in a field of wheat as it flows in a soft warm breeze. As I brush the tips of the chaff with one hand, shielding my eyes from the bright midday sun with the other, a man walks up the neat rows toward me. He's tall, thick, and walks with an air of superiority. His face is shielded from me by the sun, highlighting his form, walking with intent.

"Where were you?" he asks in raspy sort of way as he stalks closer and closer to me, moving until he's mere inches away. I still can't see his face, but he smells like warm vanilla and cinnamon.

Thinking about his question, I wonder who he is and why he wants to know where I was? Who is he? Where are we? Why am I in a field of wheat? Why does he seem know to me?

Reaching out to stroke the skin on my face, I jolt awake, leaving the lovely dream. Sullivan's tiny feet are prodding my cheek as his body lays sidelong on the bed, taking up the whole space.

That felt so real. Lovely. I grieve for it to return, even though I know the dream will never be the same.

That sucks.

Chapter THREE

Fates Return

Shoan

The memories are raw and almost palpable. Like a serial killer's flashbacks of past crusades, conquests, and confrontations. They drag me under the water, forever engulfing me in despair and regret as they remind me of the horrors I've endured, created, and avoided recreating over and over. I've tried for years to forget them but they're phantoms, poking and prodding me as I close my eyes, never to have a moment's peace. I would have considered myself an insomniac long ago if I didn't require sleep; I haven't slept in centuries. I don't really need it, but I enjoy the rest on my mind. With thousands of thoughts running rampant at any given moment like a Ritalin dosed child, I'm constantly in the *on* position. The side effects, or cause and effect of what I am, or what I've done to others are those final moments, and they leave a lasting impression on my psyche.

My life would be a great Hollywood movie. The wicked plot of a villainous and heinous character, except I've always found myself to be the victim in this historic comedy, not the instrument of death that I portray. Some twisted, fucked in the head God played out their fantasy of creation and I'm the product of that insanity. The cut and paste, scraped together leftovers of humanity, immortals and Gods alike. That's all I am; junk spliced up to make a being. I never asked to be this. I never asked to enforce what they expect of me, but I had no way to avoid it either.

A great person once said, '*But effort and courage are nothing without purpose and direction.*' Ain't that the truth. I've had the effort, the courage, the purpose, and direction, but it was removed from me by one incredulous moment in my past. Since then I've no direction to go other than revenge, retribution, and retaliation.

Reaching across the bed to the vapid, yet absolutely insatiable body of Calliope, I think of the things in the past that torture my future. It's just another night and another woman I don't care to know.

As I stroke the soft skin of her neck, tracing down her spine to the small of her back, I remove the blankets, causing her to groan into the pillow, exposing the subtle curves of her body. She reaches for my hand and halfheartedly pushes it away, tugging on the blankets to once again cover herself. Tracing across the soft curve of her spine— slowly, meticulously, down to the hard plane of her hips— elicits a hitch in Calliopes' breathing.

"Not now, Shoan. I need sleep before I go to work in a few hours," she says with heavy lidded eyes. Turning her perfect tits towards me, she tucks herself into my chest as my aching erection pulses against her naked form.

"What would you like? You know it's impossible for me to resist a request."

I've tried over the centuries to lose my Irish brogue by curbing the elongations and shortening certain words or phrases, but it's like a virgin's panties; hard to remove.

"Sleep? I don't think that's what's on your mind," I tell her as she reaches back to brush my swollen head. I might have left her alone, but not anymore after that game changer. "Calliope, darling, sleep has been taken off the menu."

Slipping past her silk teddy to her slick centre, I prepare her, like all the others before, to accept my engorged size. The feel of their warm bodies against mine and the slick travel of my cock sliding back and forth is exquisite. I try to be gentle. Many times, I've harmed more than pleasured.

Calliope screams out my name, asking for more thrust, more contact, more stroking and teasing. Hell, more *everything*. I'm a master of sexual prowess and release. Like the perfect symphony played expertly from start to finish, I'm the conductor. I know where, when, and how to adjust for the perfect pitch, tenor, and feel. The curse made this happen and by the Gods, I have hated and relished it all at once. Regardless of her needs or wants, mine are insatiable.

Harder and harder I stroke myself inside her. Feeling the tightening and the rise as one would when reaching the point of release, she let's go. It's always the same for me, and it's a bloody wretched, sick fuck's idea of torture because I never climax or release. I've had to fake it over the centuries. That fucking curse made me need this and despise it all the same. Always for me, it's a *When Harry Met Sally* moment of fake sounds, movements, and acts.

"Oh, Shoan! Yes, Shoan there, faster," Calliope screams out as she digs her nails into the headboard, before falling boneless to the bed spent and satisfied for the fifth time tonight.

"Ok," she laughs awkwardly, "I'm totally awake now."

My cock pulses in response, needing more still. It's never done. I've never finished off, so as always, it's ready for another round.

"Wanna join me for a shower?" she asks.

"No, dear. You go, I'll see you before you leave," I tell her as she steps from the bed. Stripping off her petite, twisted and torn blush pink negligee, she tosses it in the trash with a wink.

With my erection still pointing skyward, as if asking *next* like a lineup in a dime-store checkout, I sit and stare at the ceiling of my expansive room. I'm reminded of a time when my erection was the least of my troubles. For the first hundred years or so, I'd been angry and cruel, taking it out on anyone stupid enough to cross paths with me, be it man or woman. I was not gentle or careful as I wrestled to find my release. One fated night created the sick and twisted need to find my own orgasmic release, and I have tell all of them the same thing -- this is how it is; I can't finish. Some see it as a waste, others see it as a challenge. Other's hope they can fix me.

They're not the instrument of my repair, unfortunately. I wish it were that simple. I need sex to stop the ancient voices in my head for moments of peace. For a single second of blissful quiet, I'd give everything I have.

I hardly look in the mirror at myself anymore, as I find myself feeling somewhat like a tourist in my own body. I miss so many things about myself before this wretched and warped curse was set upon me. Lacking my own strength and power is probably my biggest loss. Sure, I still live an immortal life, but I'm not whole.

Time ticked by until I found I could do nothing more than accept it. Curling up in the corner and sucking my thumb wouldn't be very productive or sexy, so I curbed the idea quite some time ago. *No* fucking whining, *no* wallowing, *no* harboring regrets. My fate drew me to this point. What fate plans is not of our design, so I deal with what I've been dealt.

The curse was simple, yet overtly powerful. *You will wander the world until you find and save your true heart's love. Until that time, you will not be hale.*

I've never believed in the fairy tale dream of fate like my sister, where love is fated and found in a single meeting. With all her hoping that I'd find 'the one,' like in a Nicolas Sparks movie, I've disappointed her on the matter for quite a while. Sorry, Niamh. I roll through women like a rolodex, fucking anything that will give me a reprieve from the voices in my head. True love is something that only occurs in movies; it's a crock of shit. I'd love to believe in it, but I don't think the Fates have done one smidgen about me, as they left me to my own devices long ago.

Walking around my suite, dressing and gathering a bite to eat, I watch Calliope leave quickly for work before settling into another boring and simple day in Toronto. I've lived here for a while now and find it to be the perfect place for me. It's close enough to everything, and far enough away from dark memories that I can feel detached and alone. The sun shines outside, bright and warm, inviting me to take on another summer day.

There's nothing more settling to an unsettled mind than the sound of your feet hitting pavement in time to your heartbeat, so I decide to hit the road. With the wind in your face, bringing forth the smell of hops stewing in the brewery, and fresh baked sweetbreads coalescing in your nostrils with newly blossomed flowers from the promenade, all of it melds into an overwhelming cacophony.

I love this. The ground, the road, and the world in your face. When I run, my mind runs away with me.

I pass by young twentysomething mothers jogging with strollers, dogs in tow, and squealing children swaddled in blankets. Blue and white collar workers rush to and fro from meaningless jobs. Jobs that give them enough money to drink themselves into a stupor so they can forget why they drink in the first place.

The occasional street urchin begs for scraps and coin, sticking out their hand, wanting their next fix or meal. Things haven't changed much in over a thousand years as people are people, and their stations are always the same. Time stretches out so far that a decade—heck, a century—seems only a moment in time, like a flicker or a flash of light in the dark. I had a friend once that dreamed of such a thing; family, happiness, and growing old with those he loved. All that had been ripped from him and I didn't help. I made the matter worse, helping to fester that boiling sore. It left me to feel more alone and detached.

In this age of computers, phones, and all of its connectivity, it's caused further disconnection for me. I can search information, but most things I've experienced firsthand. Speaking of computers and technically inclined components, my personal leash rings as I round the corner on King to enter my building.

"Hey. What's up? I was just thinking about family," I answer. Depressing the penthouse button I turn the key, and the carriage starts its ascent.

"Son, have you looked at your email today?" Arif's dark voice flows through the tiny speaker, sounding tense.

The elevator rushes to my floor and as the doors open into the substantially expansive kitchen, I walk in. The Italian marble counter, the Brazilian cherry cabinets, and garish stainless steel appliances were all my sister's idea of beauty. The lack of adornment was mine. There's one couch made of rusted steel tubing with distressed leather seating, a pair of industrial airplane propeller ceiling fans, splashes of black and orange paint that creates haphazard decor on the walls, and black concrete cured floors. A guy's space. Nothing excessive or unnecessary, no trinkets or memorabilia. I don't care for the past. Who cares to display reminders of things you hope to forget?

Setting the phone on the counter and placing it on speaker, I check my email. There's the usual—junk mail, a few dirty jokes, and two emails from my sister, Niamh. The first is from her visit to Monte Carlo with Chad and the rest of the Berserkers, but nothing new. It's just the usual gaff and exploits. The second email from her is titled, **Worry Now!!!!!!**

Arif's voice cuts in as I fidget with the buttons. "Shoan, this is bad. If this happens, we'll all feel the fallout. I'm not sure about you, but I like things the way they are now. I have Anna. We have a comfortable life here, and I *don't* rock the boat. Allah, I've lived since Hatshepsut!"

When Arif starts to panic, it's never good.

I read through the email.

Shoan, this is mucho importante. I know how you are about the past and I'm sorry, brother. We're meeting at the villa. We've had word that she's after the book again. You know the consequences if we don't get involved.

As always, I miss you.

Well, that's cryptic. Thanks, Niamh. I guess the question is, what the fuck is Morrigan up to now?

"Arif, I'll meet you as soon as I can."

"May Allah keep you safe. I'll see you soon, son." With that, Arif hangs up.

Showering, dressing, and running out the door in record time, I find myself running through history that comes to mind unbidden.

Chapter FOUR

Nummy, Nummy

Thiea

So, here I sit on the patio of this little dive near lakeshore that serves cold beer and a quick lunch. I watch as a gull careens into the murky water, grabbing up a fry that the lady one bench over tossed in. It draws the attention of the hordes milling around on the roof of the pub. The woman isn't memorable. Although, if a bird poops on me, I'll not only remember her, but she'll remember my foot up her ass as I shove her into the water.

I left work earlier today to think through all the crap I heard from Garron, aka Vampire hottie, as I now refer to him as. His cockamamie story about how he's a vamp, and about how I'm somehow related in species.

Cassie, thank fuck, hadn't mentioned anything about it all week, so I didn't have to rehash the convo to her. So being the boss that I am, I left early on a Friday. Heading down here to this hole-in-the-wall, I didn't really have any other reason beyond needing a break from reality.

The last thing I want is to be found by anyone. This place is far enough away that no one I know ventures to, especially to such a shithole. Ordering the perfect, sweet, crisp bottle of golden joy, I'm hoping to either clear or cloud my mind of all of it.

That night, I expected to go out and get drunk—ok, so that was mission accomplished—but I missed out on the best part. I didn't do the waking up to a hottie that I didn't know and wouldn't care to know. I just wanted romping good sex for the end of my twenties. All I wanted was a sweaty, bare chested, big dick, nails scratching into his ass gorgeous male, above me and below me. Inside me is what really counted, because if this dry spell keeps up, I'm gonna switch teams and head for the girls' locker room. I've been told they know how to have a good time without a man. I still don't see that as a possibility, but who am I to discount the proven arousals?

With my handy-dandy laptop, I try and research some of the things Garron told me about. First on the list is my upbringing. But after a few hours of typing away, I find diddly.

What a downer. All I came across were fairy tales, hocus-pocus, damsels in distress, blah blah blah....

I did find one thing that was of interest. There was a link to a *The History of Magik* with a sublink to *The Fair Ones*. From what I gathered, they're endowed with powers from their matriarch or Goddess. Depending on who they are, they can have different things they can control or will, such as: Women touched by the Greek Goddess Narcissa are shallow, vain, and extremely beautiful. The downside of their almost obnoxious Hollywood model bodies is that they draw beauty from those around them. Cause and effect. They become more enchanting, and those around them become haggard and aged. Massive downside—they don't live long.

Huh. So that's what happened to Marilyn? Definitely not me by any means. Freckles and red hair are not starlet material, unless you have a beautiful Aussie accent.

Try as I might, I couldn't find anything I could connect with. It was becoming trial and total fucking error. Maybe this was just Garron's way of trying to mess with my head? So instead, I look up vampires.

Well, fuck, if there aren't a million and one sites to choose from on the subject. Everything from books to movies, porn to ritualistic tendencies, cravings, and signs on how to tell if a friend is. Even something about a war, impending doom, and dark vs. light.

These dorks and geeks take Dungeons and Dragons way too seriously.

With the stack loads of info available, I'd have to be immortal just to read a quarter of it. The signs on how to tell did pique my interest though, so I took the 'Cosmo test' as it were.

Does your friend have red eyes? Hell, no. Red flecks, but not red eyes.

Does your friend sleep in the day and only venture out at night? Can't say. But if the other night was any indicator, then maybe.

Does your friend ask to lick your cuts? Creepy to the power of ten, but no.

Does your friend have extremely large incisors (third from centre, out on top)? Ding ding ding! We have a winner! But one right answer doesn't make you a killer.

Does your friend seem almost unnaturally beautiful? Yeah, but so does a third of the Hollywood population.

Damn, the whole fucking test was rigged to fail. Total crap.

Thinking I could possibly find answers that would make sense from the internet was stupid. What it did do though, was make me think more about myself and less about his cryptic sci-fi life.

Deciding on another course of action that could maybe send me in the right direction, I think about my past. I'm still in contact with one of the only people that may know more, and that's Sister Jazmine. She and I had a tight relationship when I was at the orphanage, and even years later, when my foster parents disappeared, she was the one who helped with my emancipation so I didn't end up back in foster care.

Dialing the number, I wait for her typical answer.

"Hello. Mercy Home for Children, Sister Jazmine speaking. How can I help you?"

I picture her just the same as always, with her uneven punk cut of soft brown hair with colorful strands of blue, orange, and blonde sticking out everywhere. The angel and devil sugar skull tattoos that cover both lengths of her arms, and her unconventional attire of smiling skull and crossbones T-shirt and loose fitting jeans. The petite scar that runs from ear to ear along her neck makes her dangerous and sweet looking all at once. Long story on that, but needless to say, she's blessed by the big guy.

"Hey, Jaz. It's Thiea."

"Athena, nice to hear from you. What kind of trouble are you in?" Always direct, never one for mincing words. Not that I don't fit the bill, because trouble normally follows me like a black cat.

"I have a question."

"Shoot." I hear a chair scuff as she pulls it out to sit.

"Are there really devils and monsters? Ya know...like werewolves, vamps, and witches?"

"Of course there are. Why ask?" she responds in a serious tone.

"Let's just say I met someone who has a pretty impressive resume. Sharp teeth, glowing eyes, and said he was born out of this century. He also mentioned I could be like him—like his people. Do you have any idea what that might mean?"

Jaz is quiet for a moment. I picture her with one leg up on the chair, leaning back and twirling her shirt. "Thiea, you were left here with your blanket, the necklace, and that little bodysuit. I wish there were more I could impart, but if a vampire is telling you this, be careful. They *cannot* be trusted. Listen, I've gotta go. We have a bit of a mess in the nursery, sorry. Bye, darling." Without waiting for my good-bye, she hangs up and I'm left in just the same pickle as before.

I feel I've missed something, some clue that could turn the course of this search. With a mass of frustration building and the dredges of my beer appearing, I close up my computer and start heading back to my Jeep. With the lack of parking down here, I had to park a few streets over. At least I had the smarts to wear flats, otherwise I would've been cursing like a trucker on the broken pavement.

Walking past all the little shops and boutiques with designer handbags and shoes (some of my favorite creations), a pet store (my least fave), and a brightly lit travel agency, I find myself drawn in.

The travel store window pictures are of exotic places like Tahiti, Bali, and Hawaii. I probably look like a half-crazed loon staring blankly at the window of half-naked women lounging on a beach, but I haven't been on a trip in years. Decidedly, I push on the door, entering the space before I look like a nutter drooling on the windows. There's one person at the desk, stacks of books on the walls, and more pictures of beautiful places, which for some reason call to me.

"Can I help you?" The blond-haired hunk asks from behind a low to the floor kiosk.

Mmmmm. He's quite the catch. Thank you, libido, for catching on when the brain was offline.

"Uh, I'm not sure. I just…really, I'm not sure. I was walking by and decided to come in." *I wouldn't mind taking you home*, I think to myself.

All I see is the top half of his body, but from here, there's nothing wrong with the merchandise. Nice square, sturdy shoulders, soft scruffy afternoon shadow on his chin and cheeks, blond, wavy hair that frames his bright emerald eyes, with the slightest hint of dimples surrounding his tight plump lips. Damn nice specimen if you ask me.

"Did you hear what I was saying?" he asks sweetly, as I mentally shake myself from my erotic striptease moment.

"Sorry. What were you saying?"

"I asked if you've thought of a destination? Did you want sun and sand? Do you want adventure? A cruise, a spa? What type of vacation are you thinking?" He smiles at me and I almost melt.

My legs go a tiny bit wobbly as I try to rein in my sexual perusal of him. He asked destination. *Think, Thiea.* Don't go over the edge so quickly, or it'll be a short-lived orgasm. Right now, you need '*love me long time*.'

Interrupting my internal musings, I say, "I hadn't even really thought about where to go. I just found myself walking in. Can you suggest something?"

If I get away, maybe I won't have to deal with Garron's weird vampire thing. I haven't vacationed in almost five years, and even though it involved sandy beaches and sunshine, it was to bring home my mother and Father's caskets.

Dark, dire, and gloomy.

Their empty caskets.

My parents were on a cruise in the Dominican, and somehow fell overboard. Neither body was recovered, and I always thought it was foul play, but with nothing to substantiate it, I had no grounds to support it. The police wanted it covered up and the cruise liner's insurance company wanted it to go away. I just wanted them back. Guess only some of us got our wish.

Wandering around the room, perusing the various destinations and modes of transportation, I try to keep my mind on the task at hand. It's not as easy as it seems with the handsome male specimen in close proximity. The visions in my head have ventured from PG to R rating within our ten-minute conversation.

My mind has his lithe, yet sturdy body, tied to a four-poster bed with roses strewn across the floor. Then, I'm strapping him into a swing, all as he shows me various configurations of the same vacations.

Shaking it off, I say, "I'm not looking to go to the Caribbean. How about something totally off the tropical map?" As I lean over the low counter to give him a better view down my top, I reach for a pen from the holder. It's a low cut V-neck shirt, and I'm not wearing a bra today. With bee sting boobs, it's easy to be carefree when nothing jiggles.

"How about Europe?" he asks, trying to avert his eyes from my coolly protruding nipples. His cheeks are flaring the most amazing red, and I swear that if I leaned over the counter just a bit more, I'd see a slight tent in his Bermuda shorts.

"You mean, like Italy? Switzerland and all points between?" I figure after a couple more moves, I might just gain this lovely man's sexual attention. "Here," I look at his nametag, "Charlie. I have an idea. I'll let you know the amount I wish to spend, including airfare, taxes, hotel, which is five grand for the whole enchilada. You just book it to leave within a day."

"I can get you there and back with fabulous hotels and tours, no problem." He shifts his eyes from my breasts to my eyes, staring at me with a look of pure sex. I know that if I try just a tiny bit more, I might get what I want.

"Book it, and I'll be ready to go when you are." As lust clouds my judgement, I ignore my desperation as it stinks the room. I'm in need of a distraction, and if I go any longer, I'll create my own 'happy ending' in the bathroom while Charlie books the trip.

Blushing deeply, he replies, "Ah…I would love to go, but I don't think my wife would appreciate you taking me."

Damn, so close.

"That's okay. Book it anyway. I'm up for an adventure."

As he types away on the keyboard and shifts uncomfortably on his chair, I wish I could've taken his sweet ass for a ride, right there *down under* the Australian brochures.

"Do you mind if I use your restroom while you book everything?" I ask innocently.

"Sure, go ahead. It's down the hall, on the left."

Chapter FIVE

Hello? Destiny Calling

Thiea

What the hell have I gotten myself into? I just booked a fucking trip to who knows where. *Good going, Thiea.*

Here I am, hopping off to parts unknown with no one. I must be mental.

I arrived home about an hour ago, and the lovely travel agent, Charlie, mentioned that a driver service would be picking me up at nine to deliver me to the airport. I'm not even sure where the hell he booked me to, but I guess I could have asked or looked at the itinerary. Problem was, I was too busy getting myself off in the bathroom.

Clothes litter the bed as I decide what to take. A couple pairs of comfy shoes (including my precious pair of Louboutin heels), two pairs of my favorite True Religion jeans, and various shirts—all the necessities for snaring a new man. Plus, my most favorite, comfy sweater and vintage Chanel swoop back dress.

As I move to the hall closet for my travel cases, the doorbell rings.

"Hang on. I'm coming!"

Opening the door, I'm surprised to find a tall elderly gentleman. Sexy sixties.

"Ma'am, my name is Charlie. I'll be your driver service to the airport this evening. Is there anything I can help you with?" Two Charlie's in one day. Who'd a thunk?

"No, thanks," I say as I start back to my room.

"Not an issue, ma'am. I'll wait here." His Louisiana accent, bright blue eyes and lovely smile create a disarming and warm grandfather figure.

"I've just got in. If you wouldn't mind giving me a few minutes to get my things together, I'll be out shortly." Jogging back swiftly to my closet, leaving Charlie standing like an idiot in my front entrance, I start throwing everything into the bags, locking them up and wheeling them out in record time.

"Wow. If only my wife were that quick, we'd make it to events on time." He takes my bags in hand. "Your flight is in two hours, and if you are ready, we can depart." Opening the door for me, like a true gentleman, I realize how saddened I am that I feel comforted by a grandfather figure. The one thing I always missed out on was grandparents. My adoptive parents had no family. It's probably why they adopted myself and my sister in the first place; they wanted to start their own legacy. A legacy they'll never see.

I shake off the sadness. "Let's get it on," I say as I take one last look around the space.

Locking the door and stepping outside, I stop dead in my tracks and my jaw hits the ground.

Charlie's car is a jet-black, stretch MKT limo, polished to a sparkling shine. I *really* should have looked at the itinerary that the travel guy created. Now that I think about it, I'm more than likely staying in a dive. The good news is, I can scratch limo off my bucket list.

We reach the airport quickly, which if you know anything about the Toronto roadways, is sort of a freaking miracle from the downtown core. Charlie drops me at the front doors, unloads my baggage, and wishes me a good trip as I find myself adrift on the sea of mixed emotions.

Now I'm awaiting a plane to who knows where, without a single friend in the world accompanying me. I wanted to get a handle on my own destiny and this *Eat, Pray, Love* may not be perfect, but it feels right.

I left a message at the shop to let everyone know I'd be gone for a bit, and I left Cassie as head honcho until I return. It should start a flurry of questions, and Survivor Island moments as everyone tries to make her their new bestie, but I know she can handle the flock.

Charlie deposited me and my belongings at the international departure doors in front of Olympic Airlines. Entering the hall, I wander over to the lineup and grab a pole position behind an older couple in their sixties, a family with two kids screaming at the top of their lungs, and a young twentysomething's couple with backpacks. If they weren't in public, I think there'd be a serious sexual encounter as the couple grope and dry hump each other in line. It's entertaining to say the least.

I feel out of place. I'm disconnected from those who know what they're doing in life, because I let someone else decide my fate. I don't know what I was thinking. I may have been left in the Bronx and raised in Toronto, but I've never ventured into the unknown.

Reaching into my bag, I look for my phone to call someone… *anyone…*who might talk me out of this insanity. As I scramble through my bag like a crazy woman, I wonder if someone will alert the Homeland Security people. I could do with a good frisking. I'd take a cavity search if it meant a bit of arousal. Hopefully, it's not some lady named Doris or Mildred; I want a Mark or Trevor.

"Are you okay? Did you lose something?" I stumble and fall over my baggage as I crane my neck, looking for the source of the sexy, concerned, accented voice.

"Pardon?"

"Are. You. Okay?" he says again slowly, like I'm a complete imbecile.

As the owner of the amazing voice reaches out to help me up, I turn and see the tallest glass of water, with copper eyes that glimmer and shine, attached to a face that seems cut from the purest marble, like a Michael Angelo cherub.

Wide-eyed with wonder, I answer my statuesque, dangerously gorgeous man. "Yeah, I'm okay. I thought I forgot my car keys." I pull my keys from my bag, tinkling the little ring in the air. "I can't get home without these. Just a mini heart attack is all. Thanks for the hand up."

If he's on my flight, I might not need that battery-operated friend on my vacation at all. He could be the vision in my mind as I enjoy some finger action.

"No problem. Anytime. I'm Shoan, by the way, and you are?" His eyes twinkle, his cheeks flush, and his bright smile is strangely hypnotic.

"I'm clumsy—I mean, I'm Thiea."

Chapter SIX

Fun to be had by all in Technicolor

Shoan

I was looking forward to relaxing at the villa and drinking myself into a stupor while finding a few bosom buddies for an orgy or two. I needed the recharge to the system as it were, but no. Morrigan is always the black cloud wrecking my fun.

Change in plans yet again.

I booked the next flight out and here I am, helping a girl in line to upright herself after an embarrassing topple. We talk, and she tells me that this trip was decided spur of the moment. This could be just the distraction I needed.

I let out a little laugh as I undress her petite body in my mind. Seeing myself enjoying the pleasure of her company has me concentrating to keep my cock flaccid in my jeans. Stepping forward, she takes her turn at the wicket, dragging the hulking bags behind her. As I revel in her lovely pert ass, I think of how she'd be great inflight entertainment. Her red hair has coppery highlights of gold and crimson, flowing in cascading curls past her shoulders, fitting her tiny frame just right. It accentuates her bee sting nipples that are visible through the tight-fitting, plain white tee. The skinny black denim jeans are low enough I can see the rim of her blush pink lace panties that I'd bet match the bra.

"Enjoy your trip, Thiea. Maybe we'll see each other on the flight." I envision the mile high club. The wicked little thought has me hard as I try to imagine her frail body in the throes of passion. Adjusting my luggage to hide the evidence, I wave to her as she moves forward, towards customs.

She'll be just like the rest; shallow, callous, and weak. Just shells to house the pleasure I need to exist in this world.

"Why did you?"

"What did I do?"

"Help me. Help me, please..."

Oh, for Goddess' sake! Not now. Not here. I know it'll only be a matter of time before the memories of others not only haunt me, but tear me down.

I fall forward onto the luggage that I'd just used to cover up my erection. As always, my failure comes to the forefront at the worst possible time. My past drowns me every moment it can when I haven't partaken in a few hours. I need sex to keep the block in place.

Fucking curse.

I try to cover my failings from the public eye, but as my past moves and stirs to life, reaching out to drag me under, it becomes incessantly difficult as the voices of the airport patrons blur my thoughts. Gathering my luggage and ticket, I round through the kiosk and head into the departure area, hoping against hope that I can find a companion to release this mounting pressure in my head.

"You didn't have to. Why did you leave me?"

"Can't you just let me live? Please, I'll reform."

If I don't find someone soon, I won't have to worry about fucking the girl on the plane. I'll have to worry about staying sane and sober as I avoid the voices in the airport before I have a chance to leave.

Rolling through the terminal, I look at those sitting in the cafes and restaurants, the magazine stores and such. I need someone who would be up for a quick sexual encounter in the bathroom. There are very few alone. Most are travelers in groups or pairs, except for her.

Her long legs are accentuated by a pearl colored mini dress, black spike heels, and a dainty locket around her neck. Her flowing blonde hair hangs loose around her face, framing the bright blue eyes that are scanning a fashion magazine column.

I walk up behind her, lightly bumping my carry-on wheels into her expensive Louis Vuitton bag. "Oh, I'm sorry. I hope I didn't damage your luggage?" I flash her my best dimpled smile.

"No worries. There's no damage," she says as she inspects it and smiles back at me.

"I could buy you a drink? I have to wait a while for my flight anyway." She smiles and grabs her luggage, completely forgetting the magazine as we head off for the bar down the hall.

"What's your name?" she asks as we pass the milling hordes.

"Does it matter?" I clip off, pulling her into an employee's only hallway.

She shrugs. "No, not really. I just want to know if you have any names picked out for your future children." She laughs haughtily as she pushes her luggage to the side. She then rakes her finely manicured fingernails down my arm and chest.

"You have no chance of getting that from me, love." I unbutton her shirt quickly, reaching in to cup her expertly perfected double D's as she sighs into the air. The voices still threaten their way to the surface, clawing to drag me into the abyss of despair, but I won't let them.

"Lift your skirt," I tell her. "Show me what I want, gorgeous."

With a tiny laugh, she raises it slowly, inch by inch, until I see what I need. "No panties?"

With a smirk, she makes quick work of my trousers, pulling the button and zipper to free my cock. With nothing in the way of our needs, I say, "Thank you."

"For what?" she asks, moaning as I finger her moist folds.

"For this." With no warm-up or fanfare, the lucky blonde is pushed up against the wall as I thrust my cock deep inside her. She moans and grips me tighter with those painted daggers as I pull her release from her.

"More, please. Oh, yes…yeeeesssss," she cries out. I cover her mouth to lessen the noise. The last thing we need is an airport security rent-a-cop or punk Starbucks kid to come bursting through the door, worrying about a security breach.

As she crests her high I feel the dirty dark thoughts wain. No more help me's and no more memories, just a calm quiet bliss. I don't think I could have handled a flight with the thoughts screaming and shouting their pleas all the way to Athens.

Once my lady friend is finished I pull out, straighten my pants, and tuck my shirt back in as she does the same.

"Are you going to tell me your name, mystery man?" she coos, postcoital bliss.

“No.” I turn and leave, entering back into the foray of softhearted, small-minded humans towards a shitty reason to go home.

If it hadn’t been for the lovely blonde, I don’t think I could have existed through the flight. After cleaning myself up, I reached the plane just as boarding is called for the first-class passengers.

Taking my assigned seat, I’m glad I slipped the attendant a bit of coin. My seatmate is the girl I met in line.

Now that we’ve been in the air for a few hours now, and I’ve been buying her vodka and orange juice since takeoff. Her tongue has thoroughly loosened.

"So, let's see if I got this. You’re on a flight to Athens, didn't know you were going there specifically, and this is all based on a whim? What's next, the Amazing Race with a friend from high school?"

"Okay, smart ass. Listen, less than a week ago was my birthday —”

“Congratulations,” I interject.

“Thanks. As I was saying, I went out for the evening, got shit-faced, had a very short-lived fight with a chick, my shirt was ripped off by a bouncer, and I had man candy clean my teeth with his tongue. After that, I was kicked out. I still don't think I deserved it, but Cassie, of course, followed me instead of leaving me alone outside, drunk and angry." She rambles on in concise clips, visibly proud of herself. I can't wait for the inflight scuffle with the Air Marshall when they try to take her drink away.

"Okay, so you’re a bit adventurous. I would put you at the same level as wet T-shirt contestant at a frat party. You drank panty remover then danced on the pool table. So what? My cat’s probably more adventurous than you." I can't wait to hear the real story, if this is her trying to puff it up.

"I was kicked out for kissing another girl's guy. I know I won, but the bouncer dragged me out by the back of my shirt. I kinda liked that shirt too. He would've been worth it, I think. The guy, I mean. I think he would've been. Anyway, I may not be adventurous enough to climb Kilimanjaro in PJ's and flip flops, but I'm talking to you on a plane where I'm going to parts unknown with no real itinerary in mind. So I think I'm way past the wet T-shirt level."

"Fine. I'll put you at Myrtle Beach, spring break."

She scrunches up her nose, thinning her glare as she licks the rim of her glass. "Enough about me. How about we say it's time to get to know Shoan. Where are you from? Why are you on this plane? Vacation or business?" She hiccups, then takes a long drag from her drink.

"You wanna know about me? All right. When I'm done though, you have to spill the story about you." What would make her do this intrigues me.

"I'm a single white male that likes walks in the park with champagne, cute fluffy dogs named Rover, and dark milk chocolate." I adjust in my chair, signaling the stewardess for further drinks as I continue with my diatribe. Thiea gives me a glare that proves that wasn't what she meant.

"I'm from Ireland. Even though I haven't lived there in a very long time, I still consider it home. Right now, I live in Toronto, but I'm going to Athens to meet up with my sister and some friends of ours for a vacation of sorts. My sister, Niamh, is my only living relative, but I consider Arif a brother by blood, sweat, and tears. I have a cat named Margarette. She's a Calico that I found curled up in the park one winter night during a run. My sister won't let me consider getting rid of her; I'm a dog person. A big slobber puss is my top shelf any day over an annoying cat.

“I've always found it relaxing to be outside rather than in a stuffy building with a tie and jacket. I’m a sommelier by trade, so stuffy kind of comes with the territory.”

She raises her eyebrow. “I’m a—”

“Wine taster. Got it. Sorry if I looked dumbfounded, I just don’t see you as a connoisseur. You seem more like a whisky guy to me.” She licks her lips and sips from her concoction once more. Huh. She knows what I do? Not what I expected.

“Okay, you’re right. I’m not a wine sommelier, I’m a brandy sommelier to be exact. Sorry if I seemed a bit surprised. Most don’t understand the work I do. Anyway, that's me in a nutshell.” I push my chair back a bit, reclining it, as I reach for my overstuffed pillow. It’s a bit too big for the space, but it’s better than the chairs and pillows in economy.

“Now, I want the same back from you. Job, loves, likes and dislikes, favorite color, pets, plus any other basic run-of-the-mill info you feel like spilling."

Thiea takes the last gulp of her drink before handing it off to the stewardess in exchange for a fresh one. As we hit a bit of turbulence, the new drink spills over her little fingers. She licks them lazily, then sips on the drizzle going across her knuckles. The sight of her licking the rim of the cup was one thing, but with her sucking on her nimble little fingers, I’m finding I have to adjust my pants. At this rate, I'm not sure I can make the whole flight without taking her in a bathroom stall, sober or not.

I hand her a napkin. As she takes it, a pulse of energy goes through my fingers. I quickly take my hand back to shake off the feeling. It was sharp, and she didn't seem to notice what I felt. Ignoring it, she starts with her backstory.

"Irish. My friend Cassie, my only friend, really, her hubby Garron is Irish too. He’s a cop, among other things." She rubs the napkin over her hand, stuffs it in the seat garbage and continues on.

"Okay, so me. Well, I live alone in Northern Toronto, and my closest neighbor is more than an arm’s length away. I have no pets. No brothers, just a foster sister, Katherine. I grew up in foster care, but I was emancipated at sixteen when my foster parents were lost at sea. I miss my mom quite a bit, especially with shit like this. I don't like chocolate, but I can go for a great cup of tea anytime, as long as it comes in a Starbucks cup over ice with lemonade. I own my own little girlie shop, and I hate the paperwork and random boss crap. FYI, you bypassed the whole love interest part. Any girls strung up in your closet at home waiting?" She gives me a wink and a cute little smile.

The tips of my fingers are still tingling, and I can't seem to regain the feeling. It was like she shocked me…like lightning. Way worse than static electricity.

I find myself staring at her, taking in the minute details of her high cheekbones, her perfect bone white teeth and her little chin. The blonde streaks of sun bleached hair interspersed in the dark fire red shows off the freckles on her face that are perfectly positioned. It all makes her eyes stand out, like the brilliant green and red of a blood stone. I shake off staring at her before she thinks I'm a stalker.

“No girls in the closet, but I have some in other places,” I laugh. Not only two hours ago I was fucking an unknown woman in the airport. “No love interest in this storyline, but a few broken hearts along the way. Nothing substantial ever held on.”

“Oh. Good to know. I mean, sorry for the busted hearts part, but...”

“Not *my* busted heart—theirs. They all want to fix me, marry me, keep me. I’m not that kind of guy.”

“Why would they want to fix you?” she asks.

“I don’t really wanna get into it right now, but let’s just say I have some banged-up lovers in my closet.”

Thiea turns her head and mumbles something into the chair that I can’t quite hear.

“Sorry, I didn’t hear you. What was that?”

She blushes. “It’s nothing, really.”

I wait for a minute as she muses. “I doubt you would have mumbled to your cup…”

“Okay. Here’s the story of why I *really* ended up here.” She pulls herself a bit closer in the chair, wiggling her finger at me. I move in closer, wanting to hear this. “After the bar the other night, my girlfriend’s hubby told me a cockamamie story about himself. He basically said vampires and werewolves exist. I went to a travel agency by chance and Poof! Here I am, on a plane to parts unknown. I guess his revelation scared me so much, I figured getting out of town for a bit wasn’t such a bad idea."

"You don't have to lie to me. A secret rendezvous in Greece, a tryst with a married man—I get it. Really, you wouldn't be the first to do it."

"No, I'm not meeting him to have sex…though, it was a thought once or twice.” Waving her hands in the air, she shakes off the notion. “But that’s beside the point. He said some shit about a war coming, some book, and that I’m in some way “touched,” whatever that means. I figured I was touched in the head for listening to him. It seemed like a load of crap, and I still don't believe it, but it scared me enough to get out of town for some R&R."

Thiea turns, looking off to the pitch-black sky through her port window as we pass over the ocean. Taking another drink of her vodka, she peers over her shoulder at me, smiling. I know there's more she isn't saying, but I can't get a read on her.

Damn fucking curse! All the things I could find out from a single thought. This girl is deeper than what I normally find lying on the far side of my bed, and it could turn out to be more dangerous than I expect.

Why argue with it? It's never stopped me before.

"I don't think it's as big a deal as he makes it out to be." She pauses for a second, licks her lips, and sucks in her teeth. She's definitely drunk.

Again, I'm wishing we were someplace else. I envision tearing her clothes away, stripping off the petite pink panties, licking and sucking on her sweet nectar until she comes so often she's spent. I know it'll be easy to divert her from her plans, and the only thing stopping me right now from really pouring on the charm is that touch. It has me feeling a little uneasy. Normally, I would try to ensnare her to my will, but I feel as if *she's* the one trapping me in her web; like a spider on the hunt.

The whole package of this woman is like an elixir. Her humor, the way she licks her lips, and that tightly packed body makes me want her all the more.

"Garron said I have power that's probably dormant. I think it's a crock of shit, I have a hard-enough time just opening a jar of pickles."

"Why not just blow it off then? Ignore what he said and forget about it." Maybe Niamh's right. Something might be up.

"Garron said it's something I've inherited that makes me special."

She pulls back her hair into a loose ponytail and sighs as she reclines the chair further back.

"How did he think you were special?"

"Didn't say, really. He told me that there's this book. It has something to do with vampires and other things that go "bump in the night,"" she air quotes and smirks. "I didn't believe any of the shit he spewed, but Jaz told me to be wary, so I decided to avoid the whole thing for a bit."

Stunned by the conversation, I wonder…how did I end up here? Why me with her? Why would this jerk Garron think she could help out in any way? Even if she is dormant, they're never strong enough to be dangerous, and definitely never strong enough to cause problems with us.

"Hey, you okay?" she asks as she tries to reach for my forehead. I quickly pull back. "You look a little green." The last thing I need is a recurrence of that shock.

"I'll be right back. I'm gonna go use the loo." I get up, moving towards the back of the plane in economy. The further from her and the stewardesses I am, the better. I need to use my phone.

Finding the first one occupied, I step inside the second and lock the door. Pulling out my phone, I call Niamh.

No answer. Fuck.

I try Arif, and as I get his voicemail too, I decide to leave him a message.

"Arif, I think we have a problem. Maybe not as much a problem as a stroke of luck. This girl I'm on the plane with, she's a…anyway. This girl's important if they're putting out feelers to dormant ones. I won't let her out of my sight. They can't get at her, or it, without me. I'll contact you when I land."

Okay. So now what?

This trip just gets weirder and weirder. I wanted a nice little getaway, which Arif and Niamh had to screw up with the mention of Morrigan. I went from wanting to fuck anything that moved, to now wondering what she is?

Why is it when we touched did it feel like she shocked me? And that somehow a bloody vampire could feel her existence, even though Thiea doesn't know anything about it, or our world?

So now what?

Leaving the bathroom, I make my way back to my seat where Thiea is passed out. She looks so fragile, so weak and childlike as she sleeps. If I can help her figure it out, and understand what she is, then what?

I don't normally hang around after sex, even with those of our kind. I'll have to avoid her at all costs, which means no sex. She's officially off the menu until we can figure out what she is, and what she has to do with this fucking Garron guy or Morrigan.

On a whim, I touch her outstretched hand once more, hoping, needing to see if it was a fluke experience. On contact, the same occurs—a jolt of power once more flows through me.

What's so different about her?

Settling back into my seat, I find myself unusually drained. Trying to piece this together, the shock from her touch, and how or why Morrigan and her Nightwalkers would want this particular dormant, I find myself gazing out the window and drifting off to sleep.

Chapter SEVEN

Dreams, Wishes, and Parts Unknown

Shoan

I haven't slept in centuries. It's a hard-core reality that time doesn't actually have any bearing on my existence. So, the big question is; how the fuck did I fall asleep on a plane?

With no idea of what's happening to me, nor how she's involved, I decided to eat breakfast, waiting for Thiea to wake. While questions swim in my mind, like the stalker I am, I wonder what it is that makes her so different? This Garron character informed her, a mere human girl, that she's Goddess born in some way. So again, why do I feel drawn to her? Secondary to that, why do I feel different today? I'm awake and refreshed.

Fuck, this is so confusing. Maybe she's a Charge? I haven't heard of one in centuries, but she could always be one. After all, she has no idea of her parentage.

The bigger problem at hand is what can I tell her that would illicit her to stay and help me? Hell, if this guy could scent her out—

which, of course, I fucking can't—then I can't tell. Bloody fucking curse, as always, is blocking me.

Here's the biggest question of all; how did she get along all this time without others noticing her?

Picking away at the food, poking the flat eggs and moist toast, I wait for answers to come to me. Nothing. Fuck. Bloody fuck-all. As I'm sipping the warm orange juice, Thiea stirs.

She holds her head, resting her elbows on her knees. "Okay, how big was the truck that ran me over? My head feels like an over roasted marshmallow." I laugh at her analogy. "Oh, that's too loud. Don't do that again, please."

She peeks at me through her heavy lashes, trying to avoid the glare from the sun in the side window. The overhead lighting that beams down upon her swollen head must make her feel screwy. "Do you have any aspirin? I think I might need a bottle." Rubbing her hair to scuff up her bedhead causes the curls to pop and rise like tight springs.

I push my tray away. "I don't have a bottle, but I was able to get you a few."

Reaching across, I close the blind. "I know you drank more than me, and it's more than the considered legal limit. So how do you look so refreshed and chipper?"

Handing her the aspirin I'd taken from the stewardess earlier, I hand her the glass of orange juice.

"Oh no. No more of that wicked juice, unless you want me to technicolor dream that shirt of yours," she says.

Allowing a snicker of laughter, I envision her doing just that. "Thiea, I have a driver service waiting to pick me up, and I could arrange for you to get to your hotel. That is, if you don't mind taking a ride from a perfect stranger. Or if you wish, there's always the alternative. Athens has local transit, but it's kind of like TTC."

"Uh, thanks. I'm not a big fan of riding the rocket with a hang-over. I'm sure I'd miss my stop and end up in Italy," she mumbles, taking a bite of her toast.

Redirecting her and keeping an eye on her could be the best. "I have a villa here. My sister and a few friends should already be there, and seeing you don't have an itinerary, you could always hang with us for the day until your head clears. I think you and my sister would have a lot in common. She's like you; spirited, spontaneous, and a poor sport at drinking. Her affinity for all things expensive at rock bottom prices is quite extraordinary."

"I'm not a poor sport. I'm just suffering from the aftermath of Russian roulette with glasses." She's definitely hungover. "So, a villa, huh? Are we talking a house or are we talking a mansion? It'll probably make my hotel accommodations meek."

"It's just a place to stay, really, nothing special. A couple bed-rooms, a kitchen, and a garden with a view. Where is it you're stay-ing?"

She flicks through the paperwork in her bag. "I have a reserva-tion at some hotel in the Plakka, just off Ermou." Thiea's attempt at the street and area names is comical. Wiping her luscious lips with a napkin, she hands her plate to the stewardess as she passes.

"If you like, I could take you on a guided tour. I know the best spots to eat, plus you and Ni could shop once you're bored of my company." I'm positive she truly thinks the story about vampires is just a load of crap, which can play to our advantage. If Thiea's dormant, who knows what that can mean to her, to us and to the world, even if she doesn't understand it yet. She probably has enough power to kick start an engine if a Trappa vampire can detect it.

Hell, after the shock she gave me last night, I feel alive, awake, and refreshed. I'm feeling clear and alert, like every nerve is firing sequentially to the beat of my heart. Sleeping is a not a norm for me. I haven't slept in centuries. It's just so fucking weird. I can't even bring myself to consider what it can all mean. The only thing I *can* do is test the waters to see if what I feel and sense is a reality.

Conduits or Charges can ignite dormant powers. Could she possibly be powerful enough to kick-start some of my abilities?

Long ago, I could hear humans. Nowadays, I only hear snippets of past voices—those of whom I've dealt judgement on when I hadn't fucked anyone in a day, but to hear normal everyday humans? I'm not sure I have the ability.

But I'll try anything once.

Concentrating all of my energy to hear her thoughts, I'm hoping to have a positive reaction. Clearing my mind, I try to hone in, as if a giant satellite is strapped to my brain, which after a few centuries is…well, it'll be fucking insane if it works. I think of everything about her; her smell, her look, her smile. I try to think of everything and anything so that I can concentrate on her and her alone.

Great smile, good hair. I don't get what he sees in me? I bet I'm just a quick fuck before he gets back to his wife. I guess I could always do with a quick "Hello" then get back to whatever the travel agent set up. Lord does my head hurt. That's the last time I have vodka on a plane.

I hear her, I feel her emotions too. It's incredible, as her thoughts are so clear. Something definitely changed overnight, and I want more. If she's the key, then vampires be damned; I'm not letting her out of my sight. I'm signing on as her personal detail in this fucking country while she's here, and nobody will stop me. I can't let them have her. *We* won't let them.

"Shoan. Are you okay?" she asks. "I appreciate the ride to my hotel, and if you don't mind, I'd like that tour guide for hire. That is, if you have the time." *Please say yes. I really,* really, *want you to say yes.*

I can hear her thoughts as if she said them aloud. I might just break down and cry like a child. It's not sexy, but I don't give a flying duck's ass. There's definitely something powerful in her. For sure, sex is off the books. If she felt I screwed her and dumped her, she'd run straight into the arms of the enemy.

"Yeah, sure." I smile and pat her hand. It's great to know something I thought was long gone in my life has now been brought back. If I can hear her, I can possibly hear other humans as well. Honing in on other's thoughts—those of the passengers—I hope for more. If I can hear her, a Goddess born, then there's no reason why I shouldn't hear their immature thoughts.

I hope that Tomas can make it to the airport to pick us up on time...

Flaps, wind speed, altimeter is steady...

Just land so I can get this over with. Damn divorce lawyers...

I need Trevor. I hope he loves me...

If I transfer $500 to my American account, then move it...

Goddess! What the hell was I thinking? After centuries of nothing, it's like floodgates have opened during a hurricane. The din from all the soft minds and external conversations affects me worse than I thought it could. I shouldn't have tried to listen in such a confined space. Fuck, I knew better.

I *know* better. What a rookie fucking move.

"Are you sure you're okay, Shoan? You really look ghastly."

Staying calm and in control externally is becoming exceedingly difficult.

I nod, which is seemingly more difficult than I'd expected. "Yeah, yeah. I'm good." Maybe if I concentrate on just Thiea's unique signature, I might be all right.

Heck, if I'm to survive the remainder of the flight, the crowded airport, and any or all local areas, I better find a way to deal. Otherwise, this shit will be overwhelming. Also, if I can't get my shit together, this will be the best opportunity for the vampires to gain her and me as a trophy.

Taking in a deep breath, I draw in her scent. I concentrate on feeling her heartbeat and drawing in on her thoughts only. She smells of magnolia's and black pepper, with a hint of nutmeg spice.

Shopping is my favorite pastime. I have a bit of a shoe fetish, Thiea says wordlessly. Looking at me, she smiles and continues on externally. "I think shopping would be great. That's if you don't mind? After we land though, can we find a convenience store? I need more aspirin and a massive bottle of water. Hangovers rot in any country." I smile a strained and tight smile.

"Oh, I'm sure we can find you some after we get through customs." I was right to seek out only her mind; it's soothing. Like a lifeline in the storm. It eases the clamor of the passengers aboard the mental jail I've just created.

Touching down and exiting the steel jail has become my only concern. There are stars in my vision. I hear every stray thought and I'm worried that if the captain doesn't tell us to 'Have a great time in the city' soon, I'd bypass the stewardess and open the door myself. I've tried for the remainder of the trip to compose myself. The last thing I need is to alarm Thiea, but I have a feeling she's seeing how uncomfortable and antsy I've become.

As the doors finally open and we vacate the plane towards the ramp, as if the plane was on fire. Thank the Goddess that I was able to zero in on Thiea's signature and her thoughts alone. I could see this being the quickest trip to Athens; with a short stop in the rubber room.

As we exit the plane, heading up the ramp, I lean heavily on the walls. "Are you okay?" Thiea asks once more while I flounder. I haven't heard human thoughts for so long, and that small group on the plane will be nothing compared to the full airport. Not to forget, the power of millions of minds in a city like Athens. The pressure is about to become unbearable.

Without answering her, I rush towards a trash can, stumbling and tripping as if I have two left feet. I hurl into the receptacle my measly breakfast, wiping my face on the back of my hand. Rubbing my back and telling me it'll be all right, Thiea comes to comfort me like she's known me for years, not just an ocean crossing.

"I uh…I guess the breakfast wasn't agreeing with me. Can you help me? I need to sit for a minute."

"Yeah, sure. I thought I was the only hungover one. Is there anything I can do for you?"

Trying to curl my lips into a smile, I answer. "Nah. Really, I'll be okay in a minute."

"Do you want a water or anything?"

"Let's keep going," I say, taking her hand. We walk through the airport, moving until we're through customs, which thankfully went off without a hitch, and I find that holding her hand assists to quiet those around us. Human thoughts are normally tolerable.

With their monotonous daily diatribes of pointless drivel, I used to find it navigable. Now it seems that without the assistance of

Thiea's bouquet, I'd be running for the closest exit, screaming obscenities. Thank Goddess she's here to help. I still don't understand it, but I'm thankful for her.

After Thiea pulls her bags off the carousel, we head for the car with less trouble than I'd expected. My only real worry now is Dark Worlders. If any are within the vicinity, the collision of their minds mingling with the humans will turn the whole thing into a cacophony. Like a radio in-between channels.

The pall of death and destruction they create is like watching every Rob Zombie movie in montage mode. I hope to hell, heaven, and whomever else is watching that I don't run into anyone I know, or anyone that wishes to do us harm. There's no fucking way I can protect myself, let alone protect Thiea.

What good am I? The best I could do is muster up some extra spicy puke, but after that, I'd have to rely on the rent-a-cops in the airport to keep us safe. That is totally not an option; none of them would stand a chance.

"Hang on a sec, Thiea." She stops mid-stride, turns towards me and watches as I place our bags against the wall, out of the way. "I need you to trust me. I can't really explain the who's, what's, or why's, but I need you to know that I have your best interests at heart." Thiea is the anchor in this maelstrom and I need her. If I allow her to leave, this will consume me.

I don't know if I can recover.

Looking at her—like, *really* looking at her—I wonder how anyone could not fall in love with her. That hair, those sensual full lips, and those eyes...her eyes are like the deep end of a pool. In less than a day, I've found myself engulfed in her, totally dependent on her. Sure, I need her to hold the voices at bay, even though I'm sure she's the true cause of the voices returning. The shock she gave me, the rush of power I'm feeling. Hell, the fact that I actually slept, after more than three centuries of not, is just amazing.

"Listen to me, Thiea. I know what you we're talking about when it comes to Goddess born, vampires, and everything else that you so eloquently put 'goes bump in the night.' What you've been told so far isn't the whole truth though, and I need to know you trust me." My head feels like it's gonna burst wide open for all to see. As I grab my head and her hand at the same time, I feel a calm. "I promise, on my sister's life, to keep you safe. But I need to know that you trust me."

"I…Shoan?" she stammers nervously. Backing away from me, she takes my lifeline. With her out of my grip, the tone and tenor of the voices increase, both in volume and in speed, like they're all vying for my attention.

"Please, look at me. Look and you'll see the truth of it. I'm telling you what you'll learn soon enough. I won't harm you. I swear on the Goddess herself."

She's hesitant. The look on her face is of uncertainty, and I can see the internal war she's waging. After a few seconds, but what feels like hours, she takes my hand in hers. It's so gentle, that the hairs on my arm rise and my cock responds in concert. *Nice timing, buddy.* Slowly, the thoughts of others recede, falling away like the leaves on a tree, until the only thing I can hear is her sweet heartbeat and light mind.

She takes a deep breath before bending down to pick up her bags. "I don't understand what, why, or how it's true, and I don't give a shit right now, but I trust that you'll keep me safe."

Nodding is the best I can muster as I thank her for believing in me. I know it won't be the first or the last time I need her, but it's good enough for now.

As we walk up the ramp and enter into the rest of the airport, I feel them. I know there are Dark Worlders in the terminal, and whether they're here to cause trouble, or if they know about her and I, I can't be sure. But one thing I do know, I don't want her anymore afraid than she already is.

"You don't look as green." Thiea smiles, and still holding my hand in hers, she motions towards the exit, towards Athens.

"Stay with me and don't let go. I'll be fine."

Walking out the doors, I run straight into what I'd hoped beyond hope not to encounter; a waiting entourage of Dark Worlders. To boot, they're the ones I've avoided for two decades.

"Athena. Shoan. So nice to see you." With the voice of an angel and the heart of the devil himself, it's the voice I would know anywhere.

"I don't think I can say the same for you. Last I saw you, you were licking your wounds and running for the hills, Morrigan." If I had any choic, I'd tell Thiea to run the other way from this cadre of hell, but as she's the only thing keeping me sane for the moment, I need her here. As selfish as it sounds, I don't think I would fare well without her.

Morrigan's six-foot frame blocks our path, and if it weren't for her being the bane of my existence, I would almost find her attractive. Her long, flowing, platinum blonde hair, with the pitch-black streak seeping like ink along the left side near her temple, and her elegant features, make her look like a world class supermodel. Outwardly, to mortals, she possesses the poise and grace of an angel. I, on the other hand, see her true face.

I've always seen the horrific form that lies beneath the surface. The harsh planes along her jaw and cheekbones, the dark blotchy skin that looks as if it's been burned. It peels, crackles, and strips layer by layer every day. The only part of her that's not unequivocally horrific is the tell-tale sign of a Dark Worlder—her eyes. The russet with gold flecks is like glitter thrown into a kiln to give the pottery depth and dimension.

"Shoan, I appreciate you looking after Athena, but I think she should come with me." Morrigan turns to Thiea with a slight sneer, revealing her canines. Fucking vampires, always with the show. "Forcibly, if necessary."

"I'm not really into gang-banging, if you get my drift, so I respectfully decline. And it's not Athena, it's Thiea." Thiea's response is clipped, yet nasty, reserved but with an undertone of perky '*Kiss this, bitch.*'

"We'll there's your answer, Morrigan. I'm sure though, we'll be seeing you again. Soon."

"Don't worry, Shoan. We'll be around," Morrigan states crassly as she turns, leaving without even a sideways glance.

Fuck. Fuck and double fuck.

"Well that went well. Too well," I tell Thiea. I can't say I'd count my blessings yet.

Watching as Morrigan fades into the hustle and bustle of the airport, I can't bear letting go of Thiea's hand. Knowing the voices will begin anew, and that I'll collapse to the ground as a dribbling, drooling, truly sniveling certifiable mess on the floor, I realize I need her terribly. "I think we need to move and move fast. Morrigan's not the catch and release type."

Moving faster, we pass through the remainder of the hall unharmed or hindered. Finally, I see the limo and my usual driver, Auguello, standing by the passenger door. "Thiea, my driver's is directly outside these doors," I say to her quietly under my breath. "I suggest you get in as quickly as you can. Don't worry, I'll be right behind you."

Scanning the area, looking for Morrigan or her goon squad once more, I open the door of the airport for Thiea. As soon as she exits, I find myself flat on the ground from a blow to the back of my head. I don’t need to turn around to know who it is. It’s the boys—it’s always the boys. One doesn’t travel without the other; Sullivan and George.

Last time I met up with these boys I was a bit younger, and even though I may not be at full strength like they are, I'm strong enough to do some damage, escaping with dignity.

"Thiea, run for the car,” I say calmly, but with concern. “Augi, lock the doors once she's in."

Grabbing Thiea’s bag with two hands, I stand up and take a heavy-handed swing at George's head. Hitting him perfectly across his repeatedly shattered nose, he falls back into the wall, nearest the door, as Sullivan hits me square in the stomach. Knocking the wind out of me, I fall forward onto my hands and knees. Luckily, I’d already wretched out all the food in my system, or I would have once again.

Grabbing Sullivan's left foot, I pull it forward, throwing him off-balance. Sully falls on his ass, just as George comes back for a second swing. Knowing I’m on the losing side, I grab the bag, making a run for the limo door. Moving as fast as I can, I hop inside as Auguello squeals the tires.

We almost run down an older couple as we scrape the side of the car along a guardrail, weaving into the fast-moving traffic. I’ll deal with the damage to the car later. Right now, I don't care about anything except that Thiea and I are safe for the moment.

Looking over at her, she’s totally stunned. Thoroughly scared to the bone, it harms me to the core to see it.

"Are you okay?" I ask.

"Am I okay? Really, you're asking if I'm okay! Fuck, you just had your brain caved in by two UFC champs!" she yells out. Then I hear her thoughts loud and clear. *Hell, what am I getting into? This is more than I thought when I hit on that travel guy. Fuck! FUCK!*

Brushing my hand across her face, sweeping her auburn hair away, I see her tears. I don't do women's emotions well. Sex? Yes. Love 'em and leave 'em? Yes. But crying is out of my jurisdiction. Morrigan, George, and Sullivan with their penchant for violence I can handle. It was a bad way for her to meet them, but it could've been worse. Much worse.

"What just happened? And please don't lie to me. Tell me the truth."

"Thiea, it'll be okay. I promise. I'm gonna call my sister now. Hopefully, she's at the house. We're not that far away. We'll be there in a few minutes. If you can wait until we're there, I'll tell you everything."

Surprising me, she moves over from the other side of the limo where she was trying to blend into the door to snuggle into my side. Laying her head on my lap, she curls up on the seat and cries. The confusion of being something she has never heard of, and now a fight she didn't expect, is nothing more than overwhelming. Toss in a vodka hangover and you have the perfect recipe for disaster.

I'll need to distance myself from her emotionally and physically. With her head in my lap, I'm amazed she's not alarmed by my stiffy that's sticking into her neck. My body wants her—hell, I want her—but I know this isn't the right thing to do, and for once, I'm listening. I can hold off for a few more hours before I'll have to find a fuck friend in the city. I can wait. I have to.

Niamh would tell me just go for it, fuck her and get it out of your system, but two things are stopping me.

One: Morrigan wants her, and for me that's a major plus on keeping her close.

Two: It's been centuries since I've heard the calling out of minds. If she's the cause, then she's also the solution.

Which to my libido and revved cock means she's totally off limits. *You fucking peckerhead.*

Chapter EIGHT

No Time like the Present

Chad

"Listen, this was yer bet, Marcus. No backin' out now. I won't be payin' Jake at the bar 'cause ya reneged," I say, checking the straps on the back of his parachute. "Now hold still, or it'll cut into parts of ya that ya may wish to be keepin'."

"I wouldn't worry about his, so much as yerself. The straps on this are loose enough to hold two." Terese reaches around, near my ass, to pull and tug on the restraints. I don't mind, it's nice being groped. Even if it is by one of me mates.

"That's because I ain't tightened 'em yet. I was wantin' room to allow the boys to breathe till the time came to strap up." Grasping my cock, I shake it a bit. She shakes her head, walking away as the rest laugh.

"Well, boys, that time is now. Sir, you need to tighten your gear," the jump assistant Kirk says as he opens the door on the side of the tiny Cessna Skycatcher. He attaches our cables to the roof line catch. “It’s now or never if you want to hit the mark.”

“See you down there.” Marcus says with a smile so wide it accentuates his massive teeth. If Kirk didn’t know what we were before this, he does now.

Leaning out the plane door backwards, I do a final tug on all of Patrick’s straps, falling in step right behind. Turning to Terese, passing all of my things for her to place in our baggage, my phone rings.

“You’ve got five. Go.”

“It’s the book. How quick can you and the boys be ready? We’ll be at the villa.”

“Done. Nothin’ more needin’ to be said. I'll call ya in a few. Count us in.”

“The clock’s been skipped forward.” The voice on the other end says.

“I’m about to jump out of a plane behind the rest, and it's gettin’ chilly. See ya soon.” I hand my phone to Terese. She’s the only one smart enough not to do this, and without a word, she knows what we need to do.

“Ye’ll be needin’ a bit of packin’ done, I assume. Or will it be on the charge?” She puts my phone in her pocket, dialing on her own.

“Charge is fine. Now, before me bits become inverted and I’m called a chickenshit shifter, I gotta go.” I move to the door, then step out of the rigging, all while Kirk tries to stop me. Grabbing my cock, I float out into the air.

Nothing unusual for me. This is just another day. But fuck if this is the last time I jump naked in December over the Alps.

Niamh

"She wasn't there for me, Ni, she was there for Thiea. Don't ask more, I can't explain it right now. But we'll be at the house in a few minutes," Shoan says into the phone.

If I could reach through the phone right now, I think I'd be choking my big bro.

"Dump the bitch. Like you haven't had enough run-ins with Morrigan over the years." I'm worried, but there's no way I'm telling him that. He'd think I'm a pansy ass wimp. "I hope Morrigan isn't following you. That's the *last* thing we need."

"I promise it'll be okay. Really." With that, Shoan hangs up and I curse under my breath. I hate when he does that hang up shit.

Now here I am, waiting on him and his new piece of ass. A new trophy. I'm not sure I want to know why Morrigan wants her, but whatever the reason, I'm sure it's about Shoan. He's always the cause. The Alpha to the Omega, the head honcho and top dog, Lucifer to Michael. Without fail, he's always the problem.

Shoan may seem like a callous jerk, but I'm his sister and I see the truth. You don't have to be Gypsy with a crystal ball to see the writing on the walls. Like fucking anything that walks will erase the pain. It doesn't. It just holds it at bay for a while. It can't correct the past. Honestly, it just makes the sadness and his loneliness more apparent.

I'm a perfect example of that. I have a proclivity for screw and lose the dude. I avoid all strong relationships. Hell, I'm avoiding anything that could be considered a commitment. Even a goldfish is too much. There's not a chance in Hades I'll find my mate anytime soon, and I'm not looking for one. Living life and enjoying the guilty little pleasures without recourse or regret is my piece of heaven.

So here I sit, waiting, hoping this will work out once more. Laying my ass on the line to follow him blindly.

It means shit to bitch about it, I know that. Blood is blood, and he's all I have left. But dammit, if he fucks this up, we'll be in a world of hurt. The peace and quiet, the anonymity of who and what we are will all disappear.

I don't want to give it up yet.

I love this house. I love its spaciousness, the lush gardens, and the view of the Acropolis. It's breathtaking, no matter the time of day, year, or century. I love being here, and if she finds it, I'll kill him myself.

"Hey, daydreamer. You asleep?" Arif taps me on the shoulder as he passes the outdoor rattan couch I'm lounging on.

"No, I was thinking about Shoan. Did you know he's bringing someone with him? A girl. Morrigan stopped them at the airport, and for some fucking reason, she *wanted* her." I shift on the recliner to face him.

Arif is a fine example of a beautiful vampire. His appearance is that of a young thirtysomething. With his short, tight, ebony curly hair greying at the edges, a creamy chocolate tan that stands out against his stark white Tommy Bahamas shirt, and well-formed muscles that make the shirt seem almost tight, he's fucking hot.

His eyes are like any other Dark Worlder; gold with flecks of red. His bright white, massive incisors top off the whole package of dangerously seductive. But he doesn't light my fire. He's more of a George Clooney, and I like them a bit younger. More virile and easily excitable. A stallion, not an old stud.

He knows my internal diatribe can be analytical and off the map, so the quirky smile that I elicit from him is a standard response.

"Morrigan was at the airport? Shit. How long ago did he call you about this?" Arif is carrying paper bags full of food from the square. Setting them down and grabbing a perfectly ripe and juicy apricot, he brushes it against his shorts before biting into it. It sluices down his chin to the crisp shirt, leaving perfect pink trails.

"He got into a confrontation with George and Sully, *again*." It's frustrating as all fuck to not know the one answer.

WHY? Why this girl...why now? Why, why, why?

"That dirty bitch! What I wouldn't do to stake her in the noonday sun." For a vampire to say that about his own kind is nasty, but for Arif to say it, it's evil. "Shoan left me a message earlier about some girl on the plane with him, but he was pretty cryptic. We knew Morrigan was poking about for the key and the book. Maybe she had intel. I wouldn't put it past Harrison and the goon boys to have tracked it down. I mean, we've kept it hidden for decades. How would they have known it to be here? And why now?"

“I think you missed the bigger picture here, Kimosabe. Why is this *chick* important to Morrigan? I mean, if she knows where to go for the book, why the hell would she care about a random fuck of Shoan's?" Reaching into the bags, I pull out a handful of ripe dates. I rub them around like yin yang balls in my hand before popping one into my mouth.

“I think it's more than a coincidence..."

“Really. Ya think?" I say, rolling the pit against the inside of my cheek. “Of course it's more than that. She doesn't do anything half-assed. Morrigan's up to something and this girl...this random girl Shoan meets on a plane is more than he thinks."

“We don't know anything about her. Why don't we pass judgement after she's here, then we'll find out why. Right now, we know nothing, but we should still be cautious until we know more about her." Pouring himself a glass of wine, Arif puts the pit on the table and reaches back into the bag for more. When he's nervous he eats. And eats. Hell, if he wasn't immortalized in this body, he would be a sumo wrestler for the amount he consumes.

"Fine. We don't know about her, and I promise not to pass judgement on her, yet. But you better believe I'm keeping an awfully close eye on her until we know more about her. I mean, he's bringing her here! What the hell is he thinking."

"You know Shoan. His libido answers the call and he lets it lead. No waiting periods for his escapades. I hope he thinks before he tells her anything about us though. And Ni? I want you on your best behavior. Be nice, and let's see what we can find out."

"Fine. I'll be good-ish," I say, holding up two fingers, showing how much I think I will be good in measurement. Let's just say it ain't much. "Here's my question before I go overboard and turn on the *home sweet home* charm. Why again is Morrigan here? Let's say I get the whole, she knew they were on this plane, but it was totally random that Shoan met this girl. So why here, and why now?"

Arif pauses and eyeballs me. "It's here."

I take in his meaning. "What do you mean, *it's* here?"

Rising from the couch to get a bit closer, because I'm not totally sure I heard him right, I ask again. "What *it* are we talking about? If we're talking about ancient ruins and history about greek mythology, then yeah. But if we're talking *it,* as in the book is here, then—"

"Yes, *it* is here. The book has been here for ages. Shoan brought it here for safekeeping."

"Okay, this is news to me." I pace around the garden, thinking about what a stupid fuck my brother is. "I knew Shoan hid it away, but to hide it in one of his favorite haunts is a bit nostalgic, don't ya think?"

I'm actually kind of pissed off that he never told me. Me, his fucking sister. "Why was I excluded from knowing this? I mean, I was there when the last occurrence happened. I fought beside you and him to make sure she didn't get it. Did you think I'd dig it up and curse him further? Or that I'd betray him? Why keep it a secret from me?" Wandering around the glowing fire bowl in the middle of the space between me and him, I'm so stewed, I might just walk across the burning red coals instead of around them to get at Arif.

"Sorry, sweetheart. The less people who knew *its* whereabouts, the better. Plus, he knows your proclivity for destruction and mayhem. Shoan was protecting you and others from your revenge."

"Fuck protecting me! I can handle myself, thank you. When Shoan gets here, you best believe there will be revenge. The book will have shit to do with it too." I poke him in the chest, making him spit fruit juice everywhere.

"Shoan just wanted to keep its location as contained as possible. He knew that if you or I, or anyone else knew where it was, specifically Morrigan, it was the best way to get to one of us. Do you really want to hold Shoan in contempt for trying to stop another run at an apocalypse? If she knows where the key is, and if she can get the book, then Morrigan can unlock the dirtiest warfare of all time. Which I know is okay for someone like you, but for the rest of us it's bad news. Osama and Hitler would look like schoolgirl panty remover pranks in comparison."

His voice calms. "Shoan has his reasons, so let's just wait for him to get here to explain it. After all, Morrigan seems to think she's important enough to fight Shoan in public for."

"I swear to all that is unholy, I will beat the hell out of my brother when he gets here." Shoan is going to get a bullet in the chest when his ass gets through that door.

For close to three decades, he's kept this from me, and I only find out because of a girl being chased by Morrigan! If Shoan wants to see my bad side, he'll get the full-fledged God of war.

I need either a cold shower or a hot body beneath me...and I prefer the latter.

Thiea

I was sorely misled by my travel agent. I'm such an idiot for a nice body, at least when my libido runs the show. Next time, I should at the least listen to the itinerary before hopping on the plane. I'm pretty sure though, it didn't have '*Meet a guy in line. Get drunk on a plane (not such a bad idea until you're hungover). Then deal with more weird shit than what you were trying to avoid in the first place at home.*' Yep, pretty sure it had nothing about a vampire knowing who you are, and will be intercepting you at the airport with thugs.

Now it's down to the final, but crucial part of the itinerary, of which I'm sure wasn't listed, but isn't such a bad package. Meet a fabulously hot, bone chilling sexy guy, and let him stroke your hair as you cry. Which is causing me to reach a boiling over point as his acute erection is hovering just below a thin pair of jeans next to my ear. It's close enough that if I reach up to the waist of his khakis, I'm sure I could stroke the tip.

I punish myself for even thinking it, as dirty thoughts aren't going to help right now. *Thiea, get your shit together.*

Plus, right now, I'm sure I'm beyond sexy, drop-dead stunning. If

I looked in a mirror, I'm sure I'd resemble a Raggedy Ann doll at a four-year-old mascara party.

Taking a deep breath, I wipe away the tears to collect myself before I speak. "Shoan, please tell me what's going on? You obviously know the people that were there. Why do they want me? Never mind that—*how* do they know my name, or know that I was coming here? Hell, *I* didn't know I was coming here. Was there a posting on YouTube or Twitter? Did the travel agent put out an APB on the lost, sexually deprived, redhead in aisle three?" I rattle off questions so fast, he has no chance to answer even one.

I don't think I even want the answers anyway. All I want is to stay in his lap because I feel safe, and right now, safe is what I need. That fantastic pecker peeking out of his beige pants is just gonna have to wait while I get answers.

"Thiea, there's a book and Morrigan wants it. If she gains its power, it can have major repercussions for us all, both humanity and Dark Worlders alike. It's the Holy Grail, the Ark of the Covenant. It's the first Menorah and anything that you would consider the holiest of all cultural myths and truths. She's dangerous, and like most Dark Worlders who've taken from others, she's mad in the head. Centuries of stealing memories has drove her to the brink of insanity. We, myself, and those who side with me are trying to keep her from having that book." Shoan's touch is gentle, yet erotic, as he continues to drag his fingers through my hair. I tell myself to keep my shit together or this isn't going to fare well, but this bloody libido of mine has other thoughts. His erection has me a bit moist, making it even harder to concentrate on anything else.

Dammit!

There's something about Shoan's touch that ignites me, even in the face of creepy, fucked-up people. Funny thing is, even though his body has other things on its mind, he's keeping on track instead of taking me in this darkened limo. Maybe he's chivalrous? Maybe he's gay? Either way, his cock has other ideas and he's avoiding the urges.

With a clearing of his throat, he continues. "Some of the creatures from my world shut out their souls, those with the darkest souls are dead and empty shells. It's a yin and yang when there's too much take and no giving back. The darkness hollows them out." Quietly shifting in the seat so that I have to sit up, he adjusts himself.

Garron told me that others, non vampires were soulless, baby eating, kick a kitten monsters, and for some reason, I feel Garron wasn't telling me the truth, and that scares me. How much does Cassie really know? Have I left a friend to the wolves? Or is she the kind that brings the wolves dinner?

I can't think of that right now. She's the least of my concerns, the *why* I'm here is what's important.

The trip from the airport has been uneventful. Passing along the freeway, zipping in and out of traffic towards the city, the rural town disappears as the houses become closer and closer. Weaving our way through the smaller side streets, it feels like the buildings are closing in on our limo. It's almost as if the homes were built before the roads, like the landscape wasn't taken into consideration.

It's an odd thing to see after living in massive cities where history, and older homes are torn down for progress, therefore giving way to major thoroughfares and infrastructure. The ancient architecture of the once proud city looms above here like a guardian protector. Attacked by the Turks, the Romans—,heck I think everyone attacked it—it still stands the test of time, watching over the people.

The basic white washed stucco facades of the two-story buildings with bright wooden shutters and doors are inviting. Everything is painted in bright emerald greens, sapphire blues, and rosy pink reds. I find it hard to distinguish one from the next. If I was on foot, I'd be lost in the sea of white and pastels with the clean and shiny, almost marble like pavement. This is so surreal. It's like I've walked into a movie with witches, warlocks, vampires, and other creepy things. *Lions and tigers and bears, oh my!* What a story this would make if I ever live to have grandchildren.

After passing what seems like hundreds of the same house, or the same house ten times around the same block, we come to a stop.

"We're here." Shoan kicks me out of my trancelike state by patting my shoulder to interrupt my internal thoughts.

"Sorry, if I seem a bit freaked—"

Taking my face in his hands, he halts my thought as he gazes into my eyes. "I understand this is something massive to take in. Trust me, I have your best interests in mind. I'll make sure no harm comes to you." Waiting for my answer, he looks anxious and afraid.

"Yeah, Shoan, I trust you to look after me. I guess I'll go out on a limb and try for a bit of faith." Opening the door of the limo for us to exit, Shoan smiles deep, sucking me in.

As Auguello grabs our bags, we head for the front gate of a fucking mansion, and my jaw hits the ground. He opens the front gates of the house and proceeds through a massive set of double doors. To say this is a grand entrance would be an understatement. The thick ironwood doors are frosted, etched glass, intricately designed with swans, craning their necks towards two massive bronze turns. Bronze ironwork weaves its way around each swan, cradling them in place. An aura of wealth is exuded. There are lush plants surrounding the yard in little pockets, interspersed within a perfectly manicured, brilliant green lawn. Trees full of apricots, oranges, and dates line the garden walls opposite the house, giving further privacy from the adjacent homes. The house—which I'm not even sure I would call it that—is a two-story with beautiful teal shutters and massive windows conveying an air of opulence.

“So, it’s a house, huh? Summer rental? I thought you would have a one bedroom flat with window baskets and curtains flapping in the wind. This is unbelievable.” I think my jaw is actually resting on the curb as I take in the house.

“I never said it was a summer rental. I rent it out for people to use. It’s friends mostly, tourists sometimes.” As we start up to the house, Shoan looks over at me, smiling, and holds out his hand for me. Before I can take his, a girl about the same age as me bursts out the front door.

"Why not just walk up to the President of the United States and tell him you're Osama!" She charges out the front door like a banshee on the eve of war. I’m assume she’s Shoan’s sister Niamh. Otherwise, I’m hopping back in the limo and asking Augi to take me to the nearest sanitarium.

"You have a lot to explain." With a quick snap, she pops him one in the jaw, one in the shoulder, and rains down numerous smaller shots to his solar-plexus. Turning towards me, sizing me up, I feel miniscule. It's like she can see right through me. As if I’m not there at all.

"Arif has let me in on some details that you've kept from me, *dear brother*. Let me tell you, if you ever do that again, I will skewer you to a pike in the centre of the Plaka."

I like this girl. She's violent. Hopefully, I don't attract that hostility anytime soon, as I already have enough on my plate.

"Niamh, I can explain all of it once we're inside." Shoan yells toward the house, brushing past his sister. "Arif, it wasn't nice to sick the Goddess of Bitch on me without warning!"

Niamh, with a move so fast that if I'd blinked, I'm sure I would have missed it, smacks Shoan in the back of the head, causing him to fall out of step. He carries on as if nothing happened, and the only clue of a win is the smile on her face.

"It was either I tell her, or you did. I figured after the fiasco with the boys you weren't ready for war yet. This way, she had time to think rationally before beating you."

The man behind the dark and enticing voice, like a male 976 number, has silky coffee toned arms, abs and legs, bright eyes, smooth curls tight on his head, and the biggest smile. He turns towards me, genuinely shocked, before he bows his head and smiles. Looking at him, I'd swear we've met before. This will be so awkward if we've hooked up.

"This young individual must be the girl you saved from Morrigan. I am Arif al Hussein, Shoan's oldest and wisest friend." He steps in close and whispers, "No one else wanted the job, of course, so I took a pay cut to accept."

Arif turns to Shoan and tucks him in for a manly hug. If it was me, I would expect broken bones.

"Ah, yeah. That's me, but can someone explain to me what's going on? I think I might hurl if I don't get answers. And some aspirin for my hungover soul."

Arif ruffles Shoan's hair like a big brother would. "Thiea. We'll explain everything, but I suggest that you get sorted in a room. And have a shower. He looks to Shoan and fans his face. "You stink, brother. I'll have the staff prepare a platter too. I'm sure you could use a good meal."

"Terese called. She tells me you called in the boys, and they'll be due to drop in anytime." Niamh glowers at her brother, something akin to a Superman heat ray vision, burrowing into his flesh. "Next time, a heads up to your *only* sister first would be good."

Shoan nods a confirmation to his sister, then turns to me as if I hadn't really been in the room at all, like he's surprised I'm still standing here.

"Come on, Thiea. I'll get you a room." Leading me down a hall near the front door, side-stepping his sister as she attempts another round of blows, I follow behind him. Walking down a hall that makes me feel like I'm in the AGO in Toronto, I'm blown away. It's grand. Actually, spectacular would be a better observation.

The front entrance is two stories, covered with pictures of the Parthenon and the Acropolis lining the interior whitewashed hallways, where old amphorae and pieces of ancient artifacts are displayed on pedestals throughout the space. Taking my hand, Shoan leads me to a solid oak double doorway. And to think, I thought the reno to my little piece of heaven was fabulous; I have now been outdone. *He has a place.* Right, and the Queen has a residence. I'm pretty sure the whole house will be this incredible.

Psyching myself up for the…

Holy hell!

Opening the doors, I'm impressed by the most expensive space I've ever seen. The room has a massive canopy bed, with cream chiffon draping around each pillar, side tables, scones glowing on either side, woven rugs, antique arm chairs, and crystal chandeliers; a pair of them. Welcome to *Million Dollar Rooms*.

Shit, I'm afraid to touch anything now.

"Lifestyles of the rich and famous for two hundred, Alex."

Shoan smiles and ignores my blatant shock. "There's a closet tucked in on the right side. That enters into your private bathroom, and it's stocked with anything you should need. If there's something more that you don't have, just let one of us know. We'll have the staff go get it." Right. Staff. I forgot that little sidebar of lovely.

I. Am. In. Awe.

I walk over to the bed and fall backwards. Sprawling out, I take up the majority of space and release a massive sigh as I pet the bed. Walking past me to the far side of the room, Shoan opens a set of double doors that flow out into the garden. The look in his eyes is distant, and yet appealing—like he's looking past me; through me. I'm an apparition or some specter.

I try to break the awkward silence. "Wow. Shoan, this is amazing. What a place."

He pauses at the garden doors, seemingly uneasy around me all of a sudden. Do I smell that bad? As I try inconspicuously to smell myself, it's clear that…yep! It's airline and alcohol puke.

"I, uh…Thiea. I'll see you after you're refreshed. Don't worry about rushing." Stepping out to the garden, he closes the doors gently behind him, leaving me confused. He goes from warm and inviting, to formal on a hair trigger. I'm sure later I'll have time to figure him out, but my real issues don't happen to be him. It's Morrigan.

Laying back, enjoying the sweet smelling Egyptian cotton sheets, I twirl them in my fingers and quickly realize I'm totally bagged. If I don't lift my ass off this bed I'll crash, then nothing will get figured out.

Gathering a few pieces of clothing from my luggage, I walk through the closet, passing racks and racks of new clothing, shoes, and dresses. I'm not sure who's room I'm in, but they have nice taste. Checking the tags that are still attached, my inquisitive side hits. Size four and six with seven shoes. She's petite, that's for sure.

Before I start pulling things off the rack, like a Neiman Marcus sale, I pass through to the bathroom.

Holy Hanna! If I don't have a Presidential suite at the Ritz awaiting my knackered body, I'll be so sad. If I thought the bed was fantastic, then I was totally selling this room short. I've never seen something so amazing.

The shower jets protrude from all sides, as well as above. Two oversized rain heads take up the shower stall the size of ceiling fans. The tumbled stone double sinks and oversized taps have a mirror coursing the whole wall; floor to ceiling.

So how did I get here?

Dreamlike guy, nasty vampires, opulent homes, limousines, and bathrooms big enough for a whole football team? What dream have I walked into?

Shoan

I'm a mess!

Every voice and internal noise is increasing. I have no way to control it unless I hold her hand.

Great, but that means never letting her go, and that's not an option. I need distance from her or I'll bend her over, fucking her six ways to Sunday.

Then there's that dam internal conversation she had with herself in the limo. It keeps playing back like an awful earworm. All her thoughts and worries were spilling out like a teletype system into my mind.

How am I supposed to handle the whole day like this?

I wanted her to gauge my intentions, and that I intended her no harm. Well, Shoan, you got your wish. Dumbass. You got *way* more than you asked for.

I don't know how this girl changed anything, and I don't think I *want* to know. All I want is to return to my life of debauchery. At least there I knew where I stood.

After leading her to her room I sniffed my shirt. Arif's right, I stink like an airline and barf. The shower is warm and inviting, and as I let it rinse down my face in rivulets, I replay the events of today.

Why does Morrigan want her? And how did she even find out about her?

This trip was so easy. Keep the book out of the hands of the whore and her children, get home and relax. Now I have to explain to Niamh things I'd hoped were long buried. I have to keep Thiea safe but out of my reach, and somehow keep my mind intact while doing so.

Goddess, what a bloody fucking mess.

Grabbing the soap, I find myself getting aroused thinking of being near her. Holding her, rubbing the soft parts of her long slender legs and her milky white thighs that flow down to that tight perfect ass. I know she was aroused by me from the way those perky tight little tits aimed skyward whenever we were close. I imagine taking each into my mouth, rolling the pearly little nipples until they jut to the stars in anticipation.

Standing here, I decide to stroke myself, hoping it'll make my head clearer and get the urgency to bed her out of my system. Moving languidly and with precision, I stroke my cock in hard, deep throws. Back and forth, back and forth, until all I picture is her hair wrapped in my fingers. Pulling her until that back is arching, pushing her ass into my cock where I seat it tightly in her drenched pussy. I imagine her screaming my name, feeling her squeezing and contracting around my cock as it tightens and pushes towards my release.

I want all of her, and thinking of her isn't the problem. I can't fucking *stop* thinking about her. Trying to shut her out will be the real problem because I can't be with her. Hell, I don't know what being with her would do if only a touch caused me to hear things again. She was able to quiet things just as quickly.

If...if! Shit, *if* sucks. I'll just have to find numerous distractions elsewhere in town.

I can't let myself fall for her in any way. Even a slight touch could be too much.

She may be wanted by Morrigan, but that doesn't mean she's the key to my release.

After the quick shower and dissatisfying strokes, I dress and hope to have a few minutes alone to think. I always find the garden a great place to think through problems. Down the hall and into the garden, I find Arif waiting for me with two glasses and a tall pitcher of ice. I recognize the dark chocolate color immediately. It's one of the things I miss about Greece the most; Turkish coffee on ice.

"So what's new?" Arif drawls out, being sly. He knows being me is difficult. Having a willing body so close to me is excruciating. He knows I wish to pull her under me and take her orgasm in stride. Place on top of that, keeping a secret from Niamh for the past couple decades—one that I will have to explain now when it is the least opportune time—is fucking deadly.

"What a mess." Taking a glass off the table, I fill it to the brim. "Something has awakened me, my friend. I could hear her." I take a sip of my coffee, feeling it seep into every recess and crevice perfectly. Setting it on the table, I prop my feet up on the ottoman as I lay back on the soft cushions, glorying in the comfort after the awkward plane chairs.

“Believe me, I get that Morrigan could have been there for me, but for some insignificant human dormant? That I don’t get. Then top it off with a whack to the skull, a fight in public, and damaging Aug’s car?” What a predicament. Why her? Why this plain girl? I hope Arif can make heads or tails of everything because I can't. I’m just not sure of anything right now.

"Tell me the story from the beginning. Tell me what Thiea told you, and what you've had happen since meeting her. Then I might be able to understand it better."

Arif lays on the couch with his feet dangling off the end as he grabs a few fresh dates. Popping them in his mouth, he listens while I tell him everything. I tell him what she told me about herself, about Garron the vampire, about touching her and the shock, the warm wave that came over me, and how I feel now.

By the time I’m done, I’ve finished my coffee, ate a few fresh dates, some strawberries and tangerines, hoping it would all slow the churning in my stomach. Even removed from her I can feel her, I can sense her. I hear her thoughts as she tries to decipher the confusion she’s feeling. I want to be near her. I want to lead her away from all of this pain and grief. Maybe a place like Bora Bora or the Cook Islands would be good? Somewhere secluded, with a small population would be perfect, not to mention the lovely weather and hot sex on a beach.

Fuck that. I can’t think like that. I'm Thiea’s death wish. I’ve pulled her into a brutal immortal war, unintentionally, but she’s a part of it now, even if she doesn’t want it. Maybe I should just jump ahead to the easy part and let Niamh kick my ass.

"Do you know what she is? I mean, do you feel her power?” he asks so matter of fact, like we’re talking about what we’d like for dinner.

Thinking on it for a moment, I try to feel her out, reaching, stretching into the building and the immortals within it. I don't.

"Huh, interesting. You can hear thoughts again but no other gifts. Well, I'll tell you this. I can't give you what she is capable of, but she is special. Something tells me she'll be a linchpin to your resurrection."

"Great. Here I thought if I avoided her and tried to go back to the way it was I could keep her from this. Now you tell me there's no way to do that at all? Fucking sunshine and roses aren't you, Ari."

"I think you know what she is. I think you know she's important for getting you back..." Arif pauses, and looks me straight in the eyes with a smile on his lips. "You're afraid, aren't you? You're afraid you'll never be your old self. You enjoy this debauchery and carelessness, don't you? You don't want to *feel*?"

"Arif, I can't think like that. It's been centuries, almost a millennium since I was that person. I don't know if I can be who I was anymore. No more than you could be human again."

"Yeah, but I am who I'm supposed to be. You, on the other hand, are a caged lion, fearing the other side when the door is opened for your freedom. You have to try."

Sitting dumbfounded, and at a loss for a moment, I wonder. What if she is my redemption? What if she can change the course and put this broken puzzle back together?

"Have you told her the truth of what will happen to you both?"

"No, I haven't told her a thing. Arif, she's oblivious. Well, not really, as she has met Morrigan. She only knows a fraction of what our world can be. Some guy named Garron scared her enough to hop a plane to parts unknown. How well do you think she'd take knowing it all?"

"What are you intending on telling her?"

"Honestly, I’m hoping I can avoid her. It’s not like she can be the *one*. After all this time, it’s odd that an insignificant dormant could unlock my curse.”

“Shoan. Dormant or not, she seems to have awakened something. She’s living proof that even a dormant soul can awaken you.”

“Yeah, but I've had centuries to deal with my outcome. I'm not sure I can protect her. Worst part is, I don't know if I can run from her either. I’m drawn to her in more ways than I can put to words."

"I think she has a right to know what she's gotten into." Arif is right, in more ways than I care to admit. I have to tell them; all of them. Niamh will be furious, but I hope she can forgive me. She’s not known for her forgiveness.

“I don’t think you have a choice. She’s stronger than you give her credit for. Just because she’s a mortal or even a dormant Dark Worlder, doesn’t mean she’s weak.”

"I appreciate your advice, even if I think you’re enjoying this way too much, old friend."

I know there's no better time than the present to follow the path the Goddess is laying down for me.

Even if it leads to a shallow grave.

Chapter NINE

The Stories We Share

Shoan

Telling Niamh the truth about this whole predicament is the only thing in this world that scares the living fuck out of me. Firstly, she knows the binding was to stop me from returning home, but there's so much more that I've kept from her. The outcome of the next few days will either assist us in this war or seal my fate.

That's the whole thing about this David and Goliath fight we've had for almost a millennium; our battle has been mainly one-sided. My binding makes me helpless, whereas Morrigan is without remorse or compassion, and at the peak of her power. I have the book, but it doesn't make me invincible, or even stronger than any of the other Dark Worlders that are at full strength. That's why I need all hands on deck. I can't do this alone.

Thiea, though, is the wild card.

It's no coincidence that Morrigan is here in Athens now. She's here for one thing and one thing only. A powerful being like her in her prime will do heinous damage with the book in her hands. Thiea will be caught in the crossfire, or she'll be the catalyst.

What Arif said about unlocking my cage and letting out the lion, he hit that nail right on the head. I am fearful to step out. I'm deathly afraid of what can happen and what she's adjusting in me.

Crossing the garden, I watch Thiea. She glides with the grace of a queen, with her hair streaming down around her shoulders in cascades of blonde and crimson. Like a perfect cut ruby, it curls around her ears to frame her freckles, like one of Picasso's sketched masterpieces. She seems almost ethereal.

Those steel grey-green eyes unman me.

Turning away, I look to my sister. Niamh is still steaming mad at me, and it's written on her face. My sister has always been able to read my thoughts. Entering the back garden, boring into my skull with laser precision, she's reading every lurid thought that I possess. Suddenly, I feel naked and exposed.

The look on her face says it all, but it's her internal diatribe that shocks me. I hear her clearly. She and I know this is something epic. We haven't been able to for as long as I can remember.

Shoan, you know this is crazy, right? Are you sure Morrigan didn't orchestrate this? I mean, really! By chance, you meet a girl on a plane that just happens to be a strong enough dormant to undo a millennial curse that you're whoring ways couldn't touch. And to boot, you haven't told her a thing. Why may I ask?

I try to convey my thoughts coherently, which after centuries is nonetheless punishing. What could I tell Niamh? What would make sense to her this early on? I'll have to start from the beginning, and I might as well do it with everyone here.

"Wait until everyone else is here, Ni. For now, be patient," I tell her verbally.

Arif had called on Anna, his wife, earlier to join us. She walks through the kitchen and out to the garden, looking as radiant as ever. Kissing her lightly on the forehead, he brushes away a stray strand of hair, then takes her hand in his. They enter the garden with grace and poise. I envy it, but at the same time, I fear that closeness to someone.

Arif is right. Is it a coincidence that we met here at this point in time? More and more, I think not.

This will be a difficult conversation. Clearing my head, I prepare for the onslaught. Before I start, Anna addresses Thiea directly.

"Athena. It is good to see you." She sits down in a plush divan across from Arif, facing Thiea. Her face conveys what she feels. She's fully gobsmacked. I'm fully surprised too.

How does Anna know her?

"I'm sorry…I thought you were in the Bronx? I just talked to you yesterday, and you knew nothing!" Thiea steps away, yelling at Anna. I feel the pang of betrayal as it courses through her, heating her veins, increasing her heart rate.

How is this possible? I meet a guy on a plane and run into Jaz in his garden! Thiea thinks to herself. But who is it she thinks Anna is?

"Thiea, there is more at stake than you knowing about me and why I kept it from you. Please, listen to what Shoan has to say, and I will explain it all after."

Tears cascade down Thiea's cheeks, and I realize there is more than just my secrets in our little group. She wipes the dampness away with the back of her hand, staring daggers at Anna.

"Fine." she says harshly. "I came here on a whim after meeting a vampire, so I guess I can listen." Pacing back and forth in our tiny space, careful not to come too close to Anna, she says, "No. Fuck that. This is bullshit, Jaz. So far, Shoan is the only one who's told me the truth!" Glaring daggers at Jaz, she rounds the benches surrounding the fire pit, then takes a seat opposite me. "You and I will have it out." If you've never seen a more contemptuous face, the look on hers framed it like a textbook.

Cutting the tension with a knife, the doorbell rings. We all turn in the direction of the doorway, as my four massive guests enter with a petite, vivacious black beauty leading the way. Joining our unhappy group, the dealers are all together minus one, but that can't be helped.

"Hey, boys. We ready to get this started?" Patrick rubs his face against the back of his naked hand. Actually, *he's* totally naked.

"Pat, why aren't you and the boys wearing clothes?" I ask.

"Yeah, well, we made a bet with Jake at the pub. You were needin' us and we were in the air anyway. We just detoured on the wind, as it were."

Well that's a sight for sore eyes. I haven't been on many vacations, but I think this one hits the top 100 places to see. I came looking for a few good men and I found a Few. Good. Men.

Thiea can't seem to peel her eyes away from each of the scantily clad warriors. My jealousy and immediate reaction to protect her takes a front seat to the conversation. Thiea is *mine,* and I don't know why I feel so intensely jealous. I never have before. This is new.

"Terese, you poor, dear soul," Anna says as Arif attempts to hide her grinning face.

"Boys, go get dressed and stop showing off your ass-ets." Arif says breathlessly as he wrestles with Anna, who by the way, is swinging dollar bills in the air.

As my four large, yet very daft friends vacate the garden with their inhuman bits swaying in the wind, all attention is back to the reason for this meeting.

Terese pulls up a chair beside the fire bowl, curling in for comfort, quietly.

"Never a dull moment." Placing her cash back in her pockets, Anna turns back towards me. "Shoan, if you wouldn't mind."

"Okay. First, I need to apologize. Niamh, there are things I've kept from you over the years, and I did it purely for your safety and sanity. Arif knew, but only because he figured it out on his own." I kick off my shoes and pull my legs up. I sit cross legged in the chair, rolling a pair of dates in my hand.

I turn to Thiea. "A lot of this will seem fantastical, so just give me time to tell it, then you can ask questions." She nods, so I continue. "There's a book about our kind, aptly called the Book of the Dead. It holds spells and incantations of power from various mages and Gods. From that, all vampires, demigods, demon beasts, were's and shifters were created. Different Gods tried their hands at creation over their lifetimes. One such creation was me. I am what's called a Chimeric. I am the judge and jury of the immortal world, or Dark Worlders. Their fate is decided by their actions, but I hold them accountable. They, in essence, cause their own mortality or immortality." Based on the stunned looks I pause, allowing for everyone to absorb the news.

"Morrigan cursed me when it was her time to be called forward. That was almost a millennium ago. It was also when I was banished from Ireland. For years, those who should be in purgatory have been running loose on the world, without remorse or penalties. The curse bound me and my powers. To regain them, I need to return to

Ireland. Anna tried once to remove the curse, but Morrigan vowed to harm her daughter if she ever tried again."

After Anna arrived, I'd heard her thoughts. I know the truth now —Thiea is her daughter. This just makes things even more complicated and confusing.

Pouring myself a glass of ice cold coffee, I await the barrage of questions I know aren't far away.

"So why is it you couldn't remove this curse?" Thiea asks this more as a statement to Anna.

"I wanted you to enjoy a normal human life, free from all of us."

"The way the curse was written, it was very specific. Only one can remove it. *'There will be a Goddess born; they will powerful, and they will balance the scales.'* You see, the original witch that wrote the curse was my father's first wife...well, the man that I treated as my father. Morrigan knew she was in my sights, so she asked for a way to arrange my downfall. Giza was smarter than Morrigan, devising a spell that was able to bind me, but not kill me, which just pissed Morrigan off further."

"She's not only a very ancient and strong vampire, she threatened to harm Giza's daughter and any that came after. Anna is a descendant of hers, and you in turn." I pause, allowing it to be absorbed. Also, I'm afraid to venture into this next part. Yes, I'm afraid of my sister. Who wouldn't be?

"Spill it, Shoan. Now." The seething danger pulses off my sister's aura. I can feel her vengeance looming, and so can the rest of them.

"Once I was bound, I had no way to fight against her. I knew that if I left Ireland, I could save my family pain and anguish. At the time, I didn't know what you were, Ni. I thought you were a shifter. I thought you could be harmed, just like any other young Dark Worlder, not yet set into their immortality. So I left."

“Ok, so if you’re not like them, what are you?" Thiea asks. At least she's speaking to me.

"I was created and designed after the God Ammut, the Egyptian God of the Afterlife. It's not the prettiest thing to look at. I always preferred the form of a man, even back then, as it’s more appealing and easier to control. To regain my powers, I have to solve the riddle that Giza created during the spell. I know that I have to return to Ireland. After Anna attempts a few well-placed spells, I should be back in business, condemning the condemned."

"So yer tellin’ me you’ve never met yer soulmate?” Chad pipes up as he and the rest of the dealers re-enter the garden. “I get Niamh hasn’t. She avoids it like it’s a fire sale at Goodwill. But for all the dallying you do, I really figured you would have."

Grabbing the ends of one of my favorite marble benches, Pat and Chad plop it down just outside the circle, chipping edges off the corners.

"You’re a bit easier on the eyes now, boys," Arif states as he hands Chad a glass of iced coffee.

“I don’t believe in fates and soulmates. Sorry, I lost all interest in fate after my family was stripped from me.” Thiea says quietly, but her comment is harsh. She’s been hurt. She’s damaged in her assessment of life and love, just like me.

Funny.

"It’s not like the person is just wandering around with a sign, *‘waiting on Mr. Johnson’* like it does when you arrive at an airport. It's someone you have to meet. It could take centuries. Arif found his love in Anna, but he’s been alive since 4000 BC for Goddess’ sake.

Many never do. For some reason, the Fates created mates for each of us, but we don't know when it will be. I know it sounds crazy to someone like you, Thiea, but this is our reality."

And here comes the onslaught of questions.

"Okay, so what are your powers? Do you have claws like Wolverine, or a smart mouth like Deadpool?" Twirling the tiny amber necklace around her fingers. Pulling on each bead, they act almost like a balm for her. *I thought Garron's...I'm a vampire, and Shoan's 'I'm immortal' is a kick in the pants. Damn, this day just gets better and better.*

"Well, one I have back already. I can hear the thoughts of others, and hopefully soon, I'll hear Dark Worlders too. When we were in the airport and I wasn't feeling well, it wasn't from the food. I couldn't handle all the minds jockeying for supremacy. Other components, I know I won't gain back until I have the curse fully removed. It's hard magik. Not just anyone can undo the curse of someone like Giza. She was a master of light and dark. Not many are born of both."

Fine. If you're listening, I'll ask my questions soon enough. You'd better have a really compelling argument for me. Nod if you hear me, Thiea says in her head.

I still don't think this is the right thing for her, but I have to trust in the feelings I can't control. The pull I feel is colossal. If I'm going to keep her away from Morrigan, I have to prove that I deserve the trust.

"So where's this book? I mean, Morrigan must think it's in Greece. Otherwise, why would she be here?" Leaning over top of the chair, Chad looks down the open button shirt of Ni's. The two of them have had an *on again off again, screw you, screw me* relationship that I haven't quite understood. I know it's mostly 'off' because of Chad, but he's loyal to a fault. I think if the curse wasn't such a burden on the species, he and Niamh would have joined in the old ways centuries ago. She enjoys his company and he accepts her quirks.

"I hid the book here. After the last time Morrigan had it, I've been a bit cautious. There's no way I'm allowing a repeat of Hiroshima. Her and those who sided with her were like a plague of locusts, devouring everything."

"Wait. You're telling me that Hiroshima wasn't a nuclear air strike?" Thiea interjects with the most quizzical look. It's her whole world changing in a twenty-four-hour span. This is where she may just overload and run screaming out the front door. I hope that she keeps an open mind.

"No, Hiroshima was an air strike, and yes, thousands died in that blast. But it's not the full story. It was decided by those in power from the human world to work in conjunction with the allied Dark Worlders to stop the spread of her diseased clan. Morrigan was creating and killing, at will, anything that got in her way. We beat her back, but not without major casualties on both sides. We'd assumed she'd died. No one had heard a peep about her in almost thirty years."

Arif sits quietly in the massive armchair, listening to everyone's thoughts; specifically, my sisters. When she's quiet, dead quiet, hell has frozen over. I know our betrayal of her won't pass away lightly. I will pay, as will Arif.

Thiea's thoughts run wild with questions about her mother, her father, Jaz/Anna, and how Arif falls into all this. Was it a coincidence that we met, or was it a stroke of pure luck? We've lived so close and never knew of each other.

The scariest part of telling the truth is not knowing the outcome of freewill.

The first to rise off of the couch is Thiea. Brushing down the wrinkles in her outfit, she turns to me. “Okay. I think I’ve had enough Dr. Phil for one day. I feel like I’m cramming for a history quiz. I've listened and I need a walk, maybe even some therapy.” She twists her necklace. “Shoan, you offered shopping, and that's my type of therapy. I’m sure my credit card may never be the same after the fallout of this epiphany, but I need out of here."

"Yeah, sure. It’s my treat, though. We wouldn’t want the credit card company to feel you need an intervention." Right now, I feel like someone opened a can of popup snakes. I’m doing my best to get them back in before something bites me in the ass. I know it’s expected, and Niamh is leading the lineup.

Looking to my sister, she’s still deep in her own world. Niamh’s the best at blocking us; her shield is firmly in place.

"I had your best interests at heart," I tell her, hoping she grasps my regret.

"Shoan, I think I’m gonna go out for a while too. I need to think clearly without worrying about being prodded mentally. I'll talk to you later. K?" Rising up, Ni turns to Chad, the boys, and Terese. With winks exchanged, smirks fly across each face.

Slowly, each rise from their chairs. "Who's up for a bit of a chase?"

"Yeah. I’m drivin’," Terese says as she slips between the mountainous Berserkers, slapping them on the back.

"I’ll be topside,” Patrick says with a devilish grin. Without facial expressions, the rest of the boys exit the garden in their own wordless way.

"Anna and I are going to go out too. Call if you need us, kid?"

Arif knows that Niamh not talking to me or him is dangerous. She is fiercely loyal, but also deadly when crossed. She'll need room to deal with this betrayal.

"Well, you know how to clear a room. Remind me to take you to my next convention or awkward moment," Thiea remarks with a smirk.

Taking her hand in mine, the world instantly goes quiet. And as we leave the villa, walking out into the city to enjoy Athens for all it's worth, I revel in the newfound solace. It may be short-lived, but I'll accept it for now.

Chapter TEN

Um Num Num

Thiea

Everyone left the house as if it were on fire. Well, in Patrick's case, you'd think it was. He'd stripped so fast heading for the front door with Niamh and her friends in tow, I was left standing in disbelief at the insanity of this whole day. Naked men, immortals, and dangerously drunken moments. Whoa, what a day.

Turning to Shoan, I take in the minute details of him. I still wonder how the fuck Fates had this preordained?

Was I born to meet him?

Had I been walking through my life, as if it were engineered by a God with puppet strings?

Why did my parents desert me at an orphanage?

Why did Jaz/Anna—whatever her fucking name is—not tell me the truth? I guess I don't really care. Well I do, but that's beside the point. Everything else is more important right now.

This impromptu trip is slipping closely to a twilight zone moment, becoming weirder and weirder with every passing second. Shoan is an ancient God that decides the fate of immortals. Jaz is here and in love. Oh, and Vampires *are* real.

I thought Marlena from Days of our Lives had issues. This is a storyline that would keep the writer's increasing their pen supplies for centuries. With everything I know now, why can't dragons and unicorns be real too?

As we walk along, Shoan's whole body tenses, just like he did when he showed me to my room. Is he afraid I'll hate him for involving me in this? It wasn't of my choosing, and honestly, it wasn't his either. It's not like he actively tried to source me out. He didn't stalk me and leave bizarre voicemails on my cell. He hasn't done one wrong thing in this whole situation, if you ask me. He's more of an anchor in the storm. I feel that if I let go of him, I'll float away. I don't think I could do that right now. I'm positive I need the security of his presence.

"Are you ready to go? There's so many things to see," he says, pointing to the west side of the street.

"Sure." However this plays out, I hope to get shoes, the full story, and some romping great sex. I look at everything while we walk along, taking it all in. Im in awe. At home, the roads are wide enough to fit two Hummers, but here, you'd be lucky to fit a pair of Smart cars side by side. When we landed, everything went by in a split second. I didn't get a chance to look around or take in the country I'd landed in. It's warm and inviting without a cloud in the sky. The air is sweet, not stifling like Toronto's smog, and people walk everywhere. Which I totally get. Finding a parking space would be the cat's ass lucky.

The stores in the older section are small, even by Bloor Street standards. There's no more than a hundred square feet in each, all packed tightly to showcase goods for tourists. Stores with Ouzo of all sizes, side by side with magnets, trinkets of old artifacts are tucked in with jewelry stores of gold and silver. Leather shops with sandals, bags, purses and belts. Religious stores with every kind of worry beads, blessed bracelets, and crosses for holy pilgrimages.

"Shoan, this is so surreal, don't you think? I mean, really. I go out for my birthday, joking that I want to find *Mr.Right Now*. I get in a fight, have a weird convo with Garron, meet you in Toronto before boarding, then get chased out of an airport to find Jasmine here with you. It's hard to swallow."

"I don't believe this either. It's all so weird to think it's pre-arranged. I had years to expect it, but never thought I'd ever hear voices again. Now that I do, it's so strong, I can't survive without you close."

Wandering along hand in hand, I find myself eyeing Shoan from top to bottom. Fuck, he *is* good looking. When we were in the airport and on the plane, even in the car, I took notice. I saw how good looking he was. Now though, I'm seeing him in a different light.

His long slender six foot four or so body that houses a full barrel chest, strong, well-framed arms that could scare the hell out of most men I know, is sexy. His golden hued eyes are unlike anything I've ever seen. Actually, they remind me of an eagle's eyes. And the corn husk blond hair that's floppy, yet trimmed, is gorgeous. Shoan gets top marks on all my tabs for the perfect man. I could sex that body for hours. Hell, days on end.

Reminded of my predicament when he squeezes my hand, I laugh. I'd forgotten that he could hear my thoughts.

"Here, have a seat. You need the full experience of Athens." Passing an open market cafe, Shoan pulls out a chair for me, then takes the seat nearest. After ordering sweet cakes and coffee from the waitress, he swivels his body until we're mere inches apart. "This is hard, you know."

My mind wanders at that thought, and I find my eyes wandering south to his pants.

Snapping his fingers a few times, he smiles. "Up here, Thiea."

Giggling like a schoolgirl, I look up into his eyes. "I'm sorry. My mind has a dirty switch that's sometimes hard to turn off. You should have seen me booking my trip." I think back on the travel agent and the adventurous moment I had in the bathroom.

Shoan shifts in his chair and picks up his coffee, trying to avoid my dirty thoughts. For fun, I decide to crank it up.

Grabbing my drink, I lean back in the chair, remembering what it felt like to feel the wetness as it built. The rise in my own excitement when I thought of being caught fingering myself in a public washroom. The danger of thinking I was within earshot of the cute guy, as I envisioned him tonguing my clit.

Spluttering his coffee onto the table, Shoan picks up his napkin and dabs the corners of his delectable lips. I could reach out and kiss him, but I decide to let him make the first move. Well, the first physical move.

"Thiea, I only met you a yesterday, and I didn't expect anything more than casual quick sex. If someone told me that I'd find myself pulled towards you in a mental, not physical way, I'd tell them they were full of shit. I don't want you to feel obliged to stay with us, but I don't know that I can let you go either." Reaching across the table, he takes my hand in his. "Every time I touch you, it gives me a sense of peace."

"I told you how I can hear the voices of others, but it's more than that. It's their innermost thoughts…the thoughts they hold back that they're afraid to say aloud. It's quite overwhelming. When we were in the airport with so many unsaid words milling around aimlessly, it was hard to handle. That was until I touched your hand. You soothe the babble. The funniest thing is that I haven't had this happen for centuries and I wished for it; I craved it. I'd hoped that I could one day be whole again."

Pulling at his shirt, he smacks his head with the pad of his hand, "But this? To have it turn on so abruptly is like a deaf person with implants. It's excruciating and exhausting."

Thinking about what he said, what he feels, and how this affects him, I get it. I still don't get what it means to me, though. Will he just leave me once he's been fixed of this?

He hears me. "No. Nothing like that. I wouldn't just dump you like trash on the side of the road. Thiea, I don't know if you can understand how long this struggle has been for me. You're only in your twenties. I've *been* in my twenties for so long, and my life hasn't been sunshine and fucking rainbows. The worst part of the curse is something you won't see as being hard, but it is." He rakes his hands through his hair, rubbing them down his face before straightening back to his full glorious height in the chair. "The worst is I hear the voices of the past, those I've condemned. The only way to block them out and keep them at bay is sex. Lots of it. If all you want is a casual fuck, trust me, I'm the *king*."

I swear my eyes widen at that thought. Only casual sex for centuries? No relationships? Wow. Where can I sign up?

He laughs. "It's not as great as it sounds, darlin'. Without it, my head is like a bag of mushy crackers. I can't concentrate. I can't be in the company of others, and it's like the most colossal migraine you've ever had.

"I'm so sorry to bring you into this world, but apparently, Morrigan has devious plans that somehow affect you, as well as those of us who fight to eradicate the world of her blight. Even if you and I can't deal with each other's company, there's not a chance I'm leaving you to fend for yourself with Morrigan on the loose. So no. This isn't a bag 'em and tag 'em situation."

It's hard to concentrate with him stroking featherlight touches across my hand while we sit in platonic silence. I find myself staring down at my cup of joe, swirling the deep amber liquid in an effort to avert his molten gaze that's drawing me in. If I look into those eyes, I'll be a puddle of oozing wantonness.

"Come with me. I need to show you something." Shoan leads me away from the cafe and my delectable coffee. Leaving it behind, he takes me out of the modern areas to the older section of Athens.

Weaving past the stores through the milling crowds of tourists, we make our way around street vendors towards a cordoned off area of stone and ruin. I want him more than I can consider smart, and it's taking a great deal of control to hold back. I want to strip him naked while we walk.

"Stop that," he jokes, palming my neck. "Thiea, I want to show you something important. You need to know this."

"Fine. I'll be good for a bit. But I don't promise to be good for *good*."

"I'll accept that. Here. this is what I want to show you. This is the Temple of the Four Winds, and over there are the Roman baths. This was a place of meeting that teemed with politicians, deal makers and breakers, influential members of society, and various Dark Worlders like myself." Walking around the scattered history, he caresses a rock here and a stone there, like he has an intimate knowledge of all of them; as if he placed them there himself, one by one.

Walking away from me, taking his touch with him, I watch as he strolls. “I’ve been alive for centuries, watching as people leave or die. Friends and family are your strength, but if they die, there’s nothing left to live for. I’m lucky I have Ni and the boys, but when I was first condemned to this curse I had no one. I was completely alone.

“That’s when I met a mortal that accepted me for who and *what* I am. Even I failed him. This stone—this temple, I’ve helped to build and rebuild it after each of the wars. I made him a vow I would watch over his family for eternity. This is where they lie.” He strokes a particular set of stones built into the wall. “I’ve never told anyone that.”

“If they were mortal like me, how could you hold yourself responsible for their deaths?” Gazing into his face, I see the pain and regret that he’s held on tight to, like a security blanket. I've always wanted someone I’d consider a true love -- sacrifice and redemption, pain and hatred, compassion and passion; I bet he has it in spades. But he’s also mentioned he’s a type A manwhore, so I doubt that is any part of his agenda for me and him.

"I couldn't bear the thought of losing my only friend in the world, so I gave up a part of myself to extend his life. I made him immortal. It was the biggest mistake I’d ever made. He turned bitter towards me because I helped him and not his dying family. I’ve held that pain for centuries, never telling anyone. So why do I tell you? Why haven’t I told my sister or Arif? I guess because I know they’ll judge me in my failure, but I feel you won’t." Shoan lifts his shirt, and oh my God, he looks scrumptious. Perfect marble cut abs that showcase his pert pecs, and smooth skin that I’m trying really hard not to touch. In my mind, I’m slowly petting his silken skin and envisioning his godlike body with a slight path of hair, that I expect disappears into *Candyland.*

I could scream and cream at the same time.

It takes all my willpower not to reach out and unbutton his jeans.

Ogling higher up his chest, which I might add takes quite a great deal of effort, I see what he wants to show me. There's a dangerous and gorgeous tattoo of wings. One black and one white, they're surrounded by an angry purple, crimson, and poorly stitched scar. It courses right above his heart in the pattern of a warped and crooked star.

"A piece of me had to be cut out to save him. I didn't think then what it would mean to both of us or to either of our lives. In the end, though, I still lost him, and it pains me every day." Working against my better judgement, I reach out and touch the scar. Running my finger softly along it's jagged red edge, I feel the heat of it. It's like it has a life of its own. It's taken a life of its own—his.

Shoan's crystalized amber eyes see right past me, through to my soul. Pulling me apart as I caress him with my eyes and fingers, he takes me into his arms and kisses my forehead, gently and tentatively. I could see myself falling for him.

Life in an orphanage doesn't cultivate love and inclusion. Even my foster parents, my adoptive parents, and my sister have never known the real extent of my respect and care that I have for them. That's born more of a respectful obligation, not a necessity nurtured with adoration and affection. I may not have had dreams of Tinker-bell rescuing me, yanking me to Never Neverland, but I never ex-pected to possibly find something so pure and light.

Okay, check yourself, Thiea. Put on your big girl panties (like I wear any) and stop the dream sequence playing in your mind. There'll be no marrying a Cullen and driving a Maybach to the grocery store from your castle on the loch. This is reality, and there's a sexy hunk of sweet ass here with you and you're daydreaming.

Bad form.

Okay, it's like this. No light kisses for this dirty little number. I want passion. Dirty cocks, multiple orgasms, and any or all devilish things you've learned over the years that could sway my screams. That's what I'm asking you to bring forth.

The heat of my body rises in anticipation, responding as it should. I don't want to come off easy or desperate, but my body is like a nymphomaniac in a room full of naked supermodels. My needs are like a volcano. I. Am. Ready. To. BLOW!

The slightest touch and I'll go all Krakatoa on his ass.

"I can't do this here. You deserve better than a quick fuck in the middle of the Greek ruins."

Burn.

Oh, the hell you can't! He pulls away from me. His smile is playful, yet serious as he directs us out of the ruins.

"I'm not what you think, Thiea," Shoan laughs deeply. "I'm not pushing you away because I *don't* want you. I'm just not wanting it in public. At least not this time." Stopping abruptly, he pulls me in for searing kiss, his hot body tight against mine. With each delving move his tongue makes, his hands roam along my backside, down my ass, pulling me so close I feel his erection prodding me in the most delicious way.

Breaking the kiss and removing his exquisite heat with him, I pout. Fat lip out on bottom and all. "No pouting. I'll show you what happens to spoiled girls."

"Please," I chime in quickly.

His deep throaty guffaw can be felt through his hand to mine. "Come on, let's go back to the villa."

Okay.

Within moments we arrive at the villa, looking like two school kids. Kicking off our shoes as gracefully as possible, while continuing to kiss, I grasp at the corners of his shirt and raise it up and over his head. As we careen into the walls, knocking down pictures as we go, Shoan lets out a suppressed laugh as he pulls my shirt loose. I watch as buttons buzz down the hallway like confetti at a wedding.

"Uh, hi." Shit, that wasn't Shoan or I. We have company.

"Hi, Arif. Back so soon?" As the chandelier illuminates the fact that my shirt is wide open, Shoan doesn't even turn around as he smooths down the material, trying to cover my body so Arif can't see how exposed I am and he laughs. Go figure. Not even forty-eight hours have passed since I was naked in public. I think I'm in for a life of debauchery if I keep up at this pace.

"Yeah, we had a light dinner."

Arif doesn't come any closer as he stands partially in the waning light of day. I'm assuming he can read our thoughts and see where this night was headed.

Like a ripped shirt isn't a clue, stupid?

Arif laughs under his breath. "Sorry for interrupting. I see there were other things on your mind." Arif pats Shoan on the shoulder as he walks down the hall, away from us.

Brushing my hands along his hardened abs, I decide I'm taking what I want. Fuck anyone who thinks to get in my way. Garnering all the pent-up frustration I have left, I grab hold of Shoan's belt buckle as I whisper in his ear. "I may not be able to read minds, but I know where we're headed. Unless you want to leave me to my own devices with my toys, I suggest we leave this conversation for later." Lightly nuzzling his ear and nipping the tip, I take full advantage of his chest so close to mine.

I score his alabaster skin with my fingernails. “Is Niamh here?”

Arif turns back and grins like a Cheshire cat. “Not that I know of.”

“See you later then, my friend.” Shoan says huskily as we turn, heading down the hall to a room that I hope holds promise.

The door to his room seems almost light years away. Okay, that’s an exaggeration, but I’m hungry to start the exploration of his body.

Shoan must be reading my mind as he caresses soft spots I didn’t even know felt that good. Tearing and stripping each other down to the barest of clothing, I stumble across the floor, catching my feet in the legs of my jeans. Holding him around the waist, I step into his embrace to hold myself up, laughing at it all. He rights me with a grin that lights every plain on his face as I untuck the stubborn pants.

God, he's perfect. When I envision the ultimate man, he looks like this with scars inside and out; battle wounds.

Falling into the bed in a lazy heap, his featherlight caresses ignite me. Sparks fly against the banked fire within. Everything is ignited. If we stopped now, I think I’d burn down the house.

With a male appropriate giggle, I let out a whimper when he takes his hands away, smirking dangerously.

“Reminder, I can hear everything you think. Your secrets you’ve locked away into tiny tight compartments for safe keeping are gonna burst to the surface, showing me how much of a whore or prude you wish to be.”

Whore, whore, whore! No prudes here. I dare you to make me scream.

As he leans on the edges of the bed, kissing up and down the sides of my neck, tracing a path towards my nipples, I find it hard to concentrate on anything other than his touch. I don't want to come off easy, but I can hardly handle the precision of his touches. The sweet gentle movements accentuate my need as I lay there wet and uncontrollably aroused. Moving to the edge to the bed as he removes his perfectly pressed jeans, I trace the lines of his tight muscles. His low-slung jeans showcase his massive erection that peeks out the top, and I dance a jig in my mind.

He's so godlike. My oh my, what a beauty. I move to wrap my lips around his rock-hard member when he pushes on my shoulders.

"Hey, I can hear your thoughts, remember? And I decide who gets off when and how." With a smile, he picks me up effortlessly and lays me across the stacked pillows at the head of the expansive king bed.

"Now that I can hear you," he taps his head, "I don't wanna know what you want aloud; I want your thoughts. The deep dark sexual urges, the light caress or the heavy handed. I've done it all, but I haven't had *this* chance in centuries. Let me feel you. Let me hear you in here."

Okay.

Nodding, knowing I'll do as he asks, he lays a finger under the strap of my bra, unlatching it like a pro in seconds with a flick. "Told you I'm a pro." Dipping his head he licks, kisses, tastes and teases my breasts, making each bud rise at his command. My body does as he asks, responding quickly to every touch. Just when I don't want to come off as easy, it has other ideas.

I can hardly think to breathe. I don't need to tell him telepathically, directing him to what I want or need. He knows what to do as he trails kisses down my chest, past my belly to the bank of trimmed red curls. *Thank fuck I had that Brazilian last week.* Clearing my mind to think of nothing else, I try to concentrate on only his deft movements and my building orgasm.

At this rate, I'll go off before he even touches my cunt.

Please. I need your mouth, Shoan.

As soon as his tongue brushes the sensitive skin, rimming my sex and avoiding anything that will send me off, I realize holding out is *exactly* what he has in mind.

Oh, Shoan please. I can't take much more. We can always have further rounds if you're up for it, but please, I need more. Just a bit more I think as I almost give in and speak aloud. My body can't handle this teasing, even though I love it.

Nipping my pussy lips, every single moment is heavenly. With a single swipe up my core, I feel the spasms wrack my inner muscles as they tighten and release over and over.

He lifts his head. "See? You don't need as much as you think to come."

To think, I waited too long for a moment like this. All the toys, fingers, and dirty thoughts have been building like a bad porno where there was no great release, just a fake come down. But after seeing his grand cock, I want the real thing. I *need* to feel him inside me. I want him pounding and sliding back and forth while I hold him in place like a lion holds her prey.

Without a spoken word, Shoan knows. Stripping off the remainder of my clothing in a blur while I wriggle on the bed in anticipation, I can't help but gaze at the pure perfection he is. How many times can I say that before it seems only a dream? He's perfect. He is exactly what I envisioned in my head.

Creeping up the bed, he brandishes his sword like a professional. Nothing is as beautiful as his form, and as his biggest-thing-I've-ever-seen-cock stands straight and proud.

"Thiea, I don't need protection. I can't release. I mean, for centuries, I haven't been able to. I don't get sick and I'm clean."

Shit. Well, I'm going on faith so far. "I've never had unprotected, but I'm clean and on the pill."

Laying his strong body against mine, he lays kiss after kiss on my lips until they feel raw. I fall prey to his touch as his hands move across me like a pro. He knows where to stroke, where to pet, suck, lick, tease, stopping only to bring me on the verge of coming once more. Pushing me further and further to the edge of ecstasy, word-lessly, and without being enticed, I'm at the edge of abandoning reason.

"Shoan, please," I say aloud.

"Naughty, naughty girl. No talking, remember?" Slowly direct-ing his engorged cock to my entrance, he drives it within me, slowly stretching me until he's seated inside. It's exquisite. The pleasure and pain as he pushes harder and harder stretches me out. I'll be sore tomorrow.

We fit perfectly within each other's arms. Our bodies are a matched set, like we were made for this moment; for each other. The perfection of his body leaning across mine, sweating, rocking back and forth, pumping with wild abandon is euphoric.

His large cock hits every sensitive edge within me as it courses back and forth. I scream, moan, whimper and cry out at each pass, edging me closer and closer to releasing again and again, tightening all my muscles around him. I don't think I've ever felt anything like this.

In between the pounding movements, I say, "Talk to me. I can't hear your thoughts like you can mine." My words are ragged and tortured as I fight for air.

"It's ecstasy if you really need to know." He drives into me harder and harder, just like I want. "I can't believe how you feel. Your body is squeezing me so tight, it's fantastic. I've never felt this. It's exquisite and excruciating, Thiea, "Shoan grunts as he thrusts. "Oh my Gods. Fuck, I can't believe it, I'm gonna come."

I don't want him to stop. The heavens open up with a choir of angels, I swear. I've moaned and screamed so much, my voice is hoarse.

"Let go for me," Shoan pants, just as I think I can take no more. I fall apart, bucking and screaming his name incoherently.

The fabulous hours pass in a blur until we're are both satiated, spent, and any other objective that I can muster to explain the perfection of the acts we performed. The two of us acted like circus folk, and now lay out on the bed, content. Shoan is next to me, stroking my hair, raining kisses down on my engorged lips, forehead, and any other part he hadn't already punished.

I have to admit, the tension of the last few days has melted away, becoming a forgotten nightmare.

Yes, it's hard to lay here and not be aroused by his prone, impeccable body so close to mine. And as the night stretched out from one moment to the next, I decided that if immortality means expert sexual prowess, then I accept the challenge to use all of his extensive knowledge.

By the time we fell asleep, we were happily satisfied that each other's urges had been sated, and frequently. Even when no thoughts were needed, we were complete.

Chapter ELEVEN

Dangerous Dining Partners

Morrigan

That was unfortunate.

The girl Garron believes can lead us to the end of this is with Shoan, the blight of my existence. Of all the immortals, she's with him?

Being a policeman can be a handy tool. Garron persuaded the young travel agent to divulge the location of Thiea's abrupt travel plans, allowing us to intervene.

After a most wretched flight and a horrid drive through the city, I begrudgingly arrived at the hotel in Athens. There was not one measly human in first class up to my standards, so needless to say, I'm irritable and under duress after learning of Thiea's *chaperone*. Not to mention, I'm starving after such a long time without nourishment.

"Hello, darling. How was your flight?" Harrison's smirk irks me. He enjoys angering me far too easily; he always has. He knows I'm on edge about this whole ordeal and that I want to end this.

We were so close.

"You must feel superb, that once again I was thwarted by that piece of trash. I assume the boys told you about the events at the airport? I'll have to send them on errands of menial and degrading proportions as punishment." Keeping pace, walking in step behind me, Harrison depresses the button for the elevator.

"Have you found me decent entertainment? After such a disgusting day, I really would like someone with superior intelligence."

As our ride arrives, we enter the lift. "Penthouse, please," Harrison tells the operator.

"My darling, I found you a pair that I believe will be to your liking. I enjoyed their consorts; MIT candidates on vacation." Harrison reaches for my neck, pricking ever so slightly right below my ear, nibbling to arouse me. *Young blue bloods are as always entertaining,* he says within my mind.

Reaching our floor, Harrison tips the operator as I peruse the inconsequential surroundings. It's not my house in the Hamptons, or in Versailles, but it will suffice. There's plenty of room to enjoy our meals and to entice each other into further bouts of pleasure. Now that Shoan and his cohorts are involved, I'm sure that our stay will drag out.

Just thinking of Shoan and his increasing interference angers me. Why couldn't that bastard just stay out of everything and die? I *cannot* allow him to regain his strength. For centuries, I've avoided judgement. I'm not about to give up the fight now when we're so close to his annihilation.

Harrison heads directly to the kitchen to fix himself something human, as he always has food after enjoying blood. Taking in the subpar grandeur of the salon, I find it dissatisfying. Down the hall is the usual, modern opulence with overindulgent human styling, comfort, and cookie cutter design.

The bedrooms are banked off the grand room to the left, with mine being the large double door entrance at the end. As always, Harrison has marked my room with a single rose draped across the handles; his tell-tale sign of my dinner companions. Entering the room, a pair of sheepish platinum blonde, long-legged twins lay curled up on the bed in a trancelike state. They're awake and aware of their surroundings, but unable to move or run.

Lovely. It's been quite a while since I enjoyed twins, and I anticipate their connection. Uniquely tantalizing, they think as one.

Shoan can wait while I slake my need.

Chapter TWELVE

Crushed Grapes

Antonius

The pain has always been a razor-sharp edge, as it drags itself across my tender and damaged soul.

I've tried to enjoy the pleasures of women, and once or twice I felt I could love again, but it always turned out the same; they're not *her*.

After leaving Crete I never looked back. Never had I thought that choice would lead me here. The offer of immortality was too difficult to resist. Now nothing is worse than the pain as its searing anguish is also immortalized. I may portray the shell of a human, but I know underneath there is only a destroyed soul with a blackened heart.

Pain and suffering are the greatest bedfellows when there is nothing else left.

After accepting eternal life, it didn't take long for me to see the reasons for Shoan's pain. With thousands of minds thinking at the same time, your own soul is damaged. It's excruciating. Why he hopes for that back has always been a mystery to me.

For quite a long time, I blamed him. I blamed Arissa, my wife, for leaving me and taking our son with her too. But it wasn't their fault. It wasn't even Shoan's, but it took years for me to understand that. It was hard to forgive them all.

Leaving the island over two centuries ago, living in peace without human or Dark Worlder interaction has been sublime, so to see a man, clearly not of the human persuasion, walking down my grapevine rows is a shock.

"Good afternoon, sir. Are you Antonius Petera?" he asks.

"Yes. Who would be asking, *Trappa*?" I don't give a shit if I sound like an asshole; I hate their kind. Vampires are the whole reason Shoan was marooned on my island all that time ago, and why I'm not in the Elysium Fields with my family.

"My name is Garron. I have a proposition that may interest you —"

"No thanks. I have no vested interest in what the vampires are doing. Thanks for stopping by. Now, if you'll excuse me, fuck off."

Cutting him off, I turn on my heel down a row of brilliantly green hued vegetation as he calls out.

"It involves Shoan and the book." Pausing, then walking further and further away, I inspect leaves of the plants closest to me. The one thing I've been more in tune to since accepting immortality is the push and pull of nature. Tearing gently at a vine, peeling a leaf off, the rough edge and smooth face of the leaf tells me about the wine to come. The vine says it all.

I'm interested in what he says, even if I don't want to be. Fuck, I'm going to regret this. "How do you know for sure?"

"Because we traced the book back here, to Greece. I believe he knows where the book is, and with his vested interest in correcting his past, I assumed you would also be interested?"

"I'll hear you out, but only for the entertainment value, nothing more. Do you understand me? I hate vampires. The reckless Trappa like you bother me most," I tell him outright. If there's one thing I've learned, it's that there is no room for error with vampires.

"Antonius, if you'll accompany me back to the city so that we can talk with my friends—"

"Fuck no. It's here or nowhere. If you have something to say, lay it out honestly. I am still stronger than you, so keep that in mind." He knows it to be truth.

"Fine. I'm not used to the heat of Athens though, so could we at least move inside?" Garron is visibly sweating as we stand in the middle of the field. Nodding my head, I start back without checking if he's following. As we walk out of the patch back towards my house, I hope what he wants to say is worth it for him.

"I have some tea chilled in the icebox." I offer the only thing he's getting from me.

"That would be terrific." Arriving in the house, I pour us each a glass.

"What is it that you need? I know Shoan, but we haven't spoken in centuries. And before you ask, I will not betray him to you in any way. Understood?" Even if I *did* know Shoan was here, there's not a Pixie chance in hell I would help this blood bank reveler.

He clears his throat. "Shoan left a marker here. A headstone somewhere in the city that shows the way to the book. I believe it is your wife and child's tombstone," Garron says very shyly, almost fearful of mentioning their names. He should be. I don't want to talk about it, but if it makes him go away, that's all the better for me.

"If I tell you where it is, will you leave me in peace?" I await his response as he nods, albeit reluctantly.

"Telling you where the headstone is won't get you any further to the book. There's no reason not to tell you. In the Agora there is a temple to the God of Metallurgy— Hephaestus. Do you know it?" He nods and I continue. "Visit his temple and look for a stone that simply says, *Here, then gone, but never forgotten.* Find that and you will have your marker. Now, finish your drink, get out of my house and never return here unless you wish to be a permanent fixture in my grape fields."

"Thank you." Garron rises from the chair, extending his hand for me to shake, but I ignore it. Exiting, he hops in his rental and peels off quickly down the lane. I watch until he's out of sight.

After Garron leaves, I sit and think on the predicament. *I* know where the book is just as easily as Shoan does. We put it there together, and I assumed we'd never go near it again until it was necessary.

Shoan's in town, and he's trying to keep the book hidden from prying eyes. I should prepare. When the time is right, he and I will meet up again.

Soon enough, I'm sure.

Chapter THIRTEEN

Kick to the Nuts

Niamh

Hanging around, listening to Shoan talk about himself and giving me the truth after 600 years of lies is a classic kick to the proverbial gonads. Arif and Shoan both tried to reach me through their thoughts, asking how I feel.

Like I'm sitting on a shrink's fainting bench, assholes!

Good luck with listening in on me, losers. It's the *very* last thing I want right now. No one is rummaging around in my head without my say so. So I thought about kittens, oranges, the square root of pi, recipes for making bread, anything that put junk in my thoughts. I'll converse when I'm good and fuckin' ready to, pricks.

The Berserkers and I headed out to the shed, uncovered the bikes, grabbed keys and shook out the helmets before taking off. There's nothing worse than driving with a spider in your visor.

"So where we headed, sweet cheeks?" Chad reaches out to grab my ass. I bend his fingers around to kiss his wrist as he smiles psychotically.

"Well, darlin' seeing you can run faster than my bike, that Terese can port off to anywhere while Patrick flies, I'm up for pretty much anywhere that Elenor will take me over a hundred miles an hour."

I love my bike, Elenor. I ride her on the days I just need to be someplace else really fast. I can be reckless, obnoxious, and rude to everyone on the road because no one knows who you are in a helmet.

Elenor is a Ducati 1100 Monster, and she's my beautiful machine. Shoan thinks she's too much for me, but I've never had a problem with her as she handles like a formula one car. She purrs like a pampered pussy cat, screams like the demons I control are tight on her ass, but enough of a whore to do as I please when I give her room to move.

Quickly cracking the throttle, I let her loose down the streets of Athens.

I don't even have to look in my rearview to know that Chad is zipping in and out, between the stalls. Pedestrians and cars are a blur as he almost knocks over a lady pushing a stroller. They don't see him. They don't see any of us unless we want them to.

With it being such a nice night out, Syntagma Square is full of humans. It's hard to maneuver around them to really appreciate Elenor, but as soon as I'm out on the main roadways, peeling out of the tight side streets, it'll be easier to let her go.

Pushing us out towards the ocean and the Port of Piraeus, I pass the ruins of the Agora, Hadrian's Library, and the various gardens interspersed around them. I can feel the tension lifting.

Approaching a red traffic light, a flash of light catches my eye in the temple of Hephaestus. It's night, so no one should be in there at this time. The weenie security guys normally have it locked down tighter than a virgin in church for humans, so the only thing that would be there are kids or Dark Worlders.

Chad, you see that? Who the fuck would be there at this time? Motioning over to the gardens wordlessly, he comes to an abrupt stop beside me, panting and smelling pungent of sweat.

Swinging my bike around, coming up on the right side of the temple nearest the restaurants and housing complexes I park, shut off the bike, and walk over to investigate. If it was just a flick from some kid's flashlight, then it's nothing, but for some reason, I think it's way more than that. Just a sneaking hunch.

Not wanting to rip my new riding coat sneaking under the sharp chain link, I have Chad lift me over as he lightly jumps over the rickety mail. Coming up softly on the other side, I dust myself off. Starting in the direction of the building, listening in on their inaudible voices, I can make out a female and two males. They're definitely Dark Worlders, as I can hear their internal thoughts as clear as if they were standing directly beside me, shouting.

I thought I gave very specific instructions to get Antonius to Athens, Garron. I need him to lead us to the grave marker of his wife. The woman sounds like a true bitch; harsh and demanding. I can't make out their faces in the dim light, but hopefully, Chad can with his enhanced sight.

What do you see? Who are they? I ask as he shrugs.

I tried. With a loud crack, the man closest to the woman reels back from a strike across the face. *I'm sorry he wouldn't come back to the hotel, but he did direct us here.*

Rounding the bushes to come upon the far side of the temple nearer the backside of the Stoa, Terese pops up, as usual with Patrick on her shoulder. We're upwind as we all listen in on their conversation, one that I am almost certain is about my brother. I start clouding my mind again, like I had with Shoan and Arif, just in case the people below catch my wandering thoughts.

Are you sure we can trust him? What if he's lying about it's location? Another voice, this one deep and rumbling.

He didn't have to help us, but at this point, we have to trust someone and a guy who doesn't want to be what he is, well, he has an interest in us finding it as well. Now start looking at the inscriptions on all of those stones, the woman says.

Yes, Mother, they say in unison.

Mother? I mouth to Chad and Terese. I'm not totally sure, but I think the woman we're eyeballing is Morrigan. I haven't crossed paths with her since the days on Eire. That time in my life was very sketchy, the memory from that point of time is cloudy.

As the light starts to dance around the polished stones once more, we quietly retreat out of the garden. *What the fuck was that?* I ask Chad as Terese bounds off into the night with Patrick.

Hey, yer guess is as good as mine. That was Morrigan and her goons. I can smell vampire. Fucking things stink. Chad shrugs his reply, then turns back towards my stranded bike. I know I don't have to mention our night romp has been cancelled, as each of us make our way back towards the villa.

Shaking out his shaggy, jet black hair, tucking it back into a low ponytail under his collar, we walk Elenor quietly down the street. I don't want to start it right away. It would draw attention to us. We hoof it until reaching Monastiraki Station, and the centre of the Plaka.

Starting the bike, I watch as Chad shifts and tears off into the oblivious public. I consider how this is all seemingly a bit too coincidental.

Reaching the house, I park my bike and round up the gang quickly. Making a mental shout-out to everyone, neither Arif or Shoan answer. With most of the lights off, I can only hope he's at least getting it on with his new piece of tail. I'm still in a foul mood, but I grab a beer, sit in the garden, and await the rest of our friends.

"Okay, anyone else think that was totally fucked-up?" Patrick quips off as he walks in, snapping the cap off his beer with a flick. Stretching his neck muscles, snapping everything back into place, Patrick extends his naked body out to its full height. A side effect of his shift is the adjustments. They're a bitch.

"Totally," Terese interjects as she too walks in with jeans in hand for Patrick. "I know who one of those guys were, that's George. He and I have had run-ins on quite a few occasions. Let's say the bar fights and the blood spilled on both sides has been over me not wanting to hook up. Dumb ass vamp figures I should give it up for him. I don't suck cock." Terese is not *only* one of the best on our team, she's one of the meanest fighters I know. I have firsthand knowledge, and let's just leave it at that.

I'm not sure what's bothering me more, the goons and their apparent mommy issues, or Shoan and Arif lying to me. It's kind of a toss-up right now. I crack open the beer, get a bowlful of nuts and fresh dates, then sit on the couch outside.

The fire in the brazier is burning low. Tossing in a few pieces of wood to stoke it back to life, I lay back, looking to the stars for an epiphany.

"Okay. Let's recap. Shoan is not really my brother, but what does that mean anyway? None of us are blood related, and that means shit to me." Chad jumps over the back of the couch beside me, laying one arm across the back and his other on my lap. It's the common position we take up. I comfort him, he comforts me, and we both get comfort.

As I recline into his chest, I lay my feet within the fire, soaking up the heat.

"Does it mean that he'll be after me for avoiding my soul mate? Can he decide which fates are to be judged? Skipping over ones like us? Does it change who he is to me? Do I really care what he is? A few hours ago, all I wanted was for him to find his soul mate, someone to love him and vice versa. Did that change just because he's the Chimeric?"

All I've done is speak and no one seems to pipe up any answers. *Nice, you fuckers.* Just when I need to hear argumentative comments or have my thoughts bounce off the others, they're the silence of the lambs.

"Listen, Niamh. You know I'll follow yer bro anywhere. No issues on helpin' him, as he's got me out of more than one pickle since the dawn of time. It wouldn't matter if he was the devil himself. So no, it shouldn't matter to ya either." As usual, Chad has valid points. Terese upends her beer, while Patrick falls asleep on the marble bench that they dragged over earlier. At this point, I realize we are fully, completely, and utterly fucked.

Do I care who Shoan is or what Shoan is? No.

So, the only thing bothering me really is that he lied. Hiding it was ass. I would have followed him, helped him, cared for him without issue, just like Chad said.

Now, the big question is, what to do about those idiots in the temple?

Chapter FOURTEEN

So Long, Sad, Lonely Heart

Shoan

In the morning, the sun seems brighter. With its rays shooting this way and that around the room, the smell of the fresh flowers from the open doors of the garden, and the feeling of warmth in my heart, I'm sated. I'm sounding like a sentimental sap right now but I don't give a shit as I take in the happiness I feel.

Reaching towards Thiea, wanting her closer, I find the bed devoid of her. She's not here. I laugh to myself at the audacity of the moment. Normally it's me running away before the girl wakes up.

Getting up off the bed with nothing but my pride to cover me, I start for the bathroom. Peeking around the doorway in the walk-in closet, I grab clean jeans and a shirt, just as she re-enters with her arms full of food.

The smell is intoxicating.

"Don't get dressed after all the trouble I went to getting this. I don't cook so this is the best you get, even if I cheated." Thiea's balancing a bed table laden with fresh fruits, warmed honey, Greek yogurt, warm fresh bread, and Turkish coffee. What a perfect wake-up call.

“Maria said this is your favorite breakfast. I was ready to cook you hard eggs with crunchy bacon and overdone toast, so count your blessings that you have someone to stock your shelves and place me on the right path." She’s wearing my T-shirt from last night, and as it drapes around her petite frame, casting shadows of her curves through the thin material, I feel myself growing aroused. With her hair streaming around her face in soft tendrils, she smiles the biggest, brightest smile I have ever seen.

"Well, I must say, this is gourmet. How am I to top this? Do you like PB and J, or are you more of a Cheese Whiz girl?"

"Honestly, whipped cream and cherries would have sufficed for me."

She sets the tray down on the foot of the bed and crawls on her hands and knees towards me for a kiss. I feel myself stiffening against the rough jeans at the thought of her in the tee, leaving nothing to the imagination underneath. She seats herself at the end of the bed with the tray as I scooch down to sit beside her.

I never assumed that my soul would scream out when I found my mate. I assumed it was just a means to an end for my freedom, but, it’s as if the last part of me has been attached in the puzzle. If she’s it, then I’m blessed.

"I want you to try this," I tell her as I take up a bowl. Placing a fresh fig inside, I drizzle some honey on it, a dollop of yogurt is splashed on top, with a dribbling of raw sugar that lights up like bright crystals. Cutting into the ripest, juiciest looking fig, I feed the concoction to her. She closes her eyes as she eats, but the internal conversation in her head is amazing.

That's fantastic. It's like eating a...I can't even explain it. Wow! I need to visit Greek town more often if this is what they have to offer. I love that my power is returning.

I can't wait to try lunch, she mutters mentally as she pulls on my jeans, tugging down the zipper. Reaching inside, I tense as she grips me.

Some of the honey is dribbling down her lips. As she extends her tongue to reach the oozing liquid, I reach up with my fingers to smooth it towards her mouth. Licking my fingers, caressing them amorously, my cock stands fully prepared to take her.

Rising off my elbows, I reach her mouth, wanting to devour her. Pushing the tray to the floor, I upend the bowls. Anxiously awaiting me, smiling like a Cheshire Cat, Thiea smoothly strokes my cock. I lightly pinch her breast with one hand through the thin shirt while I trail the other along her smooth belly. Moving towards her lovely thighs, a soft exhale escapes her as I trace the soft patch of hair.

"Hold on there, mister. If we start this again, neither of us will leave this room." As I thumb her soft, moist folds, she pushes her hands against my chest, all the while groaning into my mouth.

"And that would be bad, *because*? I haven't enjoyed a release in centuries. Can I not have my fill in one day to make up for *at least* a decade?" I ask, lifting the shirt.

Kissing her supple nipple, tweaking it, nipping and licking it quickly, I continue until her hips rise to meet me. Delving a finger within her tight pussy, I groan in earnest against her pink bud.

"Shoan if we keep doing this, nothing will be accomplished today. I won't get to see Athens."

"Fabulous. I can go for that after..." I say as I kiss down her chest towards the sweet candy I know lies below.

"No, you and I have a date with destiny. Niamh and you need—" I cover her mouth with mine to distract and seduce her. She falls into my devious plan quite easily as I stroke her wet clit.

"Yep. It can wait," she says as she sits up, straddling my waist. I, of course, am ready to give her more.

Gripping my hard shaft, running her finger along the precum on the tip, she pulls me inside her once more. Rocking back and forth, coursing inside her lithe little frame, I find myself at utter peace. I'm fully aware of her needs, which makes this all the more enjoyable.

Guiding her up and down, I pinch her ass and kiss her marvelous breasts so that I can satisfy her every whim as we move as one.

I've never felt this before.

I don't want it to end.

A little while later, as Thiea reclines on the mass of pillows, I grab my guitar to play her something. I need to prove to her that there's more to me than just sexual prowess. The shackles of the curse are relinquishing their hold on me as I listen to her thoughts clearly. The pain of holding off my own orgasm for so many centuries is diminishing its grip on me as well.

Strumming the strings, I check the tune. "I was always fond of the guitar. About fifty years ago, I really got into it. A Stratocaster is more romantic and more sensual than straddling a baby grand," I say as I pick through the strings.

"You seem to play me like a piano. I think you hit every key without missing a beat. The guitar suits you though. It adds to the mystery, kind of like a box of cracker jacks, you just never know if it's a shit prize until you open it." She smiles and lightly kisses my scar. Tracing her hands along my tattoo, she lays down in my lap, looking up at me with wide eyes. Entrancing and exploring, they ask for all of me. When she touches my tattoo, I feel the raw power just under the skin, waiting to pounce.

"Why do you have that tattoo?" she asks while strokes her fingers lightly across the edges of my scar.

"It's a reminder of what I was. The light is the white wing. It shows the pureness and the good in the world that I know can be there. The other wing is upside down because it's the evil and the rot empowering the worst of humanity. The blood dripping shows the loss of love, compassion, and hope.

"The longer the darkness is able to continue unchecked, the darker the black will become and the white will lose its luster. It's a scale of justice. It's alive and it constantly reminds me of how much Morrigan has changed the course of my destiny. Until I can regain my power, sending those like her away from here for good, the scales will tip in her favor. There is no rebirth, no reincarnation, no deals. There's no way out for her. I'll make sure she's never heard from again."

She looks at me, sorrowfully. "You've only suffered pain and loss to this point. Have you never loved someone?"

"No. The truth is, I never expected to find anyone. After hundreds of years I gave up. I've been alive since the BC dates, and in exile from my true nature since the eleventh century."

"Damn, I'm sexing a centurion ten times over. Shoan, who knows how it'll work out for both of us? I live in the now. I can't guarantee you a lifetime or even a decade. Can you handle that we try for tomorrow?" she asks, then adds internally. *It may seem short, but at least it's the truth.*

"Of course I can. I waited this long to find someone like you, I think I can handle taking it one day at a time. Now, didn't you want to shoe shop?" I give her a devilish grin as I nibble the inside of her arm, working my way down her body once more. I'm hoping to entice her into staying here.

If you keep that up, we'll never leave. Not that I would be disappointed though. Her mind is so relaxed. Nothing hidden. Nothing masked. "By the way, while I was making breakfast, I thought about you and Niamh. I don't want to come between you and your sister."

"Can't I just avoid it for another decade or so?" After all, Niamh and I have been alive so long that all rifts repair with time. This time, of course, because I lied to protect her. She has every right to be pissed.

No.

I scrunch up my face to show my displeasure. "Fine. I'll go." As I creep to the edge of the bed, I kiss her cheek before getting dressed, but she pulls me down for a tongue lashing. The kind I love.

"Go see her."

Grabbing a fresh button-down shirt and a pair of olive colored khaki shorts, I head to the shower.

"Anyway," Thiea yells from the room as I step into the bathroom. "I can have a heart to heart with Jaz, or Anna. Fuck, whatever."

I don't understand how this is all going to play out, but I love that she's here. Thiea is strong, brilliant, funny, charismatic, and she has a twisted sense of happiness.

She is the light that will hopefully bring me out of this dark fog.

Chapter FIFTEEN

Malicious is the Mind

Garron

All right, that sucked.

I tried to do things the nice way, and boy did it bite me in the ass. Leaving the temple with no book and no trace of one ever being there, it was apparent it was just another wild goose chase. So of course it's totally my fault. In my mother's eyes, if I wasn't so weak, I would have been more convincing. I asked Antonius very nicely, and I took the information he gave at face value. Sometimes, it really bites that I don't scare anyone anymore. George is little more than a blunt instrument, but at least he's malicious. Sully is nasty, and if I'd taken him, for sure a fight would have ensued and nothing would have been accomplished.

Now, I have a large welt on my arm from a deftly tossed stone, and even though mother dearest was aiming for my face, George moved me at the last second. I would have died, and she wouldn't have had a second thought about it.

I *hate* being this soft human form. It's pathetic. It's been so long since I killed someone for the pleasure of their mind, and quite frankly, I fucking miss it. The transfer of their fears as they die, the pleading when you let them loose just before you turn on them to finish what you started is enchanting.

I've never questioned what will happen to me, if and when the curse breaks.

Will I be me again? I hope so. Can I ask my beloved Cassie to give up mortality though to join her husband and children in eternity? Will she? Call me selfish, but I hope she will. I can't stand this feeble existence, and I hope to have her for years to come.

Rounding the corner from the rail station, the swell of milling tourists grows. Their thoughts are so vivid and routine, all common random thoughts of what to eat, where to eat, what to buy, did I pay too much, did I get a deal? All of it is so monotonous.

Walking through the square, my cell phone vibrates in my pocket. Pulling it out, I see a picture of George on the screen. "Yeah, hello?"

"Listen, I don't think it's totally your fault. Mom was wrong. She's just as fed up with this life as you are—"

"Geo, I'm tired, annoyed, and ready to rip the head off anyone who gets in my way," I spit out, cutting George off.

"See, that's the point. I started thinking that if the girl ended up with Shoan, then it means we can kill two birds with one stone. Do you get me?" George talks, but he isn't making any sense. Nothing unusual there, as he's not the sharpest thumb tack.

"What the hell do you mean, Geo?"

"Shoan and Antonius know where the book is, and the girl is with Shoan, right? So that means if we find Shoan or her, one way or the other, we get the book and the key. If he was trying to keep her from us, then possibly we can get him to give up the book. Voila. We win."

Fuck, for once he makes sense. I guess there's a first with everyone at some point.

"Not bad, Geo. We would have leverage, and we could finish this all in one stroke." I switch the phone to my other ear as I pay for a soda, popping the top. "Have you seen Sully?"

"No, but I heard that he's in town enjoying some revelry."

"Okay. Night, Geo."

My night might be looking up. As I hang up the call, I immediately dial Sully.

He answers on the second ring. "What's up, little bro? You're interrupting my evening interlude with a very delicious exchange student."

At least one of us is having fun.

"Where are you?"

"Just off one of the little side streets near the Plaka. Why? Whatcha got in mind?" He's intrigued.

"Do you feel like a little hunting? You know I'm shit at tracking, and I could use you. Wanna have some fun?"

I smile to myself, 'cause I know Sullivan. He's always up for some fun. The nastier, messier, and more murderous, the better.

"Sure. I'll be finished here in just a few minutes. How about I meet you at the fountain near the church off of Ermou, say in ten?"

"Yeah, perfect. See you soon." Hanging up, I place the phone back in my pocket. Wincing from the pain in my shoulder, I start up towards where we'll meet.

I know mother. She'll be pleased. She may even stop considering me a useless walking bag of blood if we retrieve the girl from the Chimeric.

Walking along, I see Dark Worlders of all kinds out partaking in the crowd. I'm always amazed how humans pass through our world, so oblivious to us. Our kind, and the danger that we are to them should be ingrained. They are the prey.

Reaching the fountain, tossing in a coin for good luck, I toss in a second for a safe return to Cassie.

Chapter SEVENTEEN

Let the Fur Fly

Anna

"How will I explain everything? Thiea doesn't understand the decisions I had to make," I tell my love; my Arif.

"Anna, my love. Try to start with what she is, and what she is to us. She'll have questions for you about why you left, but those are questions that can possibly wait. I think that it would be best if I'm away for you two to talk without any interruptions as well." Arif pauses, turning his head towards the house. "I know that Shoan's not what you wanted for her future either, but be open-minded. I love him like a son. Treat the situation fairly, darling." Arif reaches across the table, kisses the back of my hand, then rises from the table. "I will not be far away, my love."

Watching as Thiea enters the garden with a tremendous grin that tells a thousand tales. She's wearing a brightly colored dress of gold that makes her beautiful features stand out prominently. That brilliant smile, and her radiant red hair are not to be outdone by her father's exotic eyes.

"Good morning, Thiea. I assume you slept well last night?" Arif says as he leaves.

"Yep. I slept…well. I hope I'm not intruding?" As polite as she acts, I know she's stewing inside. She's wanting and needing the truth from me.

"No, you are not intruding upon us. I'm just leaving. I need to speak with Shoan before he talks to my little Ni. He'll need a mediator, and the marines to navigate the minefield she'll erect. I'll see you beautiful women soon." Walking into the house, I watch his retreating form.

"I feel that I should explain some things first before you start with the questions. Will you give me a moment to clarify?"

Thiea nods and takes a seat on the bench.

"Would you like a coffee or tea?"

"Tea, please." I can feel her unease, and I know her well enough, she's about to ask a question. "Can you answer one question for me. What am I to you? I mean, what are you to me?"

Fuck, I knew that would be where she'd start. I would. "I'm Jazmine. I'm the same woman who looked after you at the orphanage. The same one who wiped the tears when you weren't given a home. The same one who watched your parents with excitement when they adopted you. The same one who was there for you when they died. It's still me. I haven't changed, except that my real name is Anna. You trusted me to answer questions when you called, and even though at the time I couldn't, I'll give you straight answers now."

This has been so many years in the making, and so many times I wanted to tell her the truth, but I never knew how to start. I pour each of us a tea, trying to compose myself before I start, or before I break down sobbing.

Sitting back on the couch, I take a deep breath first. "You're special, and that's the truth. I've always told you that. I had no idea I was pregnant, and I didn't know what to do when I found out I was. What I am, and whom I'm mated to, made it even harder to keep you safe. Working at the orphanage gave me an outlet to assist you without being fully involved in your life—without endangering you." Thiea ponders what I've said, scrutinizing it, calculating her next words carefully.

"So, I wasn't dropped at the home? My family didn't desert me? I wasn't unwanted? You always said I was loved, and that they cared enough to leave me in your care. If I'm yours, then why didn't you claim me as your own?" Harsh words, but true nonetheless.

"Oh, darling. I wanted you; I always wanted you. But wanting and keeping you safe from harm are two totally different things."

"What are you? What am I? And how does Arif come into this picture? Don't think I haven't seen that. And what about my parents? The people who raised me? Did they die, or did they leave me too?"

She's hurt. I expected this and I'll do my best to lessen the pain and confusion. "No, they didn't leave you, they died. They were both special in their own way, Thiea. They were both shifters. The orphanage is one of few places that takes in unusual circumstances, and those of special needs."

"What am I then? And please give me the courtesy of cutting the bullshit. I want the truth."

"Well, how about we start here." I drank so fast to keep the dryness at bay, I pour myself another glass of tea. "I'm a werewolf. I can shift anytime and anywhere at will. I started the orphanage after the Hiroshima fiasco. I thought it best to hide the children of those that lost their parents, keeping them safe. At that time, they knew their parentage, but nowadays...well, they, you included, don't. They go on living normal lives, living without fear or danger from themselves. As they gain abilities we help them, and we train them to survive with others of their species."

She's puzzled by this. The screwed-up look on her face gives it away. "So, I'm a werewolf? Wow, this shit just gets better and better. First Garron tells me I'm special and possibly have abilities that my parents may not have informed me about. I find out that my mother was with me all along, in the place I called home, and was the most trusted person in my life." Rising from the chair, Thiea storms off to the kitchen. I want to follow, but I don't want to startle her. I know that she can't handle this right now, and me smothering her would be the wrong approach, so I wait for her to return.

This is fucked! I need something stiffer than tea, I hear her mutter in her head as she rummages in the galley.

Rounding the corner, she returns with a bottle of century old whiskey. I'm sure Chad won't mind. After all, he won it in a poker game against Shoan. Walking proudly, she holds two glasses with cubes tinkling inside. Pouring a glass, she tips it to her lips, tosses the ice in the fire pit, then pours a second glass, neat.

"Oh, that shit's smooth. I might even take up cigars to finish the bottle." She adds another glass to her alcohol repertoire. "So, you're a werewolf and Arif is a..."

"Vampire. Very old, very powerful vampire."

"Like how old? Turn of the century. Ha! That's funny. *Turn of the century*. I made a funny." She smiles and it reminds me of times when we could laugh and pass the time playing chess in her room, or in the common. A time when she was carefree and oblivious.

"Like time of the Pharaohs kind of old. Sort of a powerful figure in history. He's even taken me to see some of his portraits in rooms that no one has uncovered." Setting my teacup on the bench, I motion to the bottle and the empty glass. "Mind pouring me one of those?"

She passes the amber liquid across the table to rest perfectly in my outstretched hand. "If you can turn it on and off at will, what's wrong with me?" I once knew how to answer that question, but now it frightens me. The answer, the look, and the disappointment will follow.

Buck up, Anna. Tell your daughter the damn truth.

Letting out a heavy sigh, I stare her down to give it to her straight. "Your necklace. It holds your immortal sides at bay. It keeps them from getting loose. It's spelled."

She thumbs the necklace, rolling the beads in her fingers. "Didn't you ever get suspicious when you tried to take it off and put on other things? I would tell you it suited your eyes best, and that your real parents would be disappointed if you left their most precious gift on a nightstand. Thiea, it's the *key* to unlocking yourself."

The wheels spin as she thinks it through. "Okay. You're saying if I took this off, I would become a monster? An honest to goodness monster? Like a Frankenstein or Wolfman with all the furriness and shit?"

"Yeah, pretty much. Arif and I were worried what you would be. I mean, we aren't even supposed to be mated. The curse was supposed to curb all Dark Worlder children from being born from two species. Most children are rare. Dark Worlders find them to be special in so many ways. To come from a 'mixed marriage,' one human, one Dark, is crazy difficult. You were a miracle. We were afraid you would be hunted for your uniqueness, and killed by other factions."

"So if I keep this necklace on, I'll never gain powers? And I guess that means I die as a human? I could have died never knowing you or this part of my heritage?"

I grab up the bottle and decide I need to be smashed for more of this conversation. "Sort of. Sorry. I never wanted to hurt you, only protect you."

Thiea curls up on the padded rocking chair, slightly swaying and swirling her amber drink while caressing the delicate beaded chain.

"You know, your father chose that necklace himself. He said it sang to him in his soul. I always thought it was a crock of shit, but over the years, I've learned to trust in his judgement on all things supernatural."

Thiea looks down at the ground, then swigs back the drink in her hand. "So tell me what kind of powers you and him have. Why were you so afraid? Why feel the need to cull me?"

I cringe. Not one of my favorite sayings, and said by her makes it even more hurtful. "Culling is kind of a harsh word in my species, but I'll accept it as appropriate for this conversation. We weren't quite sure what you would have. I can shift, and I'm able to feel the emotions of others. I can even project my feelings onto others. It's useful in many cases. I feel the pull of nature and I can work with the elements, both of which can be a very powerful tool when you need to know directions or need to hide. Our family is a very powerful line of witches. That's how this all started."

"Giza placed the binding curse. She worked with the vampires at the time because her daughter was being held for leverage. The one thing she knew that they didn't was that only our bloodline could release the curse. Well, the witch part of our bloodline could. Way back in our history, we were witches, not weres. I wasn't always a were. I was bitten when I was pregnant with you." I pause, waiting for Thiea's new line of questioning.

"I thought Shoan said you tried to release the curse?"

"I did, and that was before you were born. I was too afraid to try once you were. That's when I went into hiding." Thiea shifts uncomfortably in her seat, automatically reaching for her necklace as I continue. "Shoan is our family, just like you are. Maybe more so to Arif, as he has known him in this life longer than the rest of us. He reveres him like a son."

“So,” she says as she’s downs the fourth glass of whiskey. “Here’s another question. You guys were talking about soul mates and shit last night. What is that?”

“We all have a mate, someone that is destined for us. It’s also part of the curse placed on Shoan. When Giza created it, she didn’t intend on it affecting every species, every being from then until the end of time. Some go years or centuries without it. Or in some circumstances avoiding it, like Niamh.”

How do you know? she asks me mentally.

"It feels like a bolt of lightning has struck your heart. It’s as if your body is humming with unending energy," I tell her as she reaches for the bowl full of figs on the table, popping a few in her mouth. "Thiea, you are Arif's daughter. Until this moment, no one has known but me and Arif."

"Not even Shoan?”

Shaking my head, I down my glass, then go in for a refill.

“Wow, this has been a trip of a lifetime. Is there anything else I'm missing? Is there an uncle that's a dragon, or a cousin that’s a pixie?"

Thiea rises from the chair, pacing around the fountain. Running her hands through her hair, she tears at it, almost pulling some out.

I hope she understands why everything had to be as it was. As I sit silently, I await her reply. Afraid of how she'll take all, I sip on the neat whiskey.

"Jaz, I understand. Really, I do. I don't get it, but I understand it. I met Morrigan at the airport with her goons, and they were not very gentle with Shoan. If that's any indication of how things could have been for you over the years, then I get it. Protection is paramount.

"You've always been there for me without fault, and without reward. I can't say I wouldn't have liked to know, but I'm just glad I was never alone. Thank you Ja—Anna?"

"Jaz will do just fine, sweetheart." I stand up. Going around to the other side of the couch, I extend my arms out to her. She steps in and hugs me tightly, crying gently on my shoulder. Pulling away, she rubs her eyes and smiles. That bright and expressive look lets me know I haven't lost her.

Backing away, she tears at the necklace, trying to lift it off. I reach out, causing her to pause in her course. "I suggest you leave it on until we figure out the best course of action for dealing with Morrigan. We can learn what you're capable of after that. For now, let's keep you safe."

"You say that, but for some reason, I think I just need to get my freak on. Otherwise, why would Garron think I was a necessary evil in this mess?" Flopping down in the armchair again, she leans back and fists another glass of the whiskey.

"I want to find that out on *our* terms, not theirs. Let's be safe. I don't want you running into a fight without knowing your strengths or weaknesses. We'll work it out together, but trust in the person who's trained many newborn immortals."

With a sullen look, she gives me the big bottom lip. "Fine. But if there's a point when I think the tables are shifting out of our favor,

I'm pulling out the furry."

Laughing, I clink my glass to hers. "Fine. I'll let you get your freak on."

Hopefully, all is going well with Arif, Niamh, and Shoan. I have a feeling that if I can't control Thiea and stop her from doing something monumentally stupid, I hope he can at least stop them.

That is, if Niamh hasn't shredded him yet.

Chapter SEVENTEEN

Family Ties

Shoan

After dressing and leaving the insatiable, irresistible Thiea, I went in search of my deadly sister. Knocking at her door, hoping for a response that doesn't include spears, naphtha, or an army of three hundred dead souls, I wait for her to answer.

After what feels like a century of silence, I ask with trepidation. "Niamh, can we talk?"

"Come in. Tell Arif he's welcome too." I turn around, noticing Arif standing down the hall with the same fear in his eyes that I'm sure is in mine. Together we walk into Niamh's room, just as she turns down AC/DC's *Are You Ready*.

Appropriate?

"Shoan, before you start on why I shouldn't be mad at you both, and before you," She points to Arif, "start to defend his decisions, let's get this straight. I am pissed at both of you for keeping me in the dark about this for the better part of a thousand years. I am not a child; I never was. And I will never be treated that way again. Do you understand me?" The light of a thousand dead souls stirs in her gaze as she mentally peels the skin off our bodies. "If there are any other omissions in your stories between us, it needs to be aired right now, 'cause I am not about to tolerate any further fuck-ups about what you *should* and *shouldn't* tell me."

Standing in the middle of the room with a blush pink, *I Rocked the Casbah* T-shirt tight pale blue jean capris, Niamh is not really wearing the most fear inducing outfit, but she never has been a girl who looks the part that she plays.

Looking around the room, I see the various throwing stars, ancient and modern spears, javelins, a pair of AK-47's, two rocket launchers, and a Easter bunny basket full of pastel colored grenades. I haven't told her about Antonius, and before I leave this room, I'll let her know that tidbit too. "Arif. I need someone else in the firing line for a second or two." *There is way too much ammo in here to be lobbed dangerously,* I say internally.

"I heard that. Whatever you've done with Antonius, you bet your ass you'll be telling me before we leave this room." Niamh scowls and picks up one of the grenades, of which I forgot to mention has been painted pink with a black smiley face, and flips it in the air like a tennis ball with the pin swinging around her pinkie finger.

Damn. I have to remember that she can read my thoughts way better than I can hers.

Fine. At least everything will be out in the open. No more secrets.

"Okay, I'll go first." Arif speaks up as he glides around, silently. I've never understood how such a big guy can move that quietly. Slinking into a chair on the far side near her stereo, he turns to shut it off, then pauses as Niamh glares his way. Turning it down a notch, he sits silently for a moment, considering how to start.

“I've kept something from the both of you. I was protecting the person involved, and yourselves as well." *Now that you've all met my daughter Athena, I guess the cat is out of the bag,* he says to us wordlessly, and with a stupendous grin. Both our jaws drop open.

"You're serious, aren't you?" Niamh asks before I can gather my wits to do the same. I know the answer to be true, as Arif doesn't make jokes, at least not that often. When he does, they’re the driest, corniest, and worst groaners you can imagine.

Both Niamh and I sit stunned.

The woman that has me twisted in knots after centuries, just happens to be his daughter? I better keep those dirty thoughts about her to myself, especially if I don’t want to be at the end of his saber.

"Your daughter? Thiea is *your* daughter? You're telling me that your daughter is also my mate? The one who can break the curse and help me to defeat Morrigan? She can help us regain the power balance?” I flop down on the bed beside Niamh, stretching my arm over my face. *Dude, I am at a loss for words.*

“Fabulous! I love it. Both of you end up with your mates, so I end up the oldest of us because of two weres. Shit!” Niamh laughs so hard, she falls off of the bed.

"Yep. It’s true. Anna is out in the garden, explaining it to Thiea right now. I’ve wanted to tell you, to tell her, and openly announce she is my daughter for almost thirty years." He sighs and relaxes as he sits back in the chair.

You and I have been brothers in arms since Napoleon. What the Fates decide sometimes is a bit off, but fuck if this isn’t awesome! Standing back up to move towards him, I grin wildly.

“Thank you, Shoan, for not telling me all the gory details of last night. For future reference, I really don't need the visual either." Arif releases the breath he'd been holding as he stands. We embrace by clasping each other's forearms. He nods his head and smiles.

"Niamh, the curse never stated that any of us become mortal when the curse breaks, so nice try. You're not off the leash yet, little girl. I'll be here for centuries still. Why worry anyway? Once the curse is gone, the whole soul mate pairing should end. You will be able to—"

"Okay. Another topic, please. What I want to know is what we do about the book and Morrigan?" Arif voices.

"Ooh! I almost forgot about that." Niamh rises off the floor, brushes down her clothes and sits back down beside me. "When I went out last night on Elenor with the gang, we ran into Morrigan and her boys. George and some guy named Garron. I expect Sully was there too, but I didn't stick around to find out."

"Where'd you see them?" I ask.

"They were at the temple of Hephaestus, poking around monuments, looking for a block that Antonius told them was the key to finding the book. The majority of their conversations were internal, but Morrigan was pretty pissed at this Garron guy for not bringing Antonius to Athens. She really wanted him there personally. He wouldn't come with Garron, but he told him the book was located at the temple."

"So Garron's here now? He's the one who started this whole shitstorm with Thiea. He's Morrigan's son you said?"

"Yeah. She called him son and he called her mother, so I have to assume it wasn't a codename." Niamh smirks as I tug on a few strands of her hair. In retaliation, she pinches my side.

"Ouch," I snap before smacking the back of her head.

"I guess that means they're trying to go a different route, now that they don't have Thiea?" Arif asks us quizzically as he scratches his chin.

"I don't think Antonius would give anything up. He sent them on a wild goose chase. He knows where the book is. He helped me decide the location, and if he wanted to give it to them, he would have directed them to it, not away from it."

"All right, here's that truth part again, bro. Not only were you keeping secrets, but now you tell me Antonius knows where it is, even though I don't? Wow, you're just stacking up the shitstorm like Jenga. How about today is a get out of jail free card for you on secrets, but tomorrow, no more hiding. You can't look after the whole world like Atlas did. And speaking of a pass, how do we get ahold of Antonius? Second to that, do we take the book out of hiding?"

"No, definitely not. We leave it right where it is. As long as it's safely tucked away, they're screwed. Indirectly, the book staying where it is keeps us safe; no one can get it. Antonius didn't tell them where to go so he isn't working for them." Just thinking about Morrigan and her sons burn me. To know they tried to use Antonius to get to me makes me itch. I can't wait to condemn that bitch.

"Let's get the team back. We'll eat and decide a course of action. After, you tell me what that quip about Antonius was about. Spill it before I spill you." Niamh leans across the top of the headboard, cross legged, with a glare full of hatred. I haven't seen her truly upset since…well, let's just say since Korea.

You know that Antonius is an immortal, but I kind of neglected to tell you he's that way because of me. I turn away from her, expecting a barrage of damaging blows to the head.

Ni has never been noted for being calm.

What did you do, Shoan?

Okay, she's pissed. Niamh using her mind instead of her voice is scary. She reaches over to the Easter basket and grabs two grenades. I thumb the AK-47 for my own protection, but know that it will *not* save my ass at all.

She tosses the dangerous lobs into the air, giggling maniacally. She scares me.

Shoan, I think you have to explain what you're talking about. Great. Arif has reverted to speaking in his head as well. I cringe with fear, pulling myself closer to the door, hoping distance will assist. I figure I might as well show them with thoughts instead of dragging it out by speaking aloud. Once they've had enough time to see it for themselves, I speak, tentatively.

"I'm not about to apologize for saving Antonius. At the time, he was the only family I had left. His wife and child had died, he wanted to die, and I couldn't lose someone else dear to me. I couldn't. You weren't there, so don't judge me. It took so much out of me.

"I took a month of recovery, and I had to teach him how to deal with the pain of human thoughts, to live with them and around them. I left him twenty years later when we both came to Athens from Crete. I didn't see him again until I went to hide the book after the Japanese fiasco. That's all of it. Nothing more. Everything laid bare, so if you're going to toss a grenade, Ni, give me a moment to clear the human in the building first."

Waiting for a response from either of them seems to take an immeasurable amount of time. Niamh hands Arif a pink polka dotted grenade. As they're both extremely quiet, focusing all their attention on the pins, pushing and pulling them in and out, I visibly sweat.

"Say something, please. The silence is excruciating." This is stressful.

"Well, dearie, if I didn't love this house, then I'd lob a cherry red smiley face at your ass. I'd stand back drinking rum and coke, watching how long it takes for you to repair for fun." I know she would too.

Thank Goddess she likes the house. Saved by the tangible possessions once more.

"How about we ignore the mistakes and get back to the things we can fix," Arif interjects.

"Sure, easy for you to say, *Dad*. You weren't just hiding skeletons, you hid a whole other being." Placing a pin back in the red grenade, Niamh tosses it into the basket without a care for the consequences if it blew. There's times I wish she didn't enjoy strife and confrontation as much as she does.

I step towards the door. "I'm starved and parched. I need beer and good company. Let's round up the gang and go out for dinner."

Arif nods his head and curls his lip up just enough to show his bright white canines, then tosses his grenade in the basket. Even though Arif and I have been compadres, pals and buds for so long, I still get chills seeing those teeth glaring back at me.

Opening the door, Arif taps me on the shoulder in a move to say silently, *you're safe for now*, as Niamh and I step out of her bedroom.

"Shoan, I understand your reasoning behind what you did, and I'm sure you understand mine. Niamh will take time to deal with our betrayals, and we'll both just have to be patient."

Walking out into the brightly lit garden where Anna and Thiea sit, Chad, Terese, Marcus, and Patrick join us. Niamh grabs a drink with Anna and Thiea, who I think have been polishing off one of my favorite whiskeys. It's a century old corked Irish whiskey bottle that's almost empty.

"Anna suggested we get dinner at Hermion. Are you guys up for it?" Thiea asks as she hiccups.

Looking as radiant as ever without having to do a thing, her hair is tied back at the base of her neck, pulling it away from her face, but hangs loosely around her shoulders. She has on a plain white pair of linen pants and a crisp blue crepe shirt that complements her features impeccably. I'm finding it hard to cloud my thoughts. After all, it was only a few minutes ago I promised to keep things on the down low for a bit.

Good luck with that when she looks so edible.

"Okay, Okay! That's just about enough of that. You might have forgotten what it's like to hear thoughts, but the rest of us have had years of listening to your X-rated escapades. You need to keep things to yourself, Shoan!" Niamh shouts at me from the front door as she wraps her arms around Chad's waist, pretending to cover her ears in his expansive chest.

I suppress a laugh, thinking about what she's endure over the years. All the porn, hard-core sex, and momentous orgies. Now, for the sake of Arif and Anna, I'm trying to PG it.

"Sorry Arif," I say. It's not as easy as it sounds.

"Don't think on it too much. Really—don't." Arif's eyes glow dangerously as he takes Anna's hand, leading her out to the street.

As the rest take off into the night towards the restaurant, I pause in place as the most beautiful woman stands there waiting for me. Me? This vivacious beauty is waiting for me.

It feels so surreal.

Smiling, she takes my hand and places a chaste kiss on my cheek before we walk out to enjoy an early evening meal.

I know the ball has to drop soon. I never get this kind of good luck for long.

Chapter EIGHTEEN

Table for One?

Thiea

After talking with Jaz, I mean Anna? Mom? For hours, we ate all the fresh fruit and nuts, drank about a litre of tea, then polished off the ancient scotch.

I was feeling pretty good.

Thinking back on it, I've always felt different. I guess that clears up tons of questions. My dad is a vampire and my mom is a werewolf, and I'm falling for a man that I just met who's almost as old as Christ. What could be more exciting than that?

I always thought of soul mates as garbage, until I saw Garron and Cassie. The pain of separation, the searing heat of being together, entwined as one, the fear that if you were to lose one another, the death of your soul would be instantaneous. You hear stories on the news every so often of a man who dies and his wife who dies days or hours later. Once again, I see the truth of it, and it's not as surreal or as fantastical as Disney made up anymore.

With Shoan, I'm starting to see how it could feel. It's permanency. How it's ingrained on you like a tattoo. I had never thought of myself as someone's soul mate, as someone's everything, let alone anything. All I know is that I don't want to change it. I definitely don't want to go home to Toronto without figuring this out, that's for sure.

As we wait in line at the restaurant, I stand beside Shoan and take his hand in mine, relishing the feel of someone wanting to hold my hand.

Nice.

"What's the deal with your necklace?" Shoan asks.

"I guess you'll have to stay tuned to see the real me. Anna... Mom? Whatever. She wants me to wait so I don't go all freaky-deaky when we don't know the outcome."

Arif bends down in front of me to gather the tiny beads and the frail chain to inspect it. "I'm glad you're dealing with this so well, darling. I had to trade something precious to a very damaged sex demon to get the enchantment attached to something so intricate. I guess it was worth it, as it's lasted this long."

"We'll be waiting to figure this out," Shoan says, kissing the back of my hand, "together."

Smiling inside like a schoolgirl crush, I grin at the idea of doing something with someone else. "Honestly, I'm not one for waiting. I can't wait to release my inner bad girl. Impulsiveness is one of my worst traits. Maybe I'll overcome it with one of my other fetishes." I squeeze Shoan's hand lightly, stroking the inside of his palm. I don't remember how to breathe when he's with me. It's as if he takes all my common sense away, and all the pressures of the day disappear.

Arif smiles at me. He pulls me away from Shoan and wraps me

in a bear hug. I've never felt this close to my adoptive parents, and yet I lived with them for much longer than I've known the people in this room. It's weird, but this feels more intimate and heartfelt.

"Sorry," he says. "I've been wanting to do that since you walked into the house, and in turn, into my life."

"No problem whatsoever. I'm kinda getting used to the closeness of everyone's quirks. I can handle a hug or two," I tell him as I try to untuck my mouth from his shirt. With the nearness of him, I take a deep inhale of his scent. Arif smells like fresh cut cedar and apples. It's calming.

Turning back, Shoan stands with a grin that's erotic and teasing. Arif releases me before cuffing him on the side of the head.

"Son." I hear warning in that tone.

Laughing, I pull Shoan down for kiss. He kisses me as if he hasn't seen me in a year. It's full of passion and urgency, longing and care. If I'm going to be on the outside of people's jokes, at least I can make them count.

Releasing his mouth, he stares into my eyes. I stand there in awe of his beauty. He's gorgeous in every way. I try to read his thoughts like Jaz said we can, forgetting I still have on the necklace. For heaven's sake, I should just remove the damn thing and hope for the best. The only thing stopping me is turning into a big snarling hairy beast in the middle of Athens.

Yeah, that wouldn't go well. How do you explain that? *Oh, excuse my date. She hasn't shaved in a few weeks. She has a bit of a condition.*

The group laughs as I hide my face.

Fuck, I hope I can handle this.

As we're led into the building, the quaint atmosphere of the restaurant is fantastic. Vines dangle from wooden pillars. LED lights lend to the ambiance. Subtle lights peeking out of the vines, shooting like pinprick stars in paper, all while the smell of warm fresh sourdough bread, olives, and pungent red wine permeate your senses.

As we're led to our seats in the back near the waterfall, the waiter reminds me how long this day has been. The last thing I ate was figs and nuts while we drank. Dinner better be fulfilling; I'm fucking starving. A girl can't live off sex and whiskey. Well, I can, but only as an energy source, not nourishment.

"Groan. PG please, PG." I turn to see Niamh covering her face in Chad's shoulder as she tries not to laugh.

"*Kalispera,*" the waiter says. I don't know Greek. The phrase, *it all sounds like Greek to me*, totally comes to mind unbidden.

"Kalispera. Can we get two bottles of Chardonnay, a bottle of Pinot Noir, and a bottle of Ouzo, please," Shoan asks the waiter. Milling around the table, getting settled, our waiter leaves quite quickly to gather the wine.

Sitting on the far side, across from my mother, Shoan pulls up beside me on the left with Arif on the right. I feel a little closed in, but at the same time, warmly arranged. I smile at Arif, *my father*, hoping he understands that I don't feel any animosity towards him. I completely get the reasons for what transgressed over the years.

I mean, I've always wanted to know my parents, to know them and their reasoning for leaving me. Was I an accident that they couldn't care for? Was I loved like Jaz always told me, but circumstances justified that I was left to the system? Those were the thoughts that drifted by like clouds every day; now I know the truth.

Reaching over, Arif takes my hand. Kissing the back of it, he smiles. I know it will take some time to get used to the mind reading thing, and that everything will change as there's less hidden, more known, but for now, I'm adrift in their comments.

"It will take time, my small one, but we'll work through it," Arif says. I look into his eyes, realizing they're the same as mine. Now I get what Jaz always meant. The bright green with red peeking out, like a star-tracked night.

As we stare at one another, the waiter returns with the drinks, takes our orders, then moves on.

"How long did it take you to block out others from reading your thoughts?" I ask Jaz.

"I always could. It's second nature. For Dark Worlders it's ingrained, it's a defense mechanism. As for Shoan, well, he's just a—" Shoan interrupts her.

"Anomaly. I haven't had to block thoughts or hear Dark Worlders for almost ten centuries until yesterday. Humans are so used to keeping things to themselves that they don't understand that the internal voice is stronger; more intentionally damaging. If I was to say I hate you orally, it would come across nasty, but as an internal thought, it's worse. I'd rather be struck physically. Niamh is going to strike out at me for a while. It'll take centuries for her to forgive what I kept from her." As he looks to his sister, who's clearly trying desperately to ignore him, she's shooting him hatred in her mind at the same time.

I turn back to my mother. "Can you teach me?"

"You'll learn, I promise. We'll teach you after you're safe."

"Okay. Well, I've had enough of this crap already. Everyone loves each other and the world hasn't stopped turning. Morrigan is gonna try to kick some serious ass, and we have to work together to make this the fairy tale ending we want with Pinocchio and the cricket saying it will be just fine." Niamh stands up, brushing off her tighter than tight jeans, looking in my direction after her satirical diatribe. “Whatev. I need to go to the ladies’ room. Anyone care to join me?"

Knowing she means me, as she stares at me, I reply. "Sure. Lead on." I follow Niamh towards the bathroom, down the tight wooden staircase at the back near the bar.

Reaching the room, Niamh stops. "Listen, Thiea, I didn't need to go. I just wanted to say something without everyone craning their necks to hear.” Niamh pauses before continuing. "I think I can handle you being a part of this family. I can even handle that Anna is your mom and Arif is your father, but…” She stares deep into my eyes, like she can see straight through me. “Please, don't break his heart."

I lean up against the sink and sigh. I care for Shoan and his family, which in turn is my family too.

It’s funny. I feel like I belong here. If someone told me a week ago that I would be feeling connected in a way that seems totally immobile, transfixed and secure, I’d tell them to fuck right off and chew on dog treats.

Niamh laughs and slaps me on the shoulder. Always with forgetting others can hear my thoughts. Man, I’m going to have to figure out that blocking thing.

"I hope you trust me. I won't willingly harm him. Everything is moving at warp speed, and I’m not sure how to take all of it in without exploding. Shoan is the only thing that’s keeping me grounded right now. He’s the lifeline that I have to bring myself back to the boat from murky waters.” I slap my hand across my face at the TV evangelist sounding speech. “Wow, that sounds so needy. Niamh, I’m sure this is the norm for you, but my life normally consists of my store, shoes, wine, and looking for a date.”

“I can get this is going to be an adjustment. For us though, it’s just another day.” Niamh leans against the counter beside me, crossing her arms in front of her.

“I don’t want to be hurt or hurt anyone else, so I guess we’re on the same page. Now, I *really* do need to pee. Whiskey return trip and all. I'll meet you upstairs in a minute, okay?" I move towards the bathroom stall, awaiting her response.

“Yeah, cool. I’ll see you upstairs.” Niamh turns to leave, then calls, “Thiea?”

“Yeah?”

“If you need any help figuring out things, ya know, like how to hear thoughts, how to leap tall buildings like Superman, all that shit; I’m here for you.”

With a grin that lets me know she’s serious about helping me, I respond. “Thanks. I’m sure over the course of this clusterfuck, I’m gonna need all the help I can get.”

With that, she heads out and I do what I need to.

Washing up and starting back up the hall, I stop in the entranceway to the outdoor taverna. Watching them laughing and joking together, you can see that after years, there are unsaid comments and unwritten rules.

Who would have imagined that after only forty-eight hours, I could seem at peace with complete strangers? Even my mother and Father are strangers to me.

"Hello, Thiea."

You have got to be kidding!

Really?

Now?

A sense of dread falls across me as I hear a voice I would know anywhere. "Garron, stalk much? How ya been? How's the family? Cassie know you're an asshole? And please tell me, why is it that I decide to get out of the country away from you, yet here you are?" Antagonizing him may lead myself towards a path of certain destruction, but fuck it. Let's throw caution to the wind. He's the ass that got me into this whole new world anyway. Time to nut up.

"Thiea, I think you and I got off on the wrong foot." He's sarcastic and dangerous sounding. "If you don't come with me, I may have to persuade you in another way." Garron reaches for my arm and grips it tightly, flashing a gun from under his shirt that's neatly tucked into his belt. "How about you and I take a walk. We really wouldn't want to alarm anyone, would we?" He nods to the table where everyone is sitting.

There they are, laughing and enjoying the peace of the night. Going with Garron to talk won't harm them. It won't cause a ruckus, and I'm sure I can handle Garron. Right?

Agreeing seems right. I don't want to cause a fight in the restaurant, involving them when he's my problem, not theirs.

Resigning myself to my fate, we traipse back through the packed restaurant and out to the dingy alleyway. As we start down the street, away from Shoan, my parents and Niamh, I'm thinking this may not have been the best idea. There's nothing I can do that would be of any help as long as I have on this necklace, and as long as I don't know the outcome of removing it, I'm wrong to argue.

As we pass a few open stores, another person pops out and joins our little entourage.

"Thiea, this is my big brother, Sullivan. Sullivan, this is Thiea." The gargantuan man smiles a wide tooth grin with the biggest pair of canines I have ever seen.

Garron smirks, then winks as he pulls tightly on my arm, turning down another side street.

"Granny. My, what big teeth you have," I say as Garron and his Cro-Magnon brother laugh a deep, resonate guffaw.

Fuck me. I don't think I'm in Kansas anymore.

As I'm led to parts unknown to be pillaged, raped, and probably dumped in the nearest alley, I think dinner has been cancelled.

And damn, I was looking forward to that Ziti.

Chapter NINETEEN

The Devil May Care

Shoan

It's been so many years waiting for Thiea that it feels like a dream. I sit here listening to Arif and Anna, and yeah, it's wonderful to see that we're content without barriers or lies. Anna's been able to read our minds and hear our conversations for years. It must be making it even harder for Thiea to be on the outside of our jokes, questions, or even snide remarks. I'll have to continue to speak aloud until she can learn.

"Shoan, what do you think about Morrigan and her sons? Maybe it's a good time to find Antonius, talk to him. Get his feeling on the subject?" Arif asks me as we await Thiea's return.

Topping up my wineglass, I think about the situation. Antonius didn't have to lead them, or tell them anything, but he decided to send them there. Why?

"I think he sent them there to alert us. He's too shrewd to just lead them to the temple without a reason." I sip my wine, just as the waiter arrives with our dinner plates of piping hot food.

"Where's Thiea? She should've been back by now." Looking over to Arif, I feel that something is amiss.

“I left her in the washroom,” Ni says as she rises from the table. “She said she was just gonna be a sec. I’ll go look.” Walking off to check while we silently send our thoughts back and forth between each other, Arif leaves the table and enters the restaurant, scenting the air, touching surfaces for traces of her. Arriving back, the look on his face has all of us worried.

"She’s gone, but she didn't leave alone. There's a vamp with her. I can smell his blood at the entrance of the restaurant. He reeks. Bloody trappa.” Arif walks back over to where the rest of us are preparing to leave.

“Niamh, did you get any idea where they were staying when you ran across Morrigan the other night? I think we have to assume it's one of her boys." Arif pulls out enough cash to cover the meal and drinks as we all head for the door without touching our meals.

"No, they made no mention when I was there. I just happened upon their internal conversation. Remember, they were trying to be discreet."

"Shoan, I think you need to call Antonius and find out what he told them. We need some direction—" Anna says as she’s cut off.

"No need to look, my good friend," Antonius states as his large frame blocks the way to the street.

"How did you know we were here? I mean, we didn't even call you yet?"

"I came looking for you at the villa. Maria told me you were here tonight. She actually told someone else that you were here too. They left their mark on the poor girl.” Waving his meaty hands in the air, he says, “Don’t worry. She's alive. Though a little depleted of blood. I would have been here earlier, but I waited for the ambulance first." Showing us with his thoughts how she looked, Maria didn't deserve what she went through. The visions of her in my mind, how it felt, how Sullivan debased her, used her, engorged himself on her is inhumanely disgusting.

"Thank you for looking after Maria," Niamh tells him, bringing me out of the stupor.

"No problem. I always look after family; yours are mine. Now, who is this girl you’re all worried about? Garron told me you had the book and the key, but said nothing of a girl," Antonius asks as we all start to answer him with our thoughts. I'm sure it’s overwhelming, but it’s quicker than trying to say it aloud.

"So let me get this straight. This girl is the key, and she just happens to be the daughter of a vampire and a werewolf? Your daughter?" he says, directing his questions to Arif and Anna. "Don’t answer.” Antonius puts up his hand to halt their comments. “I can't handle you bombarding me again with answers. I can find out myself later when you’re not shouting. Niamh, you're normally the most boisterous one. Why are you and Shoan both so quiet?" He turns towards me and my sister with a quizzical look on his face.

She's my soulmate, Antonius. She already broke the first part of the curse, I tell him with my mind, showing him the past few days. Meeting her at the airport, the plane, the meeting of her parents, her and I together—

"Hold it! I don't need to see that part of your life, Shoan. It’s been about two centuries, and I don't watch porn. Some things I suggest you keep to yourself."

“See! I told him that too,” Ni interjects, grinning.

Arif and Anna look at me with contempt. Rubbing my hands

across my face in frustration, I wonder what we do? Standing here doesn't help, and we can't just call around to the hotels. What would we ask? *Hey, do you notice that you're missing guests daily*? People would hang up.

So how do we find them? Like a miracle, my phone rings. I'd almost forgot I had it with me. It's an unknown number and normally I'd ignore it, but under the circumstances, I answer.

"Hello?"

"Shoan?" Thiea's voice is clearly distressed.

"Thiea, are you okay? Where are you?" I almost shout into the phone before I hear it pulled away from her.

"Hello, Shoan. It's been a long time since we spoke last. How are you? How's the family? I must admit, Thiea's nice, but not the best company," Morrigan says teasingly as I hear Thiea scream in the background.

"Morrigan, I swear it'll be the last thing you do if she's harmed." I'm furious.

"Tsk tsk, Shoan. Don't get upset, it would be so bad for her. So far we've been genial, and we haven't partaken in her hospitality."

"What do you want, Morrigan?"

"You misunderstand me. I'm not about to give up Thiea; she's still our guest. I want the book, and you will bring it to me. You have two hours, no more, before I start enjoying the pleasures of our little girl here. Where to begin? Should I start with her mind, or her body?"

"Morrigan, if you—"

"You're in no position, Shoan. Where would be best for you? Oh, and I suggest you make it close to the book, not some other remote place," Morrigan says sweetly.

I look at my friends and family. In my mind, I see what they will do for Thiea, and what they wish to do to Morrigan.

Arif is the first to speak as I cup the speaker. "Shoan, she is my daughter. They don't know that, and we will meet them where *we* choose. They don't have the upper hand. Surprise is still on our side."

Looking at Niamh and Anna, both are quiet, but they say the same with just a look. They will stand behind my decision, whatever it is.

Putting the phone to my ear once more, I respond. "Morrigan, I'm sure you know where the temple of Hephaestus is. Meet us in the Stoa of Attalos. One hour. If you harm her, you will pay for all eternity, as will your family." I hang up the phone without waiting for a response. I know she heard me and is anxiously getting things together to leave.

"What do we do? Do we give them the book? Then what?" Anna's hysterical as she turns into Arif's chest, sobbing. "I will not lose my daughter to the hands of that monster. She is evil of the greatest proportions."

“All right, then. We need a plan of attack What do you suggest?” I ask them.

“I will do whatever it takes to keep my daughter safe,” Arif says, Anna tight in his arms.

"I was already prepared for war, so let's get the battle started. I haven't had a chance to use my new toys." Niamh sneers with a maniacal glare in her eyes. Turning to Chad, Terese, and the rest of the gang she grins. “Who's up for a bit of dirty warfare?”

“Game on, sister,” Terese cheers with a glint of excitement in her eyes. She flashes her small vampiric like teeth, and as Patrick tears off his clothing—in public, I might add—he phases out in the blink of an eye. He soars into the sky as an enormous black bird.

"Chad. How about some recon?" I ask.

"Always."

"I guess we can meet up at the chapel, just beside the Stoa?"

"No problem, buddy. Care to join the run, Anna?" Marcus asks as Chad heads off down the alley beside the restaurant, without waiting for a response.

As she kisses Arif, I smile. I know that Anna is far from gleeful; she's downright pissed off. Anna wipes the back of her hand across her face. Her stoic warrior facade is in place as she removes the trace of tears and running mascara before nodding to Arif. She follows the boys into the unlit alley. From the sound of it, all are off and running in seconds. The howling and snarling will scare the living shit out of any humans who happen across their path, not to mention, the Dark Worlders who aren't expecting a pack of werewolves in Athens central on the prowl.

"I agree. They aren't expecting all of us," Antonius says as he smacks me on the shoulder.

Looking at those still standing by, I count myself lucky to have them with me after all these years.

"They're only expecting us," I say, looking over at Antonius and Niamh. "They know I don't go anywhere without you, sis. Antonius, they'll anticipate that you and I will match up sooner or later after the little convo you had with Garron. So we have to work from the premise that Thiea is going to withhold info about us and her parent-age. Let's keep it that way."

For a while now, we've been walking away from the restaurant towards the Stoa, and as we reach the gates one by one, each of us hop over the steel bars without touching a thing. I turn to the right once we’re inside and ascend the large steps to the entrance. Anna, Marcus, and Chad are sitting with Arif on the large stone steps leading to the grand doorway, looking relaxed and ready to take on anything. With Patrick perched on her shoulder, Terese appears from the side, away from the tiny stone chapel.

"I need a full vote on this. I won't do it to jeopardize our lives for just one of us. Once was enough," I say to all of them.

My sister answers with a huge grin on her face. She’s always up for a good fight, even in no-win situations.

Goddess help Morrigan. Over the years, she’s been blessed to avoid Niamh. This time, I’m not asking her to hold back. She can bring on the full power of her charm. Well, what I find charming, others might see as deadly.

"Definitely in from both of us,” Anna states as she continues to wipe away her residual smeared mascara, redressing in her clothes.

"Antonius, you have as much at stake as I do. If the curse is lifted, we don't know what the consequences are. You’ll make or break the deal here, my good friend." Antonius quietly stares at me.

"I only ever wanted one thing, Shoan, and that was my family. I will not deprive you of your chance; not now, not ever. I stand behind you, my friend. Plus, that vampire pissed me off. I hate people walking in my grape rows." Antonius sneers as he thinks about Garron. He may not look scary with glowing eyes like the weres and vampires, and he may not have a deadly streak like Niamh, but his size and temperament should put *her* on guard.

"Fine. Well, we’ll need to be ready before she arrives. Arif, Marcus, Terese and Chad, you need to leave. We still need to keep up the element of surprise. If she or any of them know about you, this goes to shit. Hide up at the church on the hill. If something goes wrong, I'll signal you to join in. Anna, read over the sections you need. I suggest you look at Remus' notes on Dark Worlders and double bloodlines again. If they think we'll just roll over and hand them the book, and Thiea as well, then they're sorely mistaken. Ni, you know what I want from you. Enjoy." I bump fists with her as she heads off for the roof of the building.

Arif walks off towards the church after giving his love a deep, sultry kiss.

As I reach the end of the expansive veranda where the statue of Nike sits stoic and proud, Antonius flanks me. Of course, the head is missing, and only those who have seen it whole before know who it is. "Anna, can you stand on the far side. I'll need you to trip the lock as I open the tiny door."

Moving to the other side of the statue where I indicated, she waits. I move to the back of the statue's large marble base, feeling around for what I need. When the Stoa was rebuilt, I donated a sculpture—anonymously, of course—of Nike. I'd kept it hidden for centuries before giving away. Though, Antonious and I carved a base for it to rest on that has a special hiding place, no one would know that. We hid the book within it for safekeeping.

Antonius knows to hold the statue aloft as I move lower to open the box below. "Anna, run your hand down the back. There's a small symbol, a Delta. Press it in and hold." Anna nods and bends down towards the back of the statue. Within seconds, I hear a click from inside the base as the door on the side pops open. I push the corner at the top as the remainder of the door swings freely open. Exhaling, I reach in and slowly remove the ancient papyrus binding.

It's as fragile as I remember. The pages are split on the ends, crackled in the middle, and a creamy caramel color where the light had reached it over the years. The inner portion is the original color, a pallid grey. The deep ochre painting on the cover of an ankh stands proud, and as brilliant as it had the first time I saw it. This of course was meant as a cute little joke, the symbol for life even though our lives, if that's what you call it when you live a thousand lifetimes, are purely that of death. The true irony of the Gods; we are both a tragedy and a comedy to them.

I open the book to the first section, remembering it by heart. It reads, ***Forever the life, forever the pain. Reader be warned.*** How true that is for many of us.

Anna, with her hands out, sits waiting as I hesitantly hand it to her. I have always protected it. I am always fearful when it comes to messing with these spells, and she understands this more than most ever will.

"Shoan. You know I only have your best interests at heart; yours and my daughters. I won't let anything happen to either the book or her." Thinking on it, I nod my agreement, handing her the book tentatively.

Being careful not to damage the pages, Anna flips through the first few, caressing each with loving fingers, looking for the answers she needs. There are notes from Fey, the Førie folk, vampires who attempted to create others of their kind, various other Gods and Deities, and I think even the Norse tried to join their bloodlines with humans. All whom attempted to correct the failures of the past and start anew found the same; failures anew.

There's even a few pages written only about my beginnings. It tells of what was done to the past experiments, how they tweaked them, rearranged the order of the herbs and castings, and lastly, how the Oracle in Delphi put the final pin in place.

Only the blood of both can unlock the power. Only the key can turn the lock. Hide it away until it's calling upon those who are not the one. Willing be the damnation and end for all. Anna repeats the same lines that have haunted and driven me mad for centuries.

"Shoan, I think this is about Thiea and you. Everything we've done to hide her from the world will be her undoing. We never—I mean, we…" Turning to me, Anna rises off the marble floor, holding the precious book in her hands. "I can't help her the way she is. We've had her locked in her human form her whole life. The way she is, she won't be able to withstand or fight Morrigan."

"I don't care that she can't fight, as long as she's near me. It's been painful with her gone, and it's only been a little less than an hour. Imagine a year or more without her? I won't be able to function." I've been trying to hide my trembling since Thiea left, but I'm afraid it's pretty noticeable. With the floodgates open, the block removed and raw, my mind is taking a punishing from the voices, both past and present.

After all my years as a bachelor, just enjoying women and my freedom, laughing at all the poor saps who found their mates and that couldn't even go out of range without pain, here I am in the same position, feeling like I'll fall apart.

I have to keep that hidden from Morrigan and her merry band of jackasses. There's no fucking way that I'll let her see I don't have control. If she knows that Thiea's my mate, then it will make it even harder to get her back. Morrigan will stop at nothing to keep me in excruciating pain for the next millennia.

Anna pours over the pages in the book, and I realize that if we're going to save Thiea, we have to be smart. The book may be what they want, but we don't have to give them every page.

"Anna, are there some pages that would be helpful to remove?"

"I…I'm not sure I can do that. I mean, not that I'd want to, but the notes on one can lead to another. It's like high school graffiti. Everyone was a scribbler. Some notes are just notes, but there's pictographs, notations to see other pages. Others have even added clippings of herbs. I'm not sure it's possible to take a page or two out."

"I say we try. You have about fifteen minutes, maybe less. Do what you can, or memorize as much as possible." I don't want to press her and rush it, but I know if there's anything we can do to slow them down, we should.

My phone vibrates, pulling me from my wandering thoughts. It's a text from Niamh.

We r in place. Let's hope this works.

I reply back, saying that I hope it does too. If it goes wrong, it isn't just me on the line this time.

"Shoan," Anna calls out, and as I turn around, taking a seat on the cold marble steps beside her, she smiles. That's a good sign.

"Okay. Skimming over some of the notes on this page here and here, I think I might have something that can help. It could be an advantage, but at the same time, it could blow up."

I turn my attention to the pages she's peering at. Scribbles, hieroglyphics, ancient Greek, Latin, and something that looks like Sanskrit.

"What the hell is that? I can't read that." Running my fingers across the strange markings on the top of the page, I try to decipher it with all the languages I've learned.

"It's Bactrian. It's Giza. She says this; ***My great daughter, I wrote this for only you. You will return him to his path, but the cost will be high for both. He will give up his humanity or you will give up yours. Choose carefully. Remember it is something you cannot take back.*** Why write it in Bactrian though? Why not in Gaelic?" Anna asks.

"My only guess is that she intended it to be for whom she knew could read it. It would need to be someone with a talented mind to read it in another language other than the native tongue of Ireland. That way, it's out of the prying eyes of Morrigan and those like her."

"My feeling is…you're not going to like it, Shoan. We have to let the *cat* out of the bag." *It's time to stop hiding her,* Anna states internally.

As if on cue, there's a rustling of feet behind us. At the end of the porch are two people I hate the most in this world. Their heavy jackboots rattle on the pristine marble floor, breaking the night's serenity. The cacophony causing the small rodents in the surrounding area, and birds in the trees nearest to flee. Anna rises to stand beside me, blocking the book behind her.

Damn fucking jackals, the whole lot of them, I say to Anna unspoken. She nods her agreement.

The tension is tangible as Thiea wanders in, guarded by Sullivan, George, and a man I don't know. Following behind regally and proud is Morrigan. I know all of them intimately, except the one. His tall frame, platinum blond hair, and good looks tell me he's related to Morrigan. Especially as he's cut from the same mold as Sullivan. I guess there was more than two brothers after all.

Pressing his fingernail to the base of Thiea's jaw, keeping her inline, he grins, showing off his canines. One small movement of pressure and her blood would course down her neck. Not a fabulous idea in a pack of vamps.

"Morrigan. How about we cut the bullshit and get on with it. I want you to die and for you to take your children with you. Let the girl go. She's of no consequence, just a girl I met on a plane and fucked for a few hours. I don't see how a mere dormant could affect the course of our fight. Or are you reduced to grasping at anyone who shows a drop in their bloodline?" I say sweetly, all the while grinding my teeth to stop from reaching across and killing her on the spot.

"Tsk tsk, Shoan. Thiea may be dormant, but she's caught your eye. You really should keep your thoughts blocked better. And yes, I knew once I saw you in the airport that she was destined to be another notch on your bedpost. Now let's make the night uneventful and quick. My children, unlike the company of mongrels you keep, are hungry and very anxious to taste this lovely lady. What do you say we get this going?" Brushing down her outfit, as if the mere closeness to us is no more than speck of dust on her clothing, she sneers, showing me her pearly whites. She's always felt her race was superior, and that she was above all—the Queen Bitch.

"No matter your paltry thoughts about my kind, Shoan. I see you are still in this form, so that means this," she turns her nose up in disgust at Anna, "she-wolf beside you hasn't removed the curse. What do you say we give her a shot at the book once more, Shoan?" I hold Anna back with a look.

Not yet. Wait, I tell her.

Morrigan sneers and signals the one holding Thiea to push his nail into her neck harder, drawing blood. Thiea struggles under his grip, trying to get away. Morrigan places her finger along Thiea's neck where the blood trickles down her neckline and sniffs the air. Holding back from leaping at her, I watch in disgust as Morrigan licks Thiea's gorgeous neck.

I want to tear the fucking vampire she-witch from stem to stern. What she's doing is awful and expected, but I hate it.

I know about bloodletting. The taking of one's blood is unconditionally erotic, and Thiea can no more help the feelings she has from it, as she would feel if I were stroking her breasts with my tongue.

Listening to Thiea's moan from the contact, Morrigan stares at me, licking the corners of her mouth with a grin.

"Ohhh. I hit a sore spot, eh', Shoan? Oh Athena, don't worry. I'll leave something of you if Shoan cooperates with us *fully*."

Taking a deep breath to calm myself, I stare into Thiea's eyes, trying to find solace. "Morrigan, I may not be as strong or as powerful as the rest of you right now, but I will guarantee that I will take your life. Soon."

"Now, Shoan. If you don't want anything to happen to sweet, sweet Thiea, then don't do anything stupid. After all, we came here to talk civilly."

"I don't want to talk to you, I want to kill you." I'm furious with her, but I know it would put Thiea in harm's way if I try an attack too quickly, or at all.

"I have a proposition. I think that we have fought for enough years without a way out of this miserable curse, and I will admit, it was my fault that you are as you are. But I couldn't allow you to judge me then, and definitely not now."

"You're right, it is your fault. If you had just left things the way they were, I would have moved on after judging you to the next, and the next after that." Being this close to Thiea, but out of reach is excruciating. I can hardly contain myself as I visibly start to shake like a leaf in the breeze.

Sullivan crouches defensively, protecting his mother and the weaker trappa beside her, whom I suppose is Garron, his brother.

"You're right. This man here is no longer immortal. That witch Giza made that happen. You want to be as you were and I want him back. So my proposition is this; I want my son to live eternally once more. He has two beautiful sons that I want to see live to their full potential without the worries of them having to find a human mate, and I want to remove the curse. For that, *you* must become your previously, yet horrid looking lovely self. If you don't go ahead, I can tell you this dormant will not live till morning." Morrigan reaches over and presses her nail into Thiea's neck further, eliciting a small squeal. Morrigan pounces, biting fully on her neck. Thiea slouches into the embrace, falling prey to the endorphins that make her pliant.

After that moment, pretty much everything became a blur. Patrick, Marcus, and Terese engaged a surprising number of vampires that were hiding around the ruins, and Arif skidded gracefully down the roof of the church to attack the hulking form of Sullivan. The two were intertwined in an embrace, like two grizzlies fighting over a honey hive. Niamh, in all her glory, tossed her pink and blue grenades, swinging machetes and howling like the war Banshee she is. Antonius appeared on my left, protecting me, but it also stopped me from reaching Thiea.

All I cared for was her, and for that, I needed to stop Morrigan.

The transfer of thoughts from Thiea's blood would not only leave her in a weakened state, unable to fight back, but as she is still human, it could kill her. I had to stop it.

Making my way around Antonius' grip, I grasp Morrigan's shirt in one hand and her hair in the other, causing her to release Thiea. Thiea falls to the ground, motionless, in a heap, as I attempt to destroy Morrigan in any way possible.

"Enough!"

Holding up her hands, Morrigan halts the advance of her sons and those fighting with her, like a queen's command. Immediately, they all stop.

Turning around, I see Anna is down on her knees cradling the book tightly to her chest, while trying to shield Thiea's prone form.

Garron holds a gun to Anna's craned neck, leaving her exposed and vulnerable. She's unable to shift to protect herself.

"Release my mother, and I'll let the were live. You don't really have a choice, Chimeric, as you're outnumbered, outgunned, and outfought." He shouts out with a gleam of insanity flashing across his angelic features.

My friends, my brothers in arms, and my family are all in peril. I have no control over the situation, and everything once again is dependent on Morrigan. Sullivan holds Arif by the hair, fingernail to his neck. Antonius is knocked out cold from me vaulting over him to get at Morrigan. Patrick has flown off—thank the Goddess for that—but Marcus and Chad are both held by large vamps with their boots holding them in place at the scruff of their necks.

I have no way out of this. Relinquishing my hold on Morrigan, I stand there watching as everyone recovers; everyone but Thiea. She's passed out on the ancient marble floor, lifeless and still.

"Shoan, you disappoint me. I want us to get along." As she pats down her clothing, straightening her hair into a ponytail down her back, she motions for her consort, a prick I haven't seen in years, to move forward.

Harrison removes the book from Anna's grip, handing it to Morrigan. "My dear, Anna. I know you can read the book, and I want you to release the curse on Shoan. My wish is for him to return to Ireland. I know that sounds bizarre, but as I said before, I want the curse removed. I feel this is a fair trade. Don't you think it's magnanimous of me? A trade for a trade? The life of my son for the life of your daughter." She peers down at the idle body on the floor.

"I would rather you were rotting in the ground with bugs in your eyes. *My daughter*," she sneers, "is none of your concern. If you harm her again, it will be me looking at you from above as Shoan judge's your ass," Anna says spitefully.

"Let's get this straight. I don't give a damn about any of you, and if you try anything like that again, Thiea will not be the only one that pays the price."

She turns to me. "Shoan, what's the verdict? Do we ask our dear friend Anna here to perform the reversal? I promise, no harm will come to the girl now if you agree."

Everything has been for this and this alone. I'd be released, but I don't trust Morrigan an inch. As Antonius stirs, I reach down, grabbing his hand helping him to his feet. Morrigan signals Sullivan to release Anna.

"Time is ticking, Shoan. We need an answer. Yes or no?" Sully says as Garron holds the book back out to Anna.

I sigh, resigning that we've lost…for now. "Anna. Do as they say, please." Anna gives me a look that says what words can't, while she moves away from me to sit on the edge of the limestone stairs.

Fingering the pages one by one and locating the passages she needs, Thiea slowly stirs. She's still frail, exhausted, and depleted from the bite, but she'll survive, which makes me grateful and scared in earnest. She moves over beside Anna and sits down, shaking off the sleep as she gazes upon the book.

"Do you know what you're looking for?" Thiea asks in wander, touching the pages.

"Yes, I do, darling. And I need you for this, okay?" Anna's still thumbing through countless notes and ancient writings when she stops on an area, pointing at a note on the top. "Here, this is what you need to read."

Thiea looks at the notation, then back at her mother. She seems unsettled by what Anna has asked. "Are you kidding me? I don't know how to read this. I sell shoes. Do I look like a linguist?"

Anna flips to the previous page, reads a line, then looks back at her daughter. "Try it now."

Pouring over the words, she replies, "Christ on a Cracker! How the hell did you do that?"

"I'm special, love. Please, read it for me," Anna implores.

"Not a flying, fucking Dutchman, will you get me to say that! No fucking way." Glaring at me, she turns to Garron with contempt lighting her eyes. "I won't make you immortal again. Shoan can continue in this life until you're dead. I would rather die than let you, or any of the other blood sucking vampiric morons become immortal again."

I step up to her, holding her face in my hands lovingly, as I look into her eyes. I know she's afraid. I need her to know that I trust everything will be all right. "Please, don't worry about me."

"Shoan, if I say this it will change everything," she whispers quietly. "They'll have the upper hand, even more than they do now. They don't deserve it. It isn't right." Staring imploringly at me, I can feel her terror at the idea of releasing the evil that has been culled for so long. She worries that we won't be able to handle them and control it.

"Please. I beg you. I can't stand seeing any more harm come to you, especially not for the likes of me. Just say it," I plead.

Thiea sits quietly, and it seems that everything else moves in slow motion, like a movie montage. After all these years of nothing, everything is coming to fruition. I'll have my strength, my power, and as icing on the cake, my soul mate within my reach. Downside? I have to give Morrigan what she wants. The plus though, I get the opportunity to erase Morrigan from the Earth.

The landscape of our skirmish has adjusted as everyone waits with baited breath for something to happen. I get it. They're protecting what they feel is their greatest asset while I watch in horror. We're at their mercy. It's like hovering eagles, waiting for the mouse to come out of it's safe place.

Thiea takes the fragile book from her mother. Closing her eyes, she sighs.

I just hope you know what you're doing, she says in my mind.

"You," she points to Morrigan. "I hope you try to run and hide. It'll make for good sport. I don't see Shoan and his friends just lying down to die."

You have to admit, she isn't powerful, but she has an impressive attitude.

"If you would please, Thiea," Morrigan says in a rather bored tone.

"Elle fat kadimoh tah. Lost is the person who forgets his past. Illei fast maat. What is past is dead. You who has wandered without home, return now and be hale." Thiea looks directly at me as she recites the passage in ancient Arabic.

"That's it? That's all of it? Does it say anything else?" Garron asks impatiently.

"No. It doesn't say anything else. I don't have to say one more, single fucking word," Thiea grinds out.

"Come now, Thiea. You don't have to speak, but is there a deed to be done to consecrate this spell?" Morrigan flicks her tongue across her ample incisors, egging me on, knowing this is a warning of sorts.

"Thiea, does it say more?"

"It says you have to be bitten and drank from. Dry." Bowing her head in defeat, she averts her eyes from me, saying sorry internally.

Without an ounce of hesitation, Morrigan vaults over her sons and injects her teeth into my neck in a flash. I had no chance of protecting myself as she was on me like lightning. I felt the prick on my neck and the callous edge of her tongue as she licked the open wound. Digging her nails into my shoulder to hold me still, I couldn't think. I couldn’t move at all. I was held in place like a fly in a spider’s trap.

As time passed, I could feel my body succumb to the enjoyment, relishing in the heat like an orgasm. I had no control over the arousal, even as I was warring with my own libido. It’s true, it was massively erotic.

As my cock pulsed and strained against the confines of my jeans, I envisioned Thiea sprawled out on the bed, touching herself with wild abandon, caressing her clitoris and licking her fingers after she came. I wanted to be there. I ached to seep into her, delve my fingers inside her, pumping within her roughly, embracing her; it was more than I could handle.

I understood immediately how vampires were able to entrap their prey to their will, to enjoy the moment before death. I could hear everyone screaming my name as she devoured me, but I could do nothing about it.

Once she released me, I felt weak and exhausted. I was knocked to the ground with the sheer lack of blood circulating in my body, and the last thing I saw was Thiea’s regretful face as I felt my knees give way.

Before passing out.

Chapter TWENTY

Fear and Loathing

Thiea

"I'm telling you, the unmitigated power of the Chimeric was exquisite. No, I can't explain his flavor, exactly. It was a filet mignon with the perfectly paired Sancerre. It popped as it hit my senses. It was fantastic."

"Argh, Morrigan! Really, shut up. I'm getting you want to torture us, but I'd rather be water boarded." I can't handle hearing her talk about Shoan like a Michelin Five Star connoisseur.

"Chyene, hang on a sec. I have to teach our lovely guest here some manners." Cradling the phone in her hand to cover the mouthpiece, she glares at me, baring her teeth. "I understand you've never been introduced to us before, so I'll excuse your—"

"Disgust and loathing," I interject.

"I was going to say rudeness, but keep it up, and I'll ruin my appetite on you."

"Really, you think I would be that bad? Huh, I thought I'd be more of a soft, buttery, Belgian chocolate." I smirk, knowing I'm still interrupting her phone call.

"Thiea, I don't eat *dog food.* Mongrels aren't on my menu, darling. Now excuse me." As she walks off into the other room, continuing her conversation, I wait for her to leave to talk to Jaz in quiet.

"Sorry again, Cheyne, it's clearly poor upbringing the girl had that has made her like that. Yes, I know. Really deplorable. A horrific mating if you ask me. I know! A were and one of our kind? I always expected more from him. So, anyway, as I was saying…"

Once she's out of earshot, I turn in my bindings so that Jaz and I are close enough to talk without being heard. "Okay, Toto, we're not in Kansas anymore. And I'm pretty sure we can't hope for the cavalry anytime soon. Plan of attack?"

She's quiet. The badass orphanage headmistress is not in the house. "No plan yet, sorry. I say we listen. After all, we'll be the first to hear what's going on, and the first to be able to figure a way out of this. If we try, we won't make it far. We'll end up right back in their hands. Nothing will have been accomplished if we're out cold on the floor."

I think about what she says, and I hate to admit it, but fuck me! She's right. Trying to escape will gain us nothing.

"Fine. I'll be the good little girl and wait my turn. But she's pissing me off, talking about Shoan, you, and Arif like that." I reach around and put my hands in hers. It seems to soothe the hole in my soul.

"It's okay, we'll be just fine. And so will they. I'm not worried." As always, Jaz tries to comfort me. I think it's her defense mechanism. In the sight of terrible shit occurring, turn it around so that you comfort someone else, therefore forgetting your own terror.

"You know, I gotta ask you something. I still don't get how I could read that passage. What did you do to make it so I could?" I ask.

"There was a spell for opening up the mind so that you can see. The words that were on that page were a jumble of different languages, no one could have read it if they didn't know Bactrian. I do. So without that, they wouldn't have been able to unlock the passages."

"Okay, I get it. So without you reading that, I couldn't have helped? I think that would have been better. I hate what happened."

"Don't hate it, honey. You did what was necessary, and in the long run it will erase all the things done to Shoan and help him recover. Just being who you are—"

"Right, so let's get back to that. What am I? I mean, really. If you're a were and Arif is a vampire, what am I? Shit it sounds like a cartoon. I'm the wererabbit."

She laughs at my joke. "No, you're not anything like that. Here's the thing. When the curse was put on Shoan, Giza also made it that we could only find our soul mates in humans. Tying us to them made us mortal. We couldn't find one in another Dark Worlder, so technically, we couldn't live forever. Here's the twist; I was human. Arif met me when I was. Sure, I was a witch, but when I became pregnant with you it changed. I was bitten shortly after meeting him, but before you were born."

"Okay, so here's the million-dollar question. Am I a were like you, or am I a vampire like Arif? That's why you bound me and hid me away, isn't it?"

"Sort of. Like I said, I was bitten when you were not yet born, but, remember we have the blood of Giza in our family, so technically, we're of the Førie folk too. Just to throw in a dash of fun for good measure, the were that bit me was originally a Bezerker. Chad, Shoan's friend, bit me by mistake."

Fucking fabulous! So here's the real shit; I'm a mixed up bag of tricks. No wonder they put the necklace on me. Now I know why Garron could say I was from the same as him. This shit just gets better and better.

"Okay, so I get why you don't want the necklace removed now —"

"Oh no. You've made a mistake there, sweetheart. *Now* I want you to remove it. They've been thinking you're the product of a vampire with a human. They have no idea you're possibly more than that." Jaz cranes her neck around to look me in the eye with a look of pure determination. She *really* wants to let the cat out of the bag.

"So we've gone from hide it, to let's get yer freak on? I'm game if you are. Only thing is, what if I hurt someone, like you?"

"Trust me. Weres are harder to kill than you think. My scars? I always said it was a mugger, but it was Chad when he attacked me. Arif nearly tore him apart, thinking he had killed his wife and child. Imagine the shock when I awoke at his feet to grab him by the balls, before he had the chance to harm Chad. Quite spectacular, actually. I think I might have growled at him too."

Awesome.

"Fine. So if I bend down just enou—"

"What are we doing, my lovely guests? I see a heated conversation and a thought of escape. It wouldn't do you much good as there are more of us here than you think, and more than you can handle, *Dog*," Morrigan quips as she reenters the room, setting the phone on the side table. “Just because I’ve told them to keep you alive, doesn’t mean that they can’t toy with you a bit.”

“Fuck you. I may not be like Anna, but I know for sure a shit-storm will come your way. Karma’s a bitch. You opened Pandora’s box of toys, now you get to play. I’m sure Shoan and—”

“Oh, you are so mistaken if you put your trust in the losing team. Arif was easy to subdue, my Sully is still stronger and quicker. Being mated has weakened Arif, poor soul. Antonius was the only real problem outside of the other misfits that were with Shoan. He was able to outsmart Sullivan and Jackson for quite a time, but we got him too. Your other cowardly companions took off. It wasn’t long until I had Shoan, Arif, and Antonius tied in a position that I am sure Shoan will recognize when he regains consciousness. It’s almost poetic.” She bares her teeth and comes close enough to me that I smell her last meal.

“Get your rancid breath out of my face. Don’t you brush?” I laugh at the situation. “I hope you get cavities. Better yet, I hope someone neuters you, pulling out those ugly daggers.”

I seem to hit a nerve as she leans even closer. I can feel the predatory glare she gives Anna.

“Keep your pup on a leash before I teach her manners. After all, you’re my guests. I would hate to partake before you have a chance to see the grand finale. I have plans for you.” Anna gives me a look that I know well. It’s shut up and bide your time. Over the years it’s been a staple look of mine. I’ve tried her patience on more than one occasion after letting my tongue get the best of me in bad situations.

Morrigan walks away from us, over to the other side of the room where there’s a freshly opened bottle of wine. She pours a glass and turns back. "Anna, you know you should be proud of your daughter for her fearlessness. Others have been more terrified of us, especially after being—"

I interject. "Morrigan, thank you. If it wasn't for your prick of a son, I wouldn't even be here. I wouldn't have found out about my mother, and I wouldn't have the opportunity to watch as the light leaves your eyes as Shoan judges you. Oh, and don't worry, I'm sure he'll draw it out, relishing in your pain." I smile.

As if shimmering across the room, she slides to a stop at Anna's side. Grabbing her neck, she delves her nail into her harshly, drawing long trails of blood.

"Thiea. Right now, there's no one to save you. Remember who is the top of the food chain." As quickly as she appeared, she releases Anna's neck and walks away.

"I don't want to ruin the glorious taste in my system with the pungency of your diminished mental class. Weres are disgusting creatures."

"Don't worry. It won't be long before you won't have any flavors in your system at all," Anna quips.

"You know, Arif really has fallen far by mating to the likes of you. How did it happen? I mean, you are an immortal, so how is it you are his mate?" Looking into Anna's face, it isn't hard to tell she hit a nerve. "I don't need to read your mind to see the truth of it; you love him. No matter. It will make the pain that much sweeter when he dies in your arms. Oh, don't worry your little head about it either. I won't bore you with the details." Once more she licks those huge front teeth, showing off her canines threateningly, starting away as the door opens.

Harrison enters, wiping the corners of his mouth on a table napkin, changing the tenor of the room expediently. I can just barely see into the other room where he left the door slightly ajar. His *meal* is strewn across the baby grand piano like trash. He turns to me with a sideways glance, almost quizzical, like I intrigue him. I watch his movements, learning them, calculating his weaknesses.

“Darling, I must say the last meal is always the best before you leave a small town like this. I love ethnic take out. They seem to be the most fragrant.”

“I didn't need to feed, darling. My pleasure was slaked with the exotic Chimeric.” She gazes lasciviously at Harrison as he leaves a peck of a kiss on her cheek.

Disgusting. I feel the start of a meal coming back.

“Hey.” George so eloquently states as he enters the room with Sullivan trailing behind. I was only introduced to these two hulking behemoths over the past few hours. Dumb as rocks.

“Are we ready to go? I’ve had enough of this city. The people are shit. Let’s go home already.”

Appearing on my right, Garron unhitches the straps that bind me to the dais and prods us like cattle to rise with a gun to my back. “Don’t think about trying anything stupid,” he says, directing us towards the elevator doors.

I get it now. I understand that not only will we be at this performance as spectators, we’re the main attraction as we watch our friends and families’ lives end.

“Time to be off. We wouldn’t want to keep destiny waiting, would we?” Entering the empty elevator, I know what we’re doing, and I hate every moment of it. I wanted to see the world, and now as we head for another plane, to another country, I wish I was seeing it with different eyes.

Death is not something normally synonymous with Ireland.

Chapter TWENTY-ONE

Through the Looking Glass

Shoan

I'm not sure how I came to be here. Standing in front of a corroded, paint peeled mirror, where seemingly time passes in an instant and centuries pass before your eyes, I'm confused. Reliving my past and my dreams as they all blend into one is making it hard to understand reality from fiction, truth from lies, heartache from heartbreak.

How again did I find myself in this room, in this window of time?

I've always seen what *they* see when they're called forth for judgement, when they are present at their final justice. The mirror is bleak as it tells them their whole story, and how their final judgement came about.

But why am I here? Why me now?

I've always been their guide to Tartarus/Hell/Utopia/the Euphoric Lands, whatever the case may be, but *I am* the one whom shows the truth; not to whom it is shown. Fragments of tranquility and peace is interspersed with moments of horror and fascination from within the deepest recesses of the psyche. I hear and feel everything that has been passed by me judiciously in the name of keeping the peace in our land and theirs.

When I answered yes, as Giza's curse was engaged, I understood it meant I couldn't judge those who deserved the farthest levels of Hell. And with that, or anything there is a cause and effect; a yin to yang. Truly, I had no idea what I was giving up or allowing.

I knew I could handle the world full of immortal scum wandering loose, but to find I would suffer during that time as well, it seemed that I was given the raw end of the deal. Those like Morrigan, that were avoiding their judgement, they had found their piece of heaven here on earth without prosecution or conviction.

Flashes of lunacy, lucidity, clear moments of heated passions, hatred and bliss. I see it all reflected back at me. Their final moments are in my head every second of every day, without the relief of sex keeping it at bay. Giza didn't just make it that they couldn't be condemned, she made it that I was too. I was condemned to see their acts as they lived and as they died. I see vampires, weres, witches and shifts that didn't control their urges upon humanity.

This is what I try to avoid, this horror is what causes me pain. I could live without finding my sweet ending during sex, but I cannot live without the euphoria of sex and the bliss that it gives me to keep it at a distance. Without it, every waking moment is hell in my mind. I see it and I don't wish to. Moments like this; the first point when I changed my course in life.

February 14, 1145

As I hang here, upside down over a well of smelly, dingy, acrid water, I wonder about my life and the role I play. I got into a fight with a vampire who is the epitome of brute strength. The girth of his arms protruding through the seams of his threadbare shirt show his stiff shoulders and forearms, not like the handle of a battle axe. The floor is littered with feces, creating a pall within the confined space. It is truly revolting.

The gargantuan oaf on my left is Sullivan. He caught me while I was at a mortal wedding in the nearby town. I was there for protection against the likes of him, and as you can very well tell, I am the captured one, not he. Now, I have to try to outwit the vapid vampire.

"Sully, it matters not to me about you. I came looking for Morrigan."

"You are brutally daft to be wantin' to take her on in yer state! Yer hanging over a vat of rotting of bodies, you tosser. I could slit yer throat to pause yer laughin'. Remember right now she is the least of yer problems," Sullivan says while scratching the top of his balding, badly sunburnt head.

Sully had one thing right though, I had hung here for quite a while now. The blood had been rushing to my head like a torrent of rain in May, making my eyes sting and my temples sing. I knew that if Sully cut me down I'd be in no state to fight him. I'd be as wobbly a fresh born colt, lucky to stand without falling over.

The bonds on my feet had been twisted fairly tight, leaving me no room to move. Shifting my fingers around, reaching the end of the heavily knotted restraints, I do my best to poke and pull at the braided twine until I pulled the first loop of the rope loose. Quietly, I might add, so as not to alert my daft jailor.

"I don't think that this shite sees how bleak his predicament is. But what Morrigan wants, Morrigan gets. I won't take her wrath over yer sorry ass." A new voice says. It's George. The other dumbass brother.

Stepping into the barn, waving his hands in front of his face as a sign that the unearthly scent is excessive, all the while spinning a wide handled, sharp as shit knife deftly between his enormous hands.

George's eyes narrow slightly as the corners of his mouth curl up into a deep snarl, showing his predatory ways. The gleaming white of his teeth shimmers in the moonlight, reminding me I'm in quite a predicament. It's almost ethereal against the dirt and blood stains on his face. Even from this angle, the scars running across the right side of George's face show the monster below the surface where the angry and violent lesions mar his eyesight. It curves at the edge, tightening the corner of his eye, almost closing the lid.

His hardened sinewy arms connect to his broad, scarred chest. His feet (after all, I am hanging upside down) are missing a toe or two on each. His balance should be poor. All I have to do is find a way down, then I can overpower them and escape this hell. My fate is wholly in their hands unless I can best them.

Slowly, I work at the cord. Loosening the first few loops of my shackles, I release my left hand. It's not my best or first choice, but it will have to do. I pull my arm loose, just as Sully punches me square in the jaw, the resulting swing making my already strained head lurch and my stomach void violently onto the rancid floor below.

I can't help myself from laughing out loud as I must be quite the sight. Vomit dangling from the corners of my mouth and a wide toothed grin. I spit towards Sullivan to clear the traces, then wipe the rest on the back of my hand. Their sureness of winning this battle had dissipated as both realize I have unlocked my bonds. If I was able to get within range of each of them, their fates would be sealed. After all, I am the bane of their immortal debauchery.

"Listen, George. I know you're not as dumb as your brother, but you are uglier than a rotting corpse. Let me loose to settle this like

men, then we can all go our separate ways."

As I reach up to grab the rope that binds my feet, George leans in, punching my jaw a second time, sending me reeling once more.

That was when everything went black.

Coming to, it felt like only a few minutes had passed. I was no longer hanging upside down. That was good, but my head was ringing. That sucked. My eyes were burning and tight from the hits I had recently received, and as I gazed around at my newest course of confinement, I felt more in danger than I had before.

Here I was, tied to a chair in the centre of a different room, where the floors were clear of refuse. The once dimly lit room that was pallid, now was very bright. It was as if a hundred suns were shining. My right eye was heavy where George had hit me, making it tight to open. It mustn't have been long since he hit me, as it had not regenerated yet.

There are lamps and candles on the tables, windowsills, and hanging from rafters in the room. George is holding a very large candle at my face with a look of pure bliss on his disheveled one. I can see there are others, of which I assume are also vampires, standing on either side of me. Each bearing their lustrous incisors like warriors with blades at the ready for the onslaught of a war. I try to work up spit, but my mouth is dry and scratchy. I want to speak, but all I can taste is the stinging of sweat, vomit, and blood.

Gazing at my new accommodations, trying to find a hint of where I am, I immediately recognize a face. The tiny cherub like curls, and sweet, innocent, angelic face of my sister is lying on a pallet of straw, fast asleep, in complete peace. Niamh. None of these issues concern her.

I'm sure they're looking for the way to control and/or cull my prior intentions, and she is a means to that end.

"This is the scum that was attacking our family?" It is said with such contempt that I knew my troubles are just starting. It is the voice of someone who commands respect, and expects full complacency.

Looking at her, I know she is who I was trying to track. Morrigan's eyes twinkle and smile, alerting you to the innocence that may have been there before, but no more. She has the voice of an angel with the eyes of a devil. As she pulls back the hood of her dress to reveal her face, her sharp features come into view. The hawk like nose, high cheekbones, and full lips that show her flawless, ageless beauty.

George speaks an acknowledgment. "Aye, this is. We caught him the other night at the wedding. He'd taken quite a few of the new clan members before we caught him." Bowing his head while he speaks, George backs away, towards the door. The fear clearly written on his face.

Until this night, I had never met Morrigan. She had eluded me time and time again. I would call her ancient even by my terms, and I'm damn old. Her hair is that of spun silk with a streak of ebony, liken to that of a raven. It runs straight down her back, pulled taught into a ponytail at the base of her neck. Her eyes are a strange resemblance to the sun, the bright golden hue has such intensity that it makes you want to look away.

"I had you captured so that I could deal with you myself. Your escapades have caused me quite a problem, but I think I may have found a way to convince you once and for all to do as I bid."

With a nod from Morrigan, a young man about the same size as Sullivan walks towards my sweet darling sister. Unsheathing a bone handled dagger from his belt, stepping in low, he gently brushes stray curls from her face, bearing the dagger to her throat. A malicious smile creeps across his features as I watch helplessly. Niamh turns over, twitching in her sleep, unknowing of the imminent danger she is in.

Because of me. Because of who I am.

"My son has no issues killing one of your family as you have done to ours. What will it be, Shoan? Against us, or with us?"

Without very little thought for myself, I answer. "What do you want? You know this is my nature, just as yours is to do ill. I'll do almost anything to keep her safe." Deflated, sadness drips from the words. "Niamh is innocent of my fate. She has no idea what I am or what she will become."

Turning my determined gaze to the man holding Niamh, I say, "If you harm her, you will find out just how dangerous I can be." Pulling back the dagger, just slightly, he smiles darkly. I hate vampires, and this one has just jumped to the head of a list titled the men I wish to condemn.

"You've made the right decision," Morrigan says as she calls over another to stand beside her. Two vampires move to the side, making way for a stout lady that slowly shuffles forward from behind them. Morrigan directs her forward, and with gnarly hands she removes the cloak that obscures her face. It's Giza, my father's second wife. She is one of the Fey, a powerful witch.

Picking up a chalice the size of an apple, dented and scuffed with visible signs of dried blood, Giza lifts a small vial as well. Within it, there's a liquid the color of the ocean on a bright blue day, only one herb appears as such—ground blood horn. Adding the contents of the vial to the chalice, the room is immediately tainted with the scent of crushed herbs; lavender, witch hazel, and black pepper. Such a pungent odor masks the smell of decay and bloodshed that wafts through the room. Watching, she slowly swirls the concoction, swishing it back and forth.

Blending it together, Giza walks towards me. As I look straight into her eyes, I watch helplessly as they adjust, shimmering black with no iris or pupil, just an inky pitch black. I quickly become unnerved. Knowing witches—or Fey as they are called in the oldest of worlds—I know that as it occurs, changing eye coloring means that Giza is now enchanted by the Gods. At this point, there is wavering from her prey; from me.

"Shoan Mac Cathmhaoil. I cannot tell if you are destined for good or ill; but you are not meant to accomplish it here now. You are banished from the isle, being spared your death. Your blood will be your binding. You will lose your ability to pass judgement, and will lose all capability to ferry the condemned. You will nay otherwise feel the true nature of a Dark Worlder akin. You shall not pass the shores of this land again until you fulfill this all-consuming prophesy."

"You will wander the world, and the centuries will pass until you find and save your soul's true heart. You will never be hale until this passes. I speak for all Gods that have and will come to be. You are no longer welcome." *As Giza speaks, I feel enthralled, lacking free will in my own destiny.*

I'm to be bound and banished? Truly? I liked it better when Sully was going to slit my throat. But, if my leaving spared Niamh's life, and that she would have a chance at happiness, then so be it.

Giza holds that petite stone goblet like a death sentence, directing Sully to move forward. Positioning himself beside her and I, then reaching into his heavy leather belt, Sully draws out that same large knife as before. Dragging his blade alongside my forearm, it leaves a cut from elbow to wrist. I can feel the warm blood running down my arm, leaching onto my fingers before dripping to the floor. A grin of satisfaction courses across Sully's toothy face as all the other participants shift forward, drawn to the scent of my blood. Quickly flicking her hand, waving, all of the vampires withhold the advance on my ichor; it's as if they are acquiesced to her power.

As Giza places the goblet within the path of my slowly dripping blood, she ever so gently stirs the mixture, sloshing it within the cup. I watch, enamored, oblivious to Sully again. As he slices through the bindings, I am once again free to move, but still I feel restrained. Dazed and aching, I'm swearing vengeance on Sully and those he associates with. I internally curse all their rotten immortal souls as Giza steps in front of me.

"Take this. Drink it down in its entirety." As she holds out the challis to me, I look once more to my little angel on the bed. Taking hold of it as directed, I find it cold with an invigorating scent of anise and sea spray. Lifting it to my lips, expecting the same as its smells, it's bitter on the tongue, like raw meat. Drinking the concoction, a feeling liken to that of a bolt of lightning invades my senses. As I drink it down, the once loud and insistent internal thoughts quiet. There are no voices, at least none other than those said aloud. The third eye that was always so apparent on those around me slowly diminishes from the foreheads of those in attendance. I could not no longer feel the power that I once possessed either.

I was as weak; I was bereft.

Crying silently at first, then inconsolably, I realize I'm leaving everyone unprotected against the darkest demons of our world. The worst of it, I have no one to blame but myself for the loss. Honestly, I wonder what she means. How would I not be whole again until I find my true love's heart and save it? Make that my true love and soul mate. Those two are not intertwined.

As soon as the feeling of restraint leaves my body, I immediately rise from the chair and run across to Niamh. Had she truly slept so peacefully throughout all this turmoil? Had I made the right decision for her? Was giving up my powers going to keep her safe? Had I given her a chance to grow into a strong and righteous soul against the likes of these vampires?

I can't worry about that. I've done what was right for her now.

George appears at my side as I rest on the floor beside Niamh. Grabbing my arm, at first, I instinctively jerk away from the touch. Trying again, once more I look up, readying for a fight. In his eyes, I expected glee for my newfound fate, but instead, I see only sorrow.

As I slowly rise off of the floor, I look longingly once more at my tiny sister. The delicate features of my naive adopted little sister's face are serene. She will not understand this. She won't understand why I left her. Kissing her forehead, I swear to myself and all the Gods above and below that I will protect her in the years to come.

As tears well in my eyes, I feel the vow take shape in my heart. I would find a way back to her, and I would find a way to remove the curse set upon me. I would regain my strength, my ability, and my home, even if it meant defying the Gods. More than that, I would find a way to cause Morrigan the same pain.

"It's time to head out now. Sully and I are to take you to the boat," George says, motioning for me to move ahead.

Starting down the hill towards the shore and the awaiting skiff, I take in the surroundings. Nothing seems different, even though all has changed.

Lying within the boat, there is a bag of my belongings, some dried meat, fruit, and an old scabbard and sword. All of it I expect was packed by Giza and my father for the trip.

Watching the coast become smaller, I am scuttled out to a larger ship waiting in the shallows. I curse, cry, and enrage myself all the more.

It is such a hard thing to put into words, but as the years passed, banishment became a tangible living entity; a prison of my own making.

I would find the way out somehow, someway.

Chapter TWENTY-TWO

Swing Life Away

Antonius

Fuck, that hurt. My head feels split open like a ripe melon thrown at a wall. Opening my eyes to an immeasurable searing pain, I once again remember how much I hate vampires.

Raising my hands to my head, I realize they're not at my sides. They're dangling above my head.

I'm dangling down.

This can't be good. The pins and needles tingle the tips of my fingers from the blood rushing. Trying to reach up, I drop my hands back down. Reopening my eyes, I hope to find where I am, and if I'm alone.

Peering around, I see the white plainly carved pillars of ancient Greek architecture. Fuck, this is totally not cool. I sure as shit hope I'm not in the Stoa. As soon as the sun rises, I'll be found by the caretakers.

Swaying my hips, I'm able to turn myself slowly in a circle.

Great. I'm strung up in the temple of Hephaestus. Actually, *we,* because on the opposite corners, I see Shoan and Arif bound, just as I am.

Oh, this sucks on so many levels.

"Shoan! Arif! Hey, guys, wake up. We're hanging in the temple!" I shout out to them, but they're still unconscious. It's not like I have a rock close to lob at their heads, so I try the easier approach of internal thoughts.

Shoan. Arif. Wake up. The girls are gone and we're alone in a not so flattering position.

The first to stir is Arif. *What are you talking of...Oh, Holy Allah. This sucks. How do we get out of this?* He rubs his eyes, surveying the area. "Shoan. Can you hear us? Thiea and Anna are gone. We're swinging upside down, my friend," Arif tries.

Still no response.

He's still and limply hanging, looking deathly pallid.

"I think he's fucked. She drained him, and I can't think of the last immortal I've ever heard of being drained that recovered quickly. It will take a while for him to regain consciousness, I think. We need to find a way out of this. Can you reach your bindings?" Arif asks while he attempts to reach his feet.

"Hell, no. We have a bigger problem right now. How are we gonna get out of here before the tourists start to show?" I attempt to reach my fetters again to no avail.

"When someone notices us, we'll be shipped off to a police station for questions, or a hospital for evaluations. Not to mention, Shoan passed out with bite mark in his neck. That'll be fun to explain."

"Okay, well, neither of us can reach the ropes, and we have to be at least ten feet apart." Arif swings back and forth, finding himself no closer than when he started. Straining as he falls back from the various attempts towards his feet, he lets out a series of huffs and haws.

"No suggestions? We might as well wait for the authorities to release us."

Niamh steps out from around the corner of the pillar closest to Arif with a gleeful smile. *How about I undo the cords that are on the other side of the pillars, letting you down?*

This is going to suck on so many levels. Two strong immortal men, hung upside down, unable to reach their bonds, being released by Niamh. Yep, this will be something she will make us relive for years to come.

"Hi, honey," Arif says sweetly. "That would be great. Please leave Shoan. We should cut him down together."

"Sure. I can do that," she responds with a devious smirk on her face. She worries me.

"Be nice. Please, Ni."

"Fine." Niamh moves over to the ropes. Holding Arif in place, she gives it a tug to loosen the knot.

"Arif are you ready?" He nods. "One, two, three!" Arif falls like a stone to the hard marble floor of the temple, flat on his ass. Definite bruising.

"All right, big boy, you're next. Ready?" she asks, moving towards my ropes.

"Let me swing mine a bit. If I'm gonna fall, I want momentum to carry my hands and feet first." Niamh nods, waiting for me as I start to sway back and forth. She starts to count down and I prepare for the fall.

"One, two, three!" she shouts as I plummet to the stone floor. Hitting it with a decided thump, landing hard on my knees, I cuss.

I turn to her brother. I feel sorry for him.

I have half a mind to just let Shoan fall on his head.

"Arif, will you get the ropes on that side? Antonius, get ready to catch him as he falls," Niamh orders while I'm unbinding my hands and feet.

Stepping out of the ropes then reaching up, I grab the cord wrapped around the smooth lined obelisk beside me, waiting to catch my friend. Niamh tears through the knotted end and slowly drops Shoan. As I cradle him in the fold of my arms, he seems so childlike, it's hard to remember he's older than all of us, excluding Arif.

"What do we do with him now? We can't return to the house," Arif states as he strokes his hair, slicking it back to retie it down his shoulders.

"Where are your other friends? The shifter and the weres?" I ask.

"I sent them ahead to Ireland to keep an eye out for Morrigan. They were a bit banged up, but nothing they can't regenerate. They'll watch the usual haunts before we get there," Niamh answers, as Arif lifts Shoan's dead weight onto her shoulder. Not that she really needed the help.

"First, we need Shoan awake. He's the only one who knows where we need to go and what to do. You hear that, you big lug? I need you. Thiea needs you. And if you don't get up, you're of no use to any of us."

Shoan doesn't stir.

With a frustrated look, Niamh swings his ass around deftly so that they're face to face. "Listen here. You need to wake up. I can't do this on my own, and I need you!" With one hand holding him up, she slaps him across the face so hard, I feel his pain. “You punk ass motherfucker! When this shit is over…” She reaches down, grabs him around the waist and swings him up over her shoulder again like a Ragdoll.

Ni stares at me, clearly awaiting an answer or a fight, and I don’t flinch. “Are you coming? Or are you waiting on an invitation for the end of the world? Fight or flight, big boy?”

Lifting my hands aloft in defeat, I tell her mentally, *Hey, be pissed at the game maker, not the player. I’m in. I’m right behind you.*

Following behind her, I turn to Arif, wide-eyed and stunned that I somehow was taking heat for how everything was coming down.

No, Antonius, you aren’t to blame. But you are just as much a part of this as my brother. So let’s go and fix this, she says in my head.

How can you argue with that logic? Arif laughs internally and falls in step.

I may not have designed this, but I can’t say I won’t take the blame for not helping out more in the interim. I feel scolded like a child.

Walking out of the temple on the eastern side, I see the sun as it rises across the crest of the Acropolis. It envelops it in multifaceted rays of light that stream out of the pillars in awkward directions, just as it has for centuries. Arif looks up with despair in his eyes.

“I am at a loss. Anna is my soul; she keeps me complete. She keeps me sane. I can't lose her to them. I can't.” He’s almost in tears, and I understand that loss.

“More than you will ever know, I understand loss. I'm sure Shoan has told you about my family I lost all those years ago. I'm not whole, I never will be, but I promised Shoan I would help him get through this, and I will." I clasp him on the shoulder as he wipes the tears from the corners of his eyes.

"Niamh, honey," Arif says with trepidation, "it's not like we can get on a plane with a passed out body strapped to your back."

"Well of course we can't jump a plane like this, but we'll just have to wait for him to come to." Niamh shifts Shoan's weight on her shoulder before she jumps over the fence with ease.

"We'll hail a cab and take him back to my house. We can say he drank too much."

"Why don't you let me. It might seem a bit odd to the humans that the little girl is carrying around a man." Handing him over, I hold his body over my shoulder as Arif hails a cab.

"Someone obviously drank too much, but it wasn't him," Ni states matter of fact.

Fucking Morrigan.

"Yes, someone did."

Chapter TWENTY-THREE

Where O' Where

Antonius

Opening the front door to my house, I lead Niamh to the spare room at the back to lay the prone form of my friend down.

"In all your years together, had you ever seen Shoan in this state? It's totally new for me to see him helpless and weak," Niamh asks me as she lays him out on the bed with care.

"No. I can't say I ever have. Shoan has always been very spirited. I think Arif is right. Being drained like that…let's just say, it'll be up to him to recover. I don't think there's anything we can do." I say this, trying to convince us both. I'm not sure how much it hurt him to see Thiea violated like that, or to be in that position.

Closing the door quietly, we make our way out towards the front where Arif is in the kitchen. He's sitting at the table, staring out into the expansive grape fields, musing about our predicament.

"Arif, do you think that Anna can hold her own against them? I mean, she has a better understanding than Thiea of what they're capable of." I feel like I know the answer, but I have to ask it anyway.

"Anna," he exhales. "Yes, she should be okay. For years, she has lived with me, learning my strengths and weaknesses. With our daughter there, it could make her cautious, or it could make her unpredictably dangerous. Weres are known for taking the path less travelled. She knows where they're going and knows what will be asked of her. She will be protecting Thiea the whole time. Morrigan knows this. She'll use that weakness against her to get what she wants."

"Morrigan may be a bitch, but she knows not to mess with a full-grown werewolf. If they harm Thiea, it will influence Anna, and not necessarily as they want. Morrigan knows that both of them are her golden ticket to Shoan behaving in Ireland. If things go to shit, it screws up her plans, and she has no intention of losing this time." Niamh grabs a fresh mandarin from the bright blue ceramic bowl on the counter by the sink, washes it, and proceeds to eat it whole without peeling it first.

"I have to agree. Anna is smart, she'll stay calm. She's going to go along with Morrigan so long as she can keep Thiea safe. She'll give us enough time to arrive."

Rising from the chair, Arif walks up to me. "Antonius, I was afraid when Shoan told us that he gave you eternal life. I still feel it was unwise of him to do such a thing, but I also feel that it can give us an advantage. What I wonder though, what we never talked about, is can you do as Shoan can? Do you have his abilities, or are you bound as well?"

I must admit, it was something that had never crossed my mind. I'd never attempted to use his abilities as I never felt it was something I had a right to. "Why do you ask? It's not like I know how to use them."

"Well, possibly, you can get through to Shoan *where* we can't."

“Shit. I guess I never thought of that.” I’ve avoided using any gifts that Shoan endowed me with. I mean, I can read thoughts and send thoughts out like any other immortal, but other than that, I’ve never ventured beyond.

Arif smiles. “I need you to try something very simple. Shoan is a shifter of sorts. He can move between the realms of humanity and Tartarus, that’s how he’s able to ferry souls. Think of him as the boatman. Shoan sits between the realms. Maybe we can’t get through to him because he’s not here on this plane.”

“I’ll try anything, but I have no friggin’ idea how to get to a different plane.” I reach to the same bowl and pull out an apricot, rubbing it against my pants.

“Unless, if you’ve got a better idea, I’m open for suggestions. For now, I think it’s our best option.”

Arif motions for me to toss him a mandarin. I pop one over as he stares, awaiting an answer, like I’ve had some sort of an epiphany.

He catches the orb in mid-flight without a single glance. “Try clearing your mind. We’ll start with something easy. Try this fruit. Don’t think of it as fruit, think of it as inconsequential, nothing of importance in the grand scheme of things.”

“This is silly.”

“You’re right, but if you’re the only contact point, I will find a way to make you cooperate with us on the matter. It’s up to you to decide if you do it with or without limbs,” Ni chirps as she rolls a small blade around on her knuckles like a pencil.

“Fine. I’ll try the silly fruit.” Calming myself, I stare at the bright, plump, fleshy globe. The minuscule imperfections that dent around the stem, base, and that little smattering that gives away the typical clouding white of pesticides.

"Close your eyes and think of it just like meditation. I want you to calm your breathing and steady your heart rate, slowing it almost to a stop. Feel the release of stress as you let it escape through your shoulders, erasing all the other things around you. Thinking only of that mandarin."

I do as he asks, calming myself and forgetting all the stress from the past few days. Thinking of nothing but the orange in his hand, imagining the feel of the soft round fleshy rind, smelling the tangy sweetness of its pulp and the corded sour seeds that lay inside.

"Good, that's good. Now I want you to think broader. I want you to remove all the intangible objects. The chairs, the table, the bowls on the counter, the cupboards, all the pictures and rugs. Make it all fall away."

I concentrate on the rough edges of the old country kitchen chairs, the smooth top counter with the bright robin blue bowl, the fruit, the plank table with its knife marks, and the purple threadbare rug.

Great, Antonius, just great. Let's keep going. Arif has switched to saying things mentally. *Concentrate on the living—us, the mortals that work in your fields, the deep purple of the grapes, the bright green of the plants vines and leaves, the chickens, and anything else. Just forget about it.*

Pulling in a deep breath, exhaling slower and slower, I concentrate on those things outside our room, as if I'm editing a picture. First I envision Arif and Niamh. As they disappear like a fog on a warm morning, I then think of the plants, the small bright pink geranium in its clay pot sitting near the back door leading to the garden, the rows upon rows of lush fruit hanging on the vines, waiting to be picked.

It's becoming easier than I thought it would.

Arif's voice is like that of a trance under hypnotism. *I need you to think of only you and Shoan. You two are all that are here. There is nothing else. Look for him. Find him and bring him home.*

Envisioning Shoan, as if he and I are the only things left so that no sound or objects remain, I hear him. I can hear his soft heartbeat. I can see the rise and fall of his chest as he breathes. It's both rhythmic and soothing. I find myself standing beside him as a wraith, a soul-less ghost. Like a non-corporeal being.

I try calling his name, quietly at first. *Hey, buddy. Can you hear me? It's Antonius. We need you to wake up.*

Looking down on his immobile body lying still on the bed, it seems like an invasion of his privacy, but I know that we need him and his privacy will just have to take a back seat to our need. I wait for what I perceive to be only a few minutes, but again there is no answer. Trying it from a different approach, I enter within his body, molding our souls into one. If this doesn't work, I don't know what will.

Slowly, I enter him as if something from the movie *Ghost,* stepping into his body. It's so fragile feeling, so superficial, that it feels dangerous to go this far without there being a consequence. His body tenses from the contact as his toes flinch, and I can feel his fingers tingle. His heartbeat adjusts minutely to the fear of the unknown.

Shoan, my friend, it's Antonius. I need you to come back to us. I let the moment linger a bit more, hoping for a reaction, searching for recognition.

I can see into the recesses of his mind, to the deepest moments in his life. The moment we were introduced on the rocks all that time ago after his exile, as we built skiffs, triremes and sloops. The time he spent with us, my wife Arissa and my son, as he laid their bodies side by side in their graves. Every sensual pleasure with different women, and the need for them to be the one that would see past his history, his bullshit, and all his transgressions.

How hard it has become for him over the millennia.

Hoping against hope to find your life's purpose after having it taken away would be harsh. All these emotions are raw as you feel them firsthand.

Shoan has endured many things over his lifetime; pain, sorrow, anticipation, horror, and immense pleasure. All of it blends into one desperate search as he looked for that one love, then gave up after centuries of nothing.

I ventured so far into my friend's psyche, walking through door upon door of those things we keep locked up that I felt too far away. Those moments purposely locked away to keep that which is too painful in the back of your mind. Coming to the decision after what felt like an hour or more, I was on the way out after no contact. This didn't work. Just as I'm about to return to the living, I hear a small noise, a squeaky petite voice.

"Savior."

"Shoan. Tell me what you need? I'm not sure I understand you. Direct me. I need to know what you need me to do to help," I say into the nothingness that is my friends' mind.

"Help me. Please. I'm lost, I'm lost without her." Finally, I've found him.

He's here.

Now it's up to me to direct him back.

I don't even know how or where to start, but I won't leave until I try.

"Shoan, we need you back. Arif, Niamh, Anna, and—"

"Thiea?"

I tried to work with that in mind, no pun intended. "Shoan, concentrate on Thiea. She needs you. You left her alone and she needs you to fix this. She *needs* you to save her. You need to find a way back to her. I'll try to lead you, but you have to want to leave here." *Wherever here is*, I say to no one.

"Where are we?" he asks cautiously.

Suddenly, and without warning, the nothingness becomes tangible. A place within his mind. Looking from side to side, I search the surroundings that he has created. A world within.

Maybe a memory?

Everywhere I look are levels and levels of rough cut rock, dripping blood, oozing pus. It's steaming from stalactites that rise out of the landscape as thick as a man's body. And it's warm; too warm to be comfortable. The humidity is crushing and the air is acrid.

With rows upon rows of cages, gates and walkways made of bone and stone, I quickly feel horror in my soul. This is what he keeps, what I suppose is the damned encapsulated in Hell. Now I know where the devil goes once Shoan sends them on to their demise.

This is the Nether. This is what he tries to avoid. The waking dreams that makes him want to fuck anything to contain the pain. If I had to think on this all the time, I would want joy and pleasure too.

"We're in the Nether, Shoan. You left us and we haven't been able to reach you. You need to come back. Thiea, needs you. *We* need you."

"Thiea needs me?"

I feel his body as it registers his need and his hunger for her. His heartbeat races, his pulse increases, and as his breathing increasingly becomes stronger, I know he's waking from within this hell that he has imprisoned himself in. I decide it's best to be gone before I become a guest in this horrid hotel, hopefully leading him out of the darkness and back to reality.

"Shoan. We need you. You need to leave here."

All this time, he's only been a voice in the distance, nothing corporeal, nothing tangible that I can pull like a lifeline to me.

Hoping he can do this on his own, I say, "Shoan, I'm leaving now, and you need to come out."

"I'm scared. What if I can't save her? What if I save her and she's held in a whole new hell living with me? I'm nothing but a broken shell housing a dead soul. What can I give her? How can I protect her? What kind of man am I?"

"Shoan, I know you'll move heaven and earth for your friends. You brought the wrath of Olympus on your own soul when you saved me, and I know you can protect her and give her everything you are. Trust her to make the right choice for her." There's a long pause, long enough that I almost think I've lost him once again.

"Okay."

"See you on the flip side." I turn away from his voice and the hell he's shown me.

Thinking about the real world, where my body is sitting in the kitchen, I return to my bright kitchen. The mahogany, roughhewn table, the buzzing insects scurrying around on my plants, the strong vines as they reach for the sunlight and that bright blue bowl with the oranges and bunches of fresh grapes anxiously awaiting to be eaten.

As if credits are rolling, I see Arif and Niamh appear, the geranium returned to its place, and the world seems whole once more. Noisy, but whole.

Shaking off the feeling from the deathly, corrosive Nether, I survey my surroundings.

"Hey, chief. Did you reach him?" Niamh spews out without giving me a second to relax.

"Let him refocus himself before you bombard him, Ni. He's been gone for almost a day, remember?" Arif is so matter of fact that at first, I didn't catch the time he mentioned.

I'd been gone for almost a day? "Did you say I'd been away for almost a day? It only felt like a few hours." Stretching my stiff legs, I reach skyward to shake off the strain in my arms, feeling my joints pop.

"Okay, still avoiding the question. For all the time you were gone, I hope you got to him. Otherwise, darlin', you were wasting a shit load of time." Niamh stands beside me with her arms crossed and a look of disdain.

"Yeah, okay. Before you hit me, yes, I was able to reach him. Actually, it was more like I found him. He was lost in the Nether." Rubbing my head, I run my hands through my hair and down my neck, letting out a deep yawn.

"He was where? Are you sure? I mean, he hasn't been there in centuries." Ni attempts to poke me in the chest with the blunt end of a knife. I bat it away easily.

"Yes, I'm sure. I was there. Goddess help those who belong there. It's solitary and devoid of any joy. It's unimaginable how crushing it is."

"Welcome to Hell." We all turn in unison towards the voice,

finding Shoan standing in the doorway. He's disheveled looking from laying down so long, but awake and cognizant. Which is more than I expected.

"Thanks," Shoan mutters through his sleepiness.

"Don't mention it. And you're welcome. Let's just say we're even, but don't ask me to go there on a vacation."

Taking a seat on the chair next to Niamh, Shoan turns towards her as she wraps her arms around him for a massive hug. Burying his head in her shoulder, he releases her as tears wet each of their faces.

Reaching out across the table, Shoan takes Arif's hand, shaking it prominently with determination.

"So what happened? I wake up after my friend invades my mind. I was lost in the Nether. The last thing I remember is being at the temple. Morrigan jumped me, then it's pretty much a blur of nothing." Shoan takes a glass of water from Niamh, downing it in seconds.

"Oh, you know, the usual. You fought, you lost. Marcus, Pat, Chad, and Terese were tied up for a bit, but nothing compared to you and your brilliant friends here. You were all hung upside down inside the temple of Hephaestus like pigs for the slaughter. I, of course, came to your rescue before you were discovered by the mortals. Oh, and I've sent the Berserkers to Ireland ahead to keep an eye on the girls." Niamh expels on an explosive thought before finishing internally. *Morrigan said you would know where to go.*

Sitting quietly for a moment, Shoan ponders. "Hung, huh? Poetic."

"Poetic? How is us hung poetic?" Arif asks.

Showing each of us the first time he ran against Morrigan and her sons in Ireland, each of us let out a little giggle as we envisioned being in the same situation yet again after all these years.

"So now what?" I ask, "Do we have a plan?"

"Yep. The plan is to get home, get to them before they notice, kill the bitch and her ugly band of morons that follow her, rescue Anna and Thiea, and get your powers back. How's that sound for a plan?" Ni crows.

"That's not a plan, that's a synopsis of need."

"I think there might be a few loopholes. Where do we start?"

"First we need a ride. Let's get to the airport, charter a plane and get going. The rest we can figure out on the way there," Arif chimes in.

Trying to stand, Shoan smirks. "Good. We have a plan, a way to execute it, and hopefully a happy ending."

"Niamh, could you call us a ride to the airport? I'm gonna to try to get Shoan to eat before he passes out on us."

"Fuck off, Ant. I'm fine, really. I'm just a bit off balance. Toss me a few pieces of toast and some yogurt with fruit while we wait on the ride. I'll be as right as rain." Trying a bit too hard to smile, Shoan nods at me and I understand how he feels. The pain, the lancing anguish that he endures day after day, those things he's tucked away. The searing heat of the Nether that pokes and prods his psyche at all times, it's truly excruciating.

He addresses me in his mind. *I know you understand it now, but please let's keep this to ourselves. I can't share this with Ni or Thiea. They couldn't handle what I have to see, feel, and hear all the time.*

Do you? I mean, do you feel that all the time?

I do. It's not just the pull of the evil here that has been left behind to linger and taint others, it's those that are there, housed without their final judgement for the past millennia. When the curse occurred and my course changed, it not only made it that I was to find my soul mate to gain back my abilities, it made them the damned, frozen in purgatory without judgement. No one has moved on to the lower levels of Hell. They're all in a holding pattern. Trust me, if Morrigan gains control and is able to not only create more of her, but is able to unleash those in Tartarus, then we're truly doomed.

Goddess. I never knew the extent.

I need Thiea to help restore the balance within me. Without her, I can't become who I was, and I won't be whole. If I'm not, then neither are they allowed to fall. Morrigan would have the opportunity and the means to make it happen. The book and the blood of a Førie will do more than you could ever imagine.

I think for a moment, but only a moment before I answer him. *I promise not to tell them. It's your secret to keep. But don't look at me to step in the path of the War Goddess herself once she finds out. I think Niamh should know the fight that we're stepping into, and what can happen if it goes terribly wrong.*

I know. Just not right now, he tells me.

As we await our ride, I scrounged up morsels for Shoan. Niamh has arranged a private jet, and we sit quietly, awaiting fate and destiny once more.

Chapter TWENTY-FOUR

Boo!

Thiea

This is not what I signed up for when I left Canada.

Damn, my neck aches from that whore!

We've been flying for just over two hours, and I have a headache to rival that of a weeklong Tequila fest. Anna sits a few seats away from me, making it so we can't talk. Like we have anything deep to talk about with so many ears listening in?

They so graciously granted me the company of the smelly, snoring, lug of a man they call Sullivan.

He scares the shit out of me.

And it's not like I have somewhere to go on an international flight from Greece to Ireland anyway. Where would I go? And how the hell would I be an issue?

To my amazement, they didn't even comp for first class. They've been alive for centuries, and I'm sure they don't live paycheck to paycheck, so why cheap out?

Funny thing is, I still don't get how a few simple words were able to unlock a curse that was set by my grandmother's great great grandmother about ten times over.

Choking back tears, thinking of Shoan sprawled out on the floor after Morrigan feasted on him, the disaster takes shape in my mind. He seemed so helpless, limp, and lifeless. I aided in that.

How was I able to erase eight centuries of purgatory for him, and allow the opportunity for Morrigan to release the hounds of hell? Just by saying garbled-gook!

I allowed the bloodsucking witch to gain power over him. It’s all my fault. He should turn his back on me and run away as fast as his little immortal feet will carry him.

I’ve never been so scared in my whole life. Vampires, weres, and people who can shift their form. It seems like something from the books I read from time to time. I always thought I was immune to the weird and wonderful, living a life of a normal human, but now I’m smack dab in the middle of a nut-up. Best thing is, I never thought I was one of those so called paranormals.

Rolling my necklace between my fingers was always a soothing habit, but as I think on it now, I find that this is what has kept me at bay. The *real* me leashed. Kind of a catch twenty-two, really.

Keeping it on leaves me with a power they don’t know of, but on the other hand, I don’t know what it would be either. My power could be an asset. I’d hate to look like something that would alert the Air Marshals, without the opportunity to understand what the fuck I can do with this newfound glory.

Do I want to keep that to myself for now?

I think I want to keep it to myself. Maybe I don’t.

I don't know.

I'm confused, scared, wounded, discombobulated, fucked, and all while I want to unleash a warrior that I hope resides inside this strategically locked body.

Mulling all of it over in my head, the steward (I think his name is Gary) rolls his cart down the aisle with refreshments.

I touch him on the shoulder as he attempts to pass right by. "Would I be able to bother you for a soda before you make your way down to the other end? I have a cracker of a headache," I ask in a sweet, helpless, damsel in distress voice. Reluctantly he stops, grabs a Ginger ale from the ice, opens it. He pours it into a glass with ice, then hands it over.

"Here ya go. No charge. I know how you feel about a headache. I have one from sitting ten rows back. I can just imagine what it's like sitting beside it." He nods at Sullivan, who's still snoring like a freight train at full power uphill.

Talking to Gary with his lilting accent reminds me of Shoan. Hell, everything right now reminds me of Shoan. Sipping on the soda, I sit back, resuming my concentrated stare out into the blank sky.

How long will it take for Morrigan to be able to unleash her horde of demons on the world? Will we be the first to die, or will she save us for a more diabolical end game? What will these monsters do to Shoan, my family, and our friends?

Family. Wow, I never thought in a million years I'd say that again.

Thinking on it isn't going to change anything. After all, I'm the least experienced, and power is not one of my strengths. I'm more of a hindrance than an asset.

Fiddling with the necklace sitting coolly against my skin, I'm war with myself. Do I or don't I take it off? If I do, watch for the fur to fly, or maybe nothing happens. Maybe I'm gifted enough to look perfectly normal with no body changes. That would be fantastic.

Maybe, just maybe, I have nonlethal specialties. I could have inherited the ability to project myself into other places, seeming to have moved while I'm still in place. Or maybe I can destroy or maim others with a single thought or touch.

That could come in handy.

Superheroes have always been one of my favorites. Leaping tall buildings, climbing the walls without a net for security, growing eight arms, or having a super brain.

I've never been one for welching on a bet or backing out of a dare, so I guess I'll never know without trying. Stretching the elfin chain, I pull it above my head and tug it out of my hair once or twice. I pull until it comes free. Tucking it into my jeans for safe keeping, I wait to see the outcome. I want it real close just in case I get furry, gain wings, or grow fifteen feet tall.

Calmly sitting still in the cramped space, clearing my mind of all the garbage from the past few days and chilling my heart rate, I wait. What seems like hours pass as I keep an eye on my watch. One minute, five, ten, and eventually twenty minutes pass without a single apocalyptic occurrence.

Nothing happened. Nothing at all.

No claws, no fur or X-ray vision. I didn't start to float, and as I inconspicuously run my tongue over my teeth, I find that everything is just peachy. No freaky fangs.

Maybe I should try some of the fabulously extraordinary mind talking shit that everyone else was doing.

The plane is quiet, somber, and tranquil. Well, expect for the Neanderthal beside me. So what other option do I have but to try to use my mind-blowing-crazy-power shit out? I don't want anyone knowing about my wickedness, but for some reason, I feel that if I try to contact Anna, it will be hard for her to contain her excitement.

So, I change direction and try to go to the next best asshole. I mean Garron. I can't really trust him, but maybe I can gain an advantage. We could get the jump on them instead of us being the pawns on their immortal chess board.

Garron, I say to myself, trying to get his attention. The silence in my head is deafening. Possibly he didn't catch on it was me? *Garron. It's me, Thiea.*

Fuck this shit is harder than I figured it would be. Talk about a quick way to a harsher headache. My head rings from the pressure of concentrating so much.

Thiea? How the fuck are you doing that? Garron questions.

Not really sure, but it's convenient. Can I ask you a question? Truthfully?

Sure, I guess I owe you that. Fire away.

Is she your mother. Is she going to kill Shoan and the others once the curse is removed?

There's a long pause as Garron thinks before answering. *Yes. She's going to kill them. All of them. She doesn't bluff. If there's something she takes the time to say, it's important enough for her to see to completion.* Again, he goes quiet for a second or so, then adds, *Thiea, I can't promise I can save your mother or any of the others, but I will try to save you if you promise me one thing. Allow me to live if this goes horribly wrong. Mother thinks she can win, but if she doesn't, I don't want Cassie and the boys to live without me. It's selfish, I know, but I would do anything to spare her heartache. I'd still be mortal. I maybe have fifty years left with her. After centuries alone, I want every second I can.*

I'm not sure I can take comfort in that, but I understand his need to keep her safe and live out his life with the one he loves. *I'll do what I can. Do you know what's going to happen when we land? Is there a certain timeline after they land before she kills them? I guess what I'm really saying is, will I get a chance to say good-bye?*

I'm not totally sure what the plan is. I know that they, Shoan and your mother, need to be alive to remove the curse. After that, it'll be a toss-up.

Fuck. *So do you know where we're going at least?*

Yeah, just outside the Giant's Causeway in Northwest Ireland. We'll need cars, as it's a good four-hour drive from Shannon.

Well at least I know we have four hours after landing to reach this place. Hopefully that gives Shoan, Arif, and Niamh time to spring a trap.

They can't lose. If they do, I will personally kill Shoan if he leaves me in this hell without him. I want more. I never considered love or how growing old with those you love could be, but I want the chance to try.

Thanks, Garron. For being honest.

Thiea, I think we better get ready to land. Remember your promise. I will hold you to it.

Closing my mind off to him once more, I ready my ass for the fight of my life.

Chapter TWENTY-FIVE

The Lights go Down in Georgia

Shoan

"Hurry the fuck up, Ni, we have to go. Stop worrying about your goddamn fucking hair!" I shout at her across the cabin. She's been in the bathroom for over twenty minutes, and we have to go over the plan once more before landing.

"Fuck, Shoan. Kiss my ass! I wasn't worrying about my hair," she says as she steps out. "It was my makeup."

"The steward said we would be landing in fifteen minutes, so let's go over this one last time." I turn my seat towards the others, where Arif and Antonius are on the opposite side of the aircraft, looking like two marble statues. They're both stoic and cool. I'm glad that both of them are here this time. I'll need their poise and craftiness.

Hey! I wasn't here last time, unless you count asleep and nine being there. So don't go blaming me for your shortfall! Niamh cries out in my mind like a needle straight to the temple.

“All right. You didn't have anything to do with what happened, but at least this time, I know that I am not alone against the Fabulous Baker Boys.”

“We know for sure that we're landing before them. With their stopover in Paris, we should beat them by a good two hours.” We needed a bit of a head start. It was just a stroke of luck that the private plane we hired had an available flight plan from a cancelled trip, giving us the advantage over Morrigan, who’d taken commercial flights.

"Where do we go once we land?" Arif asks.

“We have to go to Beltany. It’s an old settlement just outside the Giant’s Causeway.” Remembering all those years of playing, hunting and growing up with Ni, I regret so much.

“I’ve arranged a car in Belfast to take us out there. We’ll still be quicker than Morrigan. What a bunch of twits.” Niamh smirks and leans back in her chair, resting her hands behind her head.

“Seeing as I haven’t been there for close to a thousand years, I'm pretty sure it doesn't look the same. We need to get a feel for our surroundings. If they’re able to surprise *us,* then we’re fucked. George, Sully, and Garron will be yours, along with Harrison and any extras they have planned,” I tell her. “As for Morrigan, no matter what, she’s mine.”

I have no idea how the curse will rear its ugly head once we’re on Irish soil. Will it be something gradual? Do I need someone to say something profound and epic, or will it be a shock as my feet hit the earth? So many times I tried to get back, but I was never successful in reaching what I consider to be my homeland. Whether by land or sea or hope, I never got this far, ever.

This will be an epic experiment in its own right. Will Antonius encounter the same feelings and engage the powers as I do?

Antonius, after all, is part of me. Actually, it's more like I'm a part of him, so will it affect him? These are the questions that have been swimming in my mind for hours since we left Greece. I'm sure that Antonius is feeling the same.

Leaving him to his internal interrogation, I turn my attention towards the cool drink in my hand.

Shoan, Arif speaks quietly in his head. *Do you think the girls are still safe*? I can feel the fear in the tone.

Myself, I've tried to not think of what they have, or have not done to the girls since they left our sight. I can't handle the possibilities. I try to answer his question without adding to his fears.

Arif, I hope the girls are safe. We know that Morrigan needs the knowledge that Anna has about the book, but after that, it's a toss-up. With the necklace she's hidden, she's protected for now. Thiea is smarter than we know, I'm sure of it. She won't try to poke the bear.

Knowing the concern is written on my face just as it is on his, we're both fearful for the coming storm that will be unleashed by Morrigan. Both of us have fought hordes of juvenile immortals in the past wars, and if Morrigan has the opportunity to create more, this world will not be the same.

"So, here's my thoughts." Pulling out a napkin, I draw a map of the cairn and the Giant's Causeway as I remember it. "Morrigan left us hanging in the temple. She knows that I was rendered unconscious and depleted, but she has no knowledge of our escape. She probably thinks we're in jail for defiling a monument."

"If she thinks that I'm still weak, she'll be caught off guard. As for Antonius, she knows you're immortal, but she thinks you're by design, not by making. That can work to our advantage. Ni, you know what's expected and what's necessary. And for that they'll underestimate you. It's about time we see that Goddess I know you house."

"Bang on, big boy. I have a whole new bag of tricks in mind." Niamh spins a pinstriped robin's egg blue and blush pink grenade. "Warrior princess to the rescue."

"I agree with Shoan," Antonius speaks up from the corner. Finally. "Niamh, you're the hammer. They have no idea you are what you are. They've underappreciated your skills."

"Damn right they have! I have no problem nailing the final bolt in place on Morrigan's coffin. And I'll control the Berserkers as much as I feel necessary, until I know the advantage is ours. But a lot's riding on you, brother. We won't know what you'll be like until we touch ground." Niamh shimmers and glints with anticipation. She's itchin' for the fight. I can't wait to see the look on Morrigan's face when she learns what she did all those years ago.

"It's hard to argue with her when she's in that mood." Arif winks to Niamh. They have an unwritten language. Even thoughts alone don't do it justice. Years of tag teaming me assisted in their maliciousness.

"Fine, but here's the glitch. What if nothing happens when we touch down?" I mention.

"If we stick to our little plan, then the rest will hopefully fall into place. If not, we go down in a blaze of glory."

"Please prepare for landing, folks. Welcome to Ireland," the pilot announces.

"No matter what our lives will be after this, I'm glad I spent my life with you until now. You are my family, and I wouldn't change a thing. Right now, all I care about is getting the girls out safe. Killing Morrigan and getting the book back before they have a chance to use it against the world? That will be a bonus," I say, faking being cheerful.

"We'll meet our fate with a smile at least," Antonius chimes in with a smile that's as reserved as mine.

Ni takes a fake shot at my head and nods as Arif taps me on the shoulder to let me know the same is felt by him. We're all worried.

As the plane starts its final descent towards Belfast, we all sit patiently, awaiting the unknown. As the fear creeps into the recesses of my mind, I have both feared and anticipated the return to Ireland.

I feel like an anxious little boy looking at the girl he has crush on at the dance. My heart starts to flutter and I perspire.

As the plane touches the ground, I feel a sense of relief. I actually made it back. I might not be out of the plane yet, but at least I'll have the opportunity to reacquaint myself with home.

Home.

Wow, that's such a vivid notion. All that I've worked towards for close to ten centuries has come to fruition.

"Thank you folks for flying with us from Athens. We have now reached Belfast. If you would give us a few minutes to jockey, we will turn off the light for your seat belts as soon as we dock. It was a pleasure to serve you. Enjoy your stay in Ireland," The pilot announces.

"Shoan?" With a look of true concern stretching across his furrowed brow, I feel the same trepidation as he does. Taking in a deep breath, I reach out and feel no change in my personal environment.

"Nothin' dude. I'm sorry, Arif." The disappointment is written in my eyes as I look towards the faces of my family.

"You didn't expect it would happen like that, did you? That would make it way too easy. It's not like the curse considered you on the soil when you're thirty feet above the ground in a plane. The curse started when only boats ventured off this island. I'm sure you must at least have your feet on the ground. You're in a plane, for Christ's sake, dumbass," Niamh reminds us in her more flattering way.

The light for the seatbelts turns off, and as we grab our duffel bags, the steward opens the door of the plane to the ramp. I realize this will be a homecoming, but to a home I've never been. The Ireland that I knew doesn't exist anymore. There are no rolling lands at the moor's, wild tracts of heather that you can lay your head in as a pillow, nor falling asleep without worrying about a person telling you you're a trespasser. All of that is now a dream.

I'm a tourist in my own backyard.

"No matter what you *are,* the one thing you most definitely are *not* is a tourist. It might be a different from the place you grew up in, but that's it."

"We pass through our lives, watching the humans die over and over as we stand by like spectators. The land is the only thing that's consistent; it will remember you." Antonius takes ahold of me in a massive bear hug, slapping me on the back, just before letting go.

"Right now we need to finish this little excursion. I want to kill that large oaf Sullivan for hangin' my ass in the temple, and it ain't gonna happen standing in a plane. After you," Antonius says as he holds out his hand to direct Niamh off ahead of us.

As each of us saunter up the gangway to the customs area, we exit the building after a quick stop, finding our ride awaiting us. A pristine vintage Austin Princess ecru in color with sandalwood interior proudly beams in the sea of modern gaudiness. Leave it to Niamh to travel in style.

Each of us look over at her as she mouths 'What?' With a wide smile, she steps inside to seat herself on the far end of the bench, with Antonius and Arif following close behind.

Driving through the city towards Antrim, we realize that not only myself, but the others are each a tourist in this country; excluding Niamh.

Staring off into the expanse of homes littered onto homes, buildings of the old manner, and newer pubs, high rises, grand buildings like the Hilton, all protrude into the skyline. The land I knew is alien in comparison.

How will I know where to go? Where will everything be? As we meander through the streets, time seems to slow. I find that I'm tired —tired enough that I fight to hold my eyes open.

"Are you all right, Shoan?" Arif asks. It sounds like he's talking to me through a tunnel. The voice is there, but faint.

"I'm just tired, I guess. I'm just gonna have a sleep..." My voice drifts as I pass out. Whether it's the stress of everything finally catching up, or something entirely different, I find myself unable to keep my eyes from closing.

Chapter TWENTY-SIX

Silence of the Slaughtered

Anna

No matter what, I will make sure that whore dies this time!

She will feel my claws in her spine as she takes her last look of me. I have so many bruises, and even bruises on bruises from their *gentle care*. The marks on Thiea's neck have been hidden using a bright purple scarf a woman let her borrow on the last plane. I think she felt sorry for her, somehow believing she's involved in an abusive marriage with Sullivan.

Landing in Paris without issue, we took off fairly quickly. Since then, we've been in the air for just over an hour. The plane this time is relatively small compared to the plane from Greece, so Thiea and I are close enough to talk as long as we talk over Morrigan. She situated herself between us, which made it difficult, but not forbidden. We talk across her about absolutely nothing of importance, just because we want to make her as uncomfortable as possible.

"Could you two shut up. I've heard enough drivel in the past hour that I might throw up from the verbal diarrhea you're spewing," Morrigan says through gritted teeth.

"Oh," I feign shock. "If we're bothering you, you could sit someplace else," I say sweetly to her with a sarcastic smile stretching across my face.

"No, Anna, I'm so enjoying having Morrigan here with us. We would be at a loss without her." Thiea laughs out loud and I'm glad to hear it. It will cause us issue I'm sure, but I like it.

"Don't mock Morrigan," I joke. "She's being *so* hospitable with the current circumstances as it is. I mean, how can you not love her? So you know what, Thiea? I'm thirsty and I'm sure Morrigan would accommodate us. Maybe our gracious hostess here could cop for a few drinks to ease the tension. I would *so* love a vodka, how about you? Morrigan, dear?"

Leaning over Morrigan with a corrosive glance, I wink to Thiea as the stewardess wanders up with her cart of drinks. "Our good friend here will be paying for us."

The stewardess hands us small plastic cups with a dribble of vodka in the bottom, ice, and an opened can of coke. Morrigan pays the young girl the money, scowling as we grin wide.

"I hope this won't change our flavor? I would hate for you to have a distasteful aftertaste from your meals," Thiea comments, motioning to the marks on her neck.

"No worries. The luscious taste lingers in my mouth from your boy toy, Shoan. I'd hate to change its flavor with filth." She licks her incisors, smiling at me with a dangerous glare as she taunts Thiea. "Hmm, I wonder how he is?"

I see the seething frustration alight Thiea's face as she holds herself back from what would create a larger issue.

Thiea smiles, takes a sip of her drink then pours it into Morrigan's lap. "Oh dear, how clumsy of me. The turbulence plays tricks on my weak body. I'll just have to be more careful." I watch as a massive grin creeps across her face. "Stewardess, could you please pour me another? I seem to have spilt mine."

Standing up, Morrigan moves off from between myself and Thiea towards the bathroom at the rear of the cabin. "Excuse me."

That was funny. "That was fabulous."

I'm so proud of her sadistic side.

"There's something I need to tell you." Thiea stops and sighs. *Can you hear me now? I feel like a Verizon commercial.*

The confusion is written across my face as my daughter's smile reaches from ear to ear. *I was afraid at first that your reaction would give it away. I took off my necklace on the last flight. I thought for sure I'd grow fangs and fur or start to howl for Christ's sake. I'm still scared that something will happen, but at least I can talk to you without her intrusions.*

Damn I'm proud. Thiea's always been tough, full of wicked guile and sneaky, sneaky, sneaky.

Honey, I don't know, this could backfire. I have no idea how you're holding back and when or if you could pop up and go boo! Hell, who knows? Maybe you don't at all. I'm not sure I wanna be around when you do. I've wondered this time and time again. What would be the reaction from her body as it came into its own? *You have both sides, Vampire and Werewolf, not to mention the Farie. Each are lethal to the other. One could kill you or nothing could happen. Maybe you counteract both sides and you're a dud. No power at all.*

One thing I don't understand is this. Watch. She turns to the stewardess. Her nametag says Mattie. She's pouring a drink for a portly balding gentleman about three seats down on the left. It looks like Guinness by the color and froth. Turning, Mattie stops pouring the drink into the glass and pours it onto the gentleman's head directly. The fluid plummets down his forehead, plastering his thinning hair to the top of his head. Without even a sideways glance for what she'd just done, Mattie puts the drink down on the seat tray in front of the man, then walks down the aisle to us.

"Would you two ladies care for another drink?" Mattie asks us in an almost robotic manner.

"Yes we would. Two more vodka, please," Thiea replies. Mattie turns back to her cart, puts the drinks together for us while another stewardess helps the portly man doused in amber beer. *See what I mean? I think it and people do as I want. I don't get it.*

I'm awestruck. How did she do that? Thiea made a person react without affecting them by touch. *Well that's a new one. I don't think I've ever seen someone do that. It's totally cool, but scary as shit,* I tell her, just as Morrigan arrives back.

I want to know how the hell I did that? When we were in the airport I wanted a drink. Thought about Sullivan, and suddenly he appeared with a bottle of water. Fucked-up is all I gotta say. I mean, it's not normal, right? Tell me it is and I'll feel so much better about it. Peering at Morrigan, I look for a reaction, hoping she doesn't noticed our conversation.

Nothing.

Turning to the magazine stack in the back of the chair, I take out a pamphlet on duty free purchases. I act like I'm reading it, even though I'm totally engrossed in the unspoken conversation with Thiea. *Morrigan doesn't hear any of this?* I ask her.

Nope. Not a bit. Now, do you see why I wondered about this?

Why can I have a personal conversation without anyone the wiser? Why can I make people do things just by thinking it, and why do I feel like someone hooked me up to a car battery. What the hell is going on! Thiea shouts out.

My best guess would be way off the mark, but I think it can come in handy when we meet back up with the boys. You'll be able to talk to them without anyone knowing it. I can talk to Arif and I can hear the other's thoughts, but I can't ever remember in all the years of someone who could do it without anyone else the wiser. Plus, she could make someone do things beyond their free will.

Growing quiet for a moment, Thiea grins to herself as if she's reading one of the other magazines.

Something is brewing. I know that look.

Sullivan wanders up the aisle before stopping beside us. He hands me a napkin— SMILE :) in bright pink crayon.

"What do you need, Sully?" Morrigan asks very curtly.

"Nothing. I, uh…I just came over to check on you," he says before walking away.

See! Come on, Anna. You must know something about this? Can't other Dark Worlders do this sort of mind control? Thiea's expression is that of wide-eyed surprise.

Hang on, honey. I want to find out something so bear with me, I tell her as I turn to Morrigan.

"Morrigan, mind if I ask you a question?"

She looks up from the magazine she was flipping through, perturbed. "Whatever. Sure. Do you want to know how much it will cost to clean my linen outfit from your daughter's moment of clumsiness?" she says tersely.

I ignore her. "I've always wondered. For you to influence humans, do you have to have contact with them, or can you just think it? It was something I thought of after all that we've gone through in the past few days."

Scrunching up her nose and mouth, she turns to me. "Why? Are you wanting to be influenced? You know you're not really my type. I like them younger, prettier. Girls like your daughter are more my taste, less wrinkly." She turns to Thiea as she runs her tongue along her teeth. "By the way, you know you taste like tree sap. Really, it's a rancid, icky fucking taste."

"I hope I stuck in your mouth for a while then," Thiea snaps back.

Ignoring the comment, Morrigan continues. "No, we have to have contact with a person by touch. Without it, we can't influence their visions. Now leave me alone to read this shite in peace."

Well there's your answer. So you can do something that even she *can't. I don't know what to tell you about it either. I'm only a witch turned were. We'll just have to ask Shoan and Arif when we get the chance. Morrigan is either not forthcoming or she's just daft. I personally like daft.* This is just awesome, but crazy.

Jaz, what do you think is going on? I mean with Shoan and Arif? We left them hanging in a temple. Shoan looked so helpless after Morrigan. Do you think they got away? Thiea wonders.

Morrigan really wants Shoan to suffer so she'll wait for him. They're probably trying to locate a flight out, and they'll only be about four or five hours behind us.

It may sound stupid, but it feels like a sharp knife grinding around inside me slowly. Like someone is trying to damage every part of me.

I don't tell her anything that she doesn't already know the answer to. I don't have to say, 'It'll be fine' or 'Shoan cares.' It's not something she needs to hear. It's something she feels already.

What do we do about our companions here, so we can get back to the people we love? she asks.

I think the only thing we can do is go along for now to keep ourselves alive. Once we land, we'll just have to work out a plan that will get us all through in one piece.

For Shoan to change back, he has to send that whore's ass to hell. Easy. Done. I don't see him leaving her to walk the earth much longer.

Thiea, we should have get some sleep before we land in a few hours. We're going to need all the rest we can get to keep sharp. Closing up the magazine, I place it back in the seatback and recline my chair.

Anna, no matter what happens, I'm glad I found out about you and Arif. Even with all this shit going on, I'm glad it's you that's here with me.

Morrigan may think she has the upper hand, but I'm not going down without a fight. No fucking way am I going down without her getting a good ass whooping, Thiea states sternly. Reclining her chair, she turns away from Morrigan. *I'm gonna try and rest. Beauty like this is hard ,ya know.*

Chapter TWENTY-SEVEN

Dirty Dancing

Thiea

The surprising quiet of the cabin leaves my mind careening down a dangerous path.

What's he doing? How are they faring after everything? Is he thinking of me?

God, Shoan should just run the other way from this orphan/non-orphan, sexually-deprived-crazy-chick that he's hooked up with. I'm the one-night stand from hell. OMG! I was an easy one-night stand that turned into a fatal attraction psycho! I'm a fucking stalker who helped a ruthless, soulless, harbinger of death drink his blood to the point of probably killing him.

Yeah, that's such a Disney Fairy Godmother hookup. *Hey, this girl will lead you to a fucked-up, malicious, certified serial killer that you have been fighting for centuries. Are you good with that? Because the sex will totally be worth it.*

This is so totally fucked-up, I swear. Sighing, I lean back in my chair and try to calm down before I morph into a snarling beast on an international flight.

It's not like I have other things to think of while I'm stuck here beside her High Bitch for another three hours. Adjusting in the chair, I shift towards the window and further away from Morrigan, trying to calm myself. The last thing I need is her feeling "heated" by my sexual arousal because I'm thinking of Shoan and the one time in my life that sex was fucking spectacular. I'm sure over the centuries she's bent both ways. Hell, I'm sure she's performed all the moves from Kama Sutra, and maybe even added a few to the famous picture book herself.

Thinking on that lovely book, I think more about Shoan. The way his hands caressed my skin, lighting it afire. Using my thoughts to direct him to what I wanted; what I needed. It felt like a thousand butterflies were beating wings against me, fanning every inch of my body. Closing my eyes, I make an effort to sleep. I'm hopeful for a fantastic dream to avoid the reality I'm in. I'm glad things went the way they did. Shoan and I are a perfect match, and even with her deadly games, Morrigan assisted us in finding each other.

It doesn't take long before I drift off.

The air is heady from hours and hours of passionate sex. It looks like a hooker convention happened at a porn show. Our clothes—or what's left of our clothes—are strewn around the room. My bra, panties, toys, lube, and Shoan's shorts hang limply from the lamp. Whatever remained is torn into confetti, along with the bedding that didn't fair quite well. So much for Egyptian cotton sheets; they're more like snowflakes.

I thought the proverbial tank was empty hours ago, but somehow, around second and third wind, I pushed past the barriers of my sex 'Guinness' record to keep up the pace Shoan had set. I mean, how can you ignore that perfect specimen of a man lying there like an all-night buffet?

The size of his cock is exquisite, reaching every nook and cranny inside me, filling me. I still can't believe it. The nipping, the petting, licking, sucking, bumping and dirty fucking. The sliding of his slick heat as he tried to restrain himself for fear of harming me before he finally broke. It made him even more sensual and sexually gorgeous to know he didn't have any curses holding him back.

With us both unbreakable the gloves were off, and it was GSP vs Silva; no holds barred.

At this rate, we'll need a new bed set every week. I might as well put us on a charge with the bed company and buy stocks, 'cause we're gonna be ramping up their sales way through the roof!

Lying across two busted bed springs, curling my head up on the piles of torn pillow feathers, I watch Shoan in the mirror as he once more inspects his tattoo. That living entity that moves with him, showing him the balance. It had been tipped the wrong way for a century or more, but now it's a work in progress.

"Why don't you come back to bed?" I toss over a T-shirt that somehow survived us and smile. "It's pulling again, isn't it?"

"Yeah. It's getting stronger and stronger. I'm going to have to go soon."

Shoan pushes on the top of the mirror, making it tilt towards the ceiling, bumping Margarette, his cat, awake. I knew he'd have to go shortly but I'm greedy. I want him all to myself forever.

Shoan's cat stretches out her back, purrs and pushes against his leg. It seems I'm not the only one wanting his affection a while longer.

Can I talk you into one more round? I say internally.

My legs are dangling off the bed so that I straddle his calves, showcasing my sex. "Actually, how about no talking?" I take his still hard cock in hand, stroking it gently, nipping the sensitive area around the base and bringing him back to life once more. Covering him fully, I growl my impatience. I want him to let go and rock his cock deep within my wet mouth. I love him this way, falling apart from a simple motion.

Reacting the same every time with a soft moan, he rubs my swollen budding nipples. Pinching them, he pulls ever so lightly to tease and entice me. There's no need to kick me into gear, I'm already in hyper drive as I dig the fingers of my one hand around to grip his ass. Holding a loose spring to keep from rocking off the bed, I caress his ass with the other drives him deeper and deeper into my mouth. I want all of him.

Without warning, he pulls himself free, picking me up to place me against the wall in a dizzying speed. "Come, my little wallflower. Don't let me put baby in a corner." He holds my hands above my head so I can't touch him. Villain.

"Nobody puts baby in a corner. You know the rules." I smirk and allow my tiny little fangs to descend. He's within reach, and once I have him there's no turning back. He will sing like a canary. Moaning, panting, crying out for more, all while I read it from his blood.

Striking quickly, he releases my hands so that I can take hold of his wet slick rod once more to guide it inside me. We both feel the pleasure as we rock against the wall; him inside me while I taste his blood. In no time, we come in unison over and over again. Within the next few hours, I realize he was saying good-bye.

This was a sendoff.

Chapter TWENTY-EIGHT

Pictures Enclosed

Shoan

The heavy and swollen, almost pregnant flakes drift down from the hoary, overcast sky, casting an almost heavenly pall over the day. I had anticipated this. I had awaited this moment, relished in the chance to have this snow day. The city shuts down, closing streets in, because the plows can't keep up as it falls in massive piles. Taxi's, buses, and trains are inoperable, so her store is closed.

She's home, and she's not going anywhere.

Her stimulating lithe body sprawls out like a banquet at an all you can eat Vegas hotel buffet, enticing me to enjoy every sensual, erotic inch of her. Turning over, thumbing the soft folds of her earlobe and down her neck. Feeling her strong, steady-paced pulse as I brush the harsh planes of her collarbone. Softening, she breathes in and out. Thiea is controlled and serene, without a care in the world.

For now.

It was a fight but well worth it. We won, we conquered, triumphed jubilantly and wholeheartedly after such a hard-won war.

Now she's mine. None can take her from me as long as I continue on my path. I can't give in to the danger of the power I have been given. She's too important for that.

"Hey, are you stopping there? I kind of hoped on a snow day so I could enjoy the interior of this pillow fight massacre for like, I don't know; the whole day," Thiea says groggily as she reaches around to skillfully thumb the tip of my shaft. Teasing it, caressing it before taking it in hand and gripping it tightly, stroking up and down the hilt in measured movements without hesitation, Thiea smiles into my chest. Dangerous girl. After all this time together, she knows how and where to stroke, tickle, lick, nip, and even draw blood to arouse me without reservations.

Leaning further into the plush ample pillows that lay around us, under us, and sprawled around the room, some are empty of feathers from teeth, nails, and excessive roughness last night, but it was worth every minute. The sex candles have long since burnt out, or I would have dripped the pliable liquid across her already slick kitten, licking it all up and leaving her pleading for more.

You know the rules. No words, thoughts only, I tell her through the bond of our mind.

Are you for fucking real! You screamed my name tons last night, so I'm pretty sure you lost the bet already.

Thiea, with the speed of her enriched talents, links my hands in the zebra print handcuffs, mounts my engorged cock and rubs every inch of her sexy lady lips against the already sensitive skin to entice and arouse me. The way she moves, torturing every nerve, overloading my senses is tantric.

Fuck, Thiea. Give me back my hands, darlin'. Oh my Goddess, you are amazing. Stroke it. Take it deeper. I know I lost the bet already with moaning and screaming out last night, but by the Gods, I can't hold out as she so expertly pushes me to the edges of coming, holding out my release.

"Shoan!" she yells as I manhandle her breasts, gripping them sensually, pinching the nipples until the sensitive buds turn bright red from the abuse.

Shoan. Please, I need to. I know what she wants, and I'll give my little girl anything she needs, anything she wants. I can't hold back. I won't. She knows this, she knows my every thought, and that my every movement is for our enjoyed mutual pleasure.

As she leans down, her fragile fangs extend as she anticipates the contact just before piercing my skin. As always, it's exquisite. The transfer of our thoughts together as one as we move in concert to the beat of our hearts. I'll miss it. I'll miss this.

As our pulse increases, so does the rhythm of the stroke in and out, in and out. She knows when to pull more from me, when it will increase the driving force of our uncontrollable carnal demands, and as Thiea relinquishes her hold on me and screams out......

I shudder awake. That dream was so real. I can still feel my cock throbbing, pulsing to complete what we started. There's a compelling force to come inside her tight folds. Easing my eyes open, the cold, harsh truth becomes apparent. It was a dream; an awesome, fulfilling dream. Lifting my hands to my worn eyes, I'm shocked. Maybe it wasn't a dream as I find my hands bound.

"That was for your own good, and ours," my sister says.

Shit.

"Naimh, mind telling me why I'm bound?"

"Well, dear brother, after you passed out at the airport, you started to…let's see if I can explain this without too much pomp and pretense. You started to moan, which was cool, no problem with you having a wet dream and all, but you were undressing. We, meaning the royal *we*, have never had issues with the porno thoughts and toys strewn across your apartment, but to see you starting to thumb your own junk was a breaking point for me. And needless to say, the heavy petting you were about to engage Antonius in was where we all cut the line."

Shit, that was not cool. But it was so real?

"I'm grateful you stopped me. Antonius and I, even in Greco-Roman timeline, we never did the horizontal mambo *ever*. So thanks."

"No shit, but what the F? What was going on? I've never seen someone so into a dream that they start to strip. P.S, we couldn't wake your ass for anything. We tried the water in the face trick, we tried slapping you, punching and pinching you, but to no avail." Antonius pipes up, pulling the key for the cuffs from his pocket to release me.

"I'm afraid to ask why you carry cuffs, Ant. Still, nonetheless, I'm appreciative of the intervention." Rubbing the rawness from my wrists, I adjust the fly of my jeans, covering my peeking erection back inside.

My body is still humming from the pulsing sensations that are still rocking me. "It was exquisite, fantastic, and so surreal. It was the most erotic dream I've ever felt."

"Yeah, we got that. Pictures were enclosed in the package."

"Really. I'm truly sorry. It was winter in Toronto. We were at my place, snowed in, and the war was over. I could feel everything, and I knew I had my powers back, fully. We were at peace."

"So you had a dream about what you want for the future? That's great, but Goddess, it's the first I've ever seen someone so intensely in a dream. If you could have, you would have pounced on anyone of us and drove into us like a whore on Saturday night." As usual, Niamh is the graphic one.

"I don't know, but it didn't feel like a dream. It was more like a future."

"Whatevs." Niamh blows it off with a huff. "Next time though, you're riding in the trunk if you aren't housebroken around family and friends when you sleep." She leans into the plush leather seat and stares out to the passing hills and cracks open a beer.

Conversation over.

Steadying my heart, pulse, and cock, I ease back, trying to ignore the elephant in the room.

Chapter TWENTY-NINE

Lions, Crocs, and Hippos, oh my!

Niamh

The ride from Belfast was fairly relaxed after Shoan's erotic outburst. We had the usual traffic through the city core, and the detours for summer construction. Arif and Antonius took the break to have a snooze, while Shoan and I had been awestruck by the surroundings. It was heart-wrenching to watch his despondent temperament. He misses her terribly; sexual encounter aside.

The one thing I have always expected of my brother was strength. He was the solid one. If I skinned my knee he was there. If I had a broken heart from someone dying, he was there to be the shoulder I needed. I'm having difficulty with the changes in him. The roles are reversed right now, and Shoan needs me to be the strong one.

We sat for quite a while in silence, me watching him and him watching the passing sheep as they meandered around the idling vehicle as we waited through yet another traffic jam.

“Do you think we can win? I mean, finally ending this?” Shoan asks finally, as he closes the window of the limo.

“Honestly? I'm afraid it could go either way.” There's no use in lying.

“Don't get me wrong, I believe in myself and what I can do, but I am afraid.” He tells me something I already know, but I listen. “There’s just so much more at stake this time. Last time, we only had to worry about me and Anna. You can take care of yourself, and I know that, but I worry about involving Antonius and Arif. Not to mention, Thiea. She’s bound. She’s no more powerful than a kitten at a knife fight.”

“Listen, they can all hold their own. And, besides we all know what’s at risk if we lose. Nobody wants there to be any more young hybrid vamps running around. The unpredictability of them. Their thirst for blood and knowledge is chaotic. I don't mind being immortal and living like I do, but to start an open war is suicide. Hiroshima was a disaster. Fuck, look how humans are right now? They can't even live in peace over religion. How would they handle our kind?”

“I know you're right about the others. They can look after themselves, but I still hate bringing them into this.”

“So then, we just have to make sure Morrigan doesn't win. No new harbingers of death to follow her and we get your curse removed, no big deal. We can do this.” I smile at him with a wide grin, then take a gulp of my newly opened Guinness. “Any news on the Lorry? Do you think we might be moving soon?” I ask the driver.

“It seems people are going back to their vehicles, ma’am. We should be moving soon.”

I need to break Shoan from this melancholy before he drags us all down into despair. “Do you feel any different yet?” I ask. “I thought it might happen once you were on the ground."

"No, and I'm getting a bit frustrated. I can't understand why nothing is changing. I thought for sure it would once I touched Irish soil. Don't get me wrong, I'm happy that I'm here, but after almost a thousand years, it's not home to me anymore. You know what I mean, right? The fields are all changed, the buildings are modern, even the livestock is tame. Ireland has lost its wild. I think it doesn't know the ancient powers anymore." It's as if Shoan is disappointed with the land more than himself. Like *it* has forgotten him, even though he never forgot it.

I punch him hard across the face. "Snap out of it! You're mewling like a child. The land hasn't forgotten how to be wild, it's just dormant. Not unlike you. You need to stop wallowing in pity and stop worrying about how you will get back your powers. Maybe you have to ask."

We sit quietly for a few minutes while he thinks about what I've said. Maybe he's thinking a bit about the hit too. I just thought it was about time he reacted instead of being on the offensive, waiting.

As the driver restarts the car and we start to move past the accident, our two other compatriots wake up.

"Sorry, I didn't mean to drift off like that. Nothing out of the ordinary happened, did it?" Arif asks as he yawns, stretching his arms out the car window, trying not to bump me on the head. "How long were we out?"

"About an hour. We've been waiting for the truck to be righted, and nope. No surprises."

"So what did we miss?" he wonders.

"Nothing new. Niamh hit me on the head." Shoan smirks, rubbing his wounded pride.

"Question, Shoan. Is there anyone else of your kind, present company excluded?" Antonius asks as the limo starts to weave around the upturned truck.

"Not that I know of. There were experiments in the book about me, so I suppose there could be more like me. In almost two thousand years, give or take, I've never ran into any. Why?"

"Well here's my thought. When is the last time you tried phasing? Is it something that maybe I can do too? After all, I reached you in the Nether."

Shoan huffs. "I tried just after meeting you in 1245 but since then, no, I haven't. As for the second question, I assume you can since it seems you gained some of my other more innate traits. Did you wanna try?"

"Hey, I already said once I would do what I can to help. If it means trying to be like you, then I'm up for it." Antonius reaches over and grabs a bottle of water from the cooler in front of where Arif sits, gulping down massive mouthfuls.

"I was designed after the ancient Egyptian Chimeric, Ammut. The power is routed in the ability to feel the level of good or evil in a soul's existence. It's an extension of your emotional state. What you have to do is concentrate on love, compassion, kindness, friendship, all of the goodwill in the human soul. That is what makes you, *me,* strong." Antonius closes his eyes and leans back, taking a deep breath. "Think of all the happiness that you had with Arissa, the joy you experienced when you thought of your child, of having a family. Don't think on the negative in life. Think of the laughter with friends, how your crops make you joyful when they grow. All of that will centre you in the right place."

Shoan pauses, allowing him to think without hearing any explanations as Antonius' face beams with delight. His smile reaches from ear to ear, and I must admit, it's something I haven't seen on Shoan for quite some time. If it can bring that out of him—that joy—then this will be the best thing ever.

As I sit quietly and watch my brother and his friend thinking on only happiness, it reminds me of the same, and all the things I can be thankful for.

In my head, I hear Shoan’s thoughts as he thinks of Thiea. *Thiea’s flowing red hair that shines, as if there’s a ray of light behind her head. Her striking eyes, just like her father’s. I swear they pierce your soul and see through all your bullshit. Her uncanny way of being just like my sister; opinionated, stubborn, hotheaded, reckless and insatiable in their need for enjoying life.*

Hey, truly a little unfair there. I am not opinionated.

Once Shoan’s way of thinking drifts off to the more sexual moments with Thiea, I have to shut it down. I can’t be seeing her and him naked. It will take years to get that vision out.

“Here, here. Too much for me too.” Arif hands me another Guinness. Cracking open his own, he guzzles it down.

Ant has a look of serenity and peace on his face, showing a calm I don’t think I possess. Even envisioning myself with Chad, our encounters and our torrid affair, it doesn’t compare to the pure bliss that I see.

Looking over to my brother, I’m sort of in shock. “Shoan? Are you okay?” I ask warily.

“Yeah, I’m fine. Why?”

“You’re fucking glowing.”

“Pardon? Did you say I'm—” Looking down at his right hand, he sees what we do. It’s transparent. I can see the veins like the route on a map, all of it laid out in a design, but still somewhat erratic in placement. I guess this is what he looks like phasing. I've never seen it. I heard about it from him, but seeing it in action is fucking weird.

As his fingers fuse together, they round out at the top so it looks like the pads of an animal. The hair on his arm, which is normally blond, turns an amber shade, thickening to cover his skin's surface. Looking over at Antonius, where the same thing is happening to him as well, I'm fucking shocked and in awe. Whoever thought this shit up had a fucked-up sense of humor.

I understand vamps needing thoughts to survive. After all, they are stupid (present company excluded). Weres are not the prettiest, but strength doesn't require beauty. Then there's me. What can you say, Goddess gains it all. But, this shit is all around weird.

Antonius' face changes, but his arms and body seem to stay the same thickness and broad shouldered.

"All things holy. Allah, this is a marvel of DNA for sure." Arif is awestruck. "Shoan, I always thought you were a beautiful man, but I'm sorry this changes my opinion of you with my daughter."

"I second that motion. Holy fuck, Shoan."

His arms are shapely like a lion—muscular, powerful, and fucking hairy. His hands becme that of a lion. Great massive paws with pads as large as my head, and claws the size of my hand. Shoan decides to show me with his thoughts what he used to look like as the Chimeric, and I'd say it's way different since he shared himself with Ant. It seems they've *shared* the burden.

His face, head, and neck would normally transform to that of a crocodile—scaly with an elongated snout, rows on rows of jagged teeth and eyes that are reptilian where the whites would dissipate, leaving a sea foam green as the pupils stretched out into slits. A second set of eyelids would form to protect his eyes just tops off the weird.

He tells me in his head how the worst part of the transformation was his big grey fat ass. That of a Hippopotamus, and that the whole process would occur as natural as blinking. One moment Shoan would be a human, then he wasn't.

Gazing at Antonius and my brother, switching back and forth between them, both Arif and I have a mixed look of awe and horror. It's hard to tell which takes front seat. If I was up against *that,* I'd for sure be fuckin' freaked out.

"Okay, so I know how I usually look with the head of a Croc, front legs of a Lion and back legs of a Hippo. Ant though, looks… how do I put this? Incomplete." I guess Shoan hasn't done a one-two of himself as he is the same mismatched.

"Shoan," Arif says with a bit of trepidation, "you have the hands, or paws of a Lion, but no Hippo components at all. Antonius has the head of a Croc but not the eyes; his are still human. I think that because you shared your soul to save him, your powers and shape were shared as well."

"Give me a mirror, Niamh," he growls. "You always have one in your bag. I need to see this." I hand him the small clutch.

While he's admiring his new digs, the car makes an abrupt stop in the middle of the road, screeching to a halt. The limo driver is looking at me through the rearview with a look of shock and disgust as he eyes Shoan and Ant.

"I would appreciate you getting your animals out of my car immediately, madam. We don't allow pets!" As the driver gets out of the vehicle, stepping over to the side door, I can hear his thoughts.

Mother Mary of God, Jesus Christ in heaven, help me. I have circus folk. I'd swear I ner' seen that shite before and I'm a shifter!

We proceed to exit the car as the driver unlocks the boot, unceremoniously dumping our things onto the side of the road before hopping back in after taking his money from Arif. As he squeals the tires, I see people staring at us. Normal humans, not Dark Worlders. That in itself is unusual and strange. Normally humans are unable to see us unless we allow it, as we're cloaked like a glamour to keep them unaware of our world.

Taking out my cell to text the boys, I walk a short way down the roadway. I can hear Shoan and Ant as they freak out about their looks while I send off a note to Chad.

"Ni, Arif, am I…am I fucking hideous?" Shoan pauses as I walk back. I consider what it must look like to him. He must be devastated after all these centuries. Knowing what you *will* look like, then looking completely different must be a total shocker.

"I'm hideous! My true form was ugly before, but at least it was what I was used to. Now I have arms like Popeye, but still shaped human and fucking furry as fuck! My face is human, but my eyes are reptilian. What the hell happened?" Attempting to lift his shirt using the monstrous paws, he rips it in two up the middle.

Well, his body is still the same shape. Human, but it's a steely grey color, like that of a Hippo with thicker skin like armor. Once Antonius has completed the same inspections as Shoan, he's quietly standing in shock. His head has stretched out, shaped like the Croc, but his eyes are still the sky blue as always. I guess his body was already furry enough so that didn't change much. Greeks are like descendants of minotaurs anyway.

"What the hell is going on, Shoan! I mean, it was already a bit of a shocker to deal with eight hundred years living alone, now I get to do it looking like a Circus freak! How the hell do we change back?" Antonius shouts.

"How the hell do I know? This is a bit of a fuck-up on my side too, okay! I was used to looking like a jigsaw built by a kid."

"A kid! Hell, Shoan! We look like God had scraps left over from creation. Now what do we do?"

"I suggest we get away from this road before we cause an accident. I can see a house and barn just over that ridge. We'll go there for now to figure this out." I point to the barn on the rise as each of us picks up a bag and starts walking, with the exclusion of Shoan, who can't with his enormous paws.

"Shoan, everything changed when you shared yourself with Antonius. You were one of a kind," Arif states as he tows some of my luggage up the hill.

"Okay, my bad. Now what? How do we change back? Any suggestions?"

"Well, fucktard, how did you do it before?" I reach for Shoan's arm to help me over a steep rise of rocks as I toss luggage ahead.

"Let's just get to the barn. We'll go inside and see what we can come up with. Otherwise, I think leprosy is kind of a keen idea. For the rest of our long existence, the pair of us will be hiding in dark buildings." Shoan clearly thinks this could be an eternal form? Still looking at the bright and cheery side of life, I see. I hope the fuck not. He would get zero dates. Thiea would leave his ass at the nearest zoo, and he'd be in pain for the rest of his existence.

No sex, no girls, no one. How would he handle the voices, the thoughts?

"Don't ask me."

I guess I said that thought a bit too loud in my mind.

Even through the change, the despondent Shoan still peeks through the facade. And if I wasn't afraid of him, I'd pound the living crap out of him in the only possible way I know how. Full on.

Chapter THIRTY

Who said Lightning doesn't Strike Twice?

Niamh

Goddess, help me.

I knew that Shoan was a Chimeric and I understood that would make him different, but I was not ready for what I was about to see. My brother was a good-looking guy, and even Antonius is not a bad looking, but once you see them change, all bets are off. Having scales and forearms like a Lion was just repulsive. Don't get me wrong, I wouldn't leave their side in this fight, or stop being their family. It's just kind of freaky.

Freakiest part was the look on the limo driver's face. It's been awhile since I laughed so hard. He was frightened out of his mind. He thought we'd brought live animals in the back of his car. A shifter scared of a shift is typically not cool. The next time I need a cool party trick, I'm callin' those boys over.

Twenty minutes later, after walking in muck, we reach the barn. My heels have dug in so often that they're ruined beyond repair, and

Shoan will pay dearly for that. The squat building is a low set tile roof, with stones and mortar to hold it together. The door is weathered blue, with red peeking out underneath. Rusty hinges squeak as we open it. The inside is typical; hay, straw, and horses in stalls, panting and shying away from the newcomers in their house.

Placing our baggage by the bales of hay stacked in the corner, each of the guys grab a seat on the fresh straw piled on the floor. There's one milking stool that's relatively clean, and Arif knows me well enough as he brushes it off and hands it to me. Asking me to sit on the straw would be like asking the Queen to retire to a dog house.

Not fucking happening.

"Okay. Shoan, let's try and figure this out, 'cause I'm sure as shit not staying in this form. Why the hell do you look like this anyway? What was your creator thinking?" Antonius balks.

"I can't really remember. It's been so long, and this just kind of happened suddenly. Let me try something." We see his thoughts concentrate on Thiea, picturing her in his mind like before. This time, he's envisioning all the bad in life. I see the horrors of war, man killing man for justice of religion, children dying of starvation, animals being slaughtered for sport, clearing of land for progress, and the whole thing makes me sick.

It reminds me of the past wars that I've been involved in, where the deaths of hundreds of thousands was a necessary evil for the expansion of our kind. The so called brilliant minds of politics never saw the fault in their reasoning. Hiroshima with Morrigan, Egypt with Napoleon, the Spanish in the Americas, Hitler in Germany, just to name a few. As he concentrates on these atrocious moments in time, we watch as his skin warps back to its natural brotherly mess.

"Did it work? Did anything happen?" He asks without opening his eyes.

"Yeah, you're your usual devilish self." I'm still wide-eyed and smiling ear to ear that it even happened, but it's awesome to see the transformation. There was no sloughing scales or anything. It was just as if in a puff of smoke. If I'd blinked, I would have missed it.

"Share with the group. What did you do?" Antonius questions, slurring his words over the large teeth protruding in his oversized jaw.

"Think of all the horrible things in this world; war, hunger, death, the demons who want this new war to begin. All of that is what I concentrated on. Sort of the opposite of what makes you happy, think on the dirtiest and most vile things you can." Bowing his head, Antonius tries to emulate what Shoan just accomplished.

Settling himself into the straw and closing his eyes, nothing happens, but then I see the same thing happen all over again like it had with Shoan. His elongated snout changes back, the scales dissipate and maybe, just maybe, the hair on his arms diminishes.

In all this time, I'd forgot how to shift. I'm so out of practice it's scary.

"After that, I need a beer, or a keg. Fuck." Shaking off the creep factor, as I really don't want to envision that shit ever again, I rise off the stool. Flattening down my outfit, I walk to the door with my bag in hand. "I'm not sure about the rest of you, but I'm famished and I hardly doubt we'll find a fantastic meal in this barn. So how about we find a pub? It would suck if we're exhausted at the moment it comes time to kick that witch's ass. Shall we?" I swing the door open.

"Do I look like a good looking Greek man again?" Antonius asks as he surveys himself, pulling straw out of his sweater.

"No, but you never did. Can we go?"

As the boys grab the remainder of our bags, we make the way towards the road and to Thiea, Anna, and Morrigan, I feel empowered that our course in this fight has taken a different direction.

I won't let Morrigan take those things from me. Not this time, nor any other time in the moments to come. My family is important to me. If it means I have to unleash my own powers fully, I will. I've held off so far. Actually, being honest with myself, I haven't used them to the full extent in a century or more.

I'm afraid to let it loose. Everyone should be if I have to.

Walking along, I realize we aren't far from Bushmills distillery. Finding a quaint little pub for a bite, I'm kind of scared of this reintroduction to the country. It's been years since I've been in Ireland; close to a hundred at least. This new Ireland is so different. It's like comparing a shack in the Everglades to a house in Miami. The last time there were no cars. The roads were dirt paths. Your shoes were disgusting after a few steps, and the buildings were built into the landscape, not protruding from it.

The decor inside the pub is nothing to write home about, but at least it's clean. There's a variety of clientele too. Families, old men, and even a young crowd of immortals by the bar.

"So now we have to get to Beltany? Taking a taxi should be easy as long as we don't pull a fast one again," Antonius states comically.

Yeah, you keep your scales all to yourself and we'll do fine. Arif quips, grinning.

Grabbing seats, we tuck our luggage by the door. A lovely waitress brings by a few pints as we look over the menus.

Taking a long haul of my beer before taking a seat beside Arif, he bumps me on the shoulder, putting his arm around me and smiles.

I miss this comradery. He's been like a father to me for years. When I needed a confidant, he's always been there to answer the phone. Heck, Shoan still thinks I have a constant companion in Chad, when the truth is, nothing can come of it. So why fight the fates. Chad is fun, energetic, and enthusiastic in bed, but he's not the one for me so I'd be wasting both our time. I flitter around with guys that mean nothing, and can mean nothing.

More than nothing.

Go figure. I call Shoan the player. I've never really thought of having a soul mate as the be all of end all. I know I'm not going to find a human mate like the rest. I'm *not* like the rest. I'm not a vampire, I'm not a were, and I'm sure as shit not like Shoan, so the idea of finding a mate that's going to die in less than a hundred years is a waste of my affection. I've been around long enough that that would be a potential risk to my sanity.

"When the waitress comes back over, I'll ask for the name and number of a cab," Shoan says while wiping foam off his mouth. Still seeming distant and sad, I'm thinking of how to kick his asshole attitude into overdrive. He'll need it.

Well, no time like the present.

"What's your issue? I don't get it. We're on the way to fight Morrigan, you have your abilities almost back—mind you, fucked-up—but this time you have the upper hand. So why the fuck are you so bitchy?"

"Do you recognize where we are? I promised them I would come back. I said I would, I just didn't think it would be almost a millennium later." He told our parents that he'd return, that when they saw him leave, it wouldn't be the last time. They'd see each other again. He'd told me this time and again.

"Sadly, I do remember where we are, but I'm not mewling like a child that I didn't get to see them before they died. Remember *I* saw them die. I was there, and I'll be damned if I'm gonna join them today. So don't think this is the last time you'll be here, 'cause there's no way you're dying on me. Understood? Get over yourself and your self-absorbed pity."

"I'm not self-absorbed. I have a problem with being doubtful of our winning. That is my issue, not yours."

"To hell with that! If you don't think we can, then we won't win. You are condemning all of us to your fate of loss. No way. I don't accept that. I didn't pack a Louis Vuitton bag to have someone else inherit it, all because I leave it at some backwater hicktown in Ireland. Get over yourself. First you were worried you wouldn't be strong enough, then you were worried about your powers returning, and now that they have, not to mention that you share them with someone else, you want to give up and die at the hands of the whore you have avoided for close to a thousand years! I call bullshit, Shoan!" I upend my beer, flagging down the waitress. As she appears, I ask, maybe a bit crassly, "Could you bring me a whiskey, please."

"No' a problem. What kind? We've a varied selection. Best thing I suggest is you'd go to the bar and select it yerself."

Hell, why not? I seem to be doing everything else right now. I might as well pick a decent whiskey instead of being disappointed in cheap shit.

I walk over to the bar to inspect the selection, and damn if the waitress wasn't right. There is a fuck-ton to choose from. Jamieson twelve year, twenty, and even a forty Bushmills, two Tullamore, a Red Breast, and a rare Middletons all sitting prominently behind the glass.

"Excuse me," I say to the bartender that's down the bar, chatting up a group of elderly men. Ignoring me for a moment, he holds up his finger in my direction to tell me to wait.

Well, okay. I guess I'll just wait. Stewing after the fight with Shoan, I patiently wait, which is not my strong suit, as he continues with his conversation.

"Excuse me, I'd like a whiskey." This time, I'm a bit more sarcastic. I don't want this bartender in the middle of nowhere to think he can be nasty and get away with it. I hate rude people. So when he continues to ignore me, I decide to welcome myself into his conversation.

Without turning, the bartender answers. "Mum, I'll be right there. Hold yer' knickers."

Mum? Really? Oh, it's not going to play out that way. Not a fucking chance.

"Fine. If that's the way it's going to be, game on." I walk down the far end of bar to the end where the gate is open. Grabbing a fresh whiskey glass from the pristine rack, I proceed to peruse the selection.

"Are ye' that impatient about gettin' drunk? Ye' cannae hold yer decorum, madam?" His Irish brogue is rough, growly. Definitely heavier than mine or Shoans.

Stalking towards me, I feel insignificant compared to his overall stature. I'm not really a tall person, but with heels I can reach 5'9". This man is at least a foot taller as I stand in four inch pumps. His mahogany hair, smoky blue cobalt rimmed eyes are framed with a heavy set of eyelashes. Giving me one of the sternest looks I've ever felt threatened by, I laugh aloud. Wow, not a bad looking immortal.

What's your pedigree, pretty boy?

Standing directly in front of me, he glares. "No, I'm not impatient to get drunk. I just don't have an affinity of patience while waiting on rude bartenders. Now, if you wouldn't mind getting that forty-year-old double malt poured, I'll be on my way." I give him a look of pure distaste at his smugness. I'm sure he's used to having his way with the humans in the bar, but he better not expect it from me. Flashing my eyes, I see the glimmer of fear creep across his.

The thing is I don't want to scare him. I want him to rebel and fight me. Taking the glass from my hand, the whiskey down from the shelf, he walks away from me, walking back down the bar.

"Princess, Goddess, or lowly Dark Worlder -- ye' being a might rude, missus. Now when you remember yer manners, I will gladly serve ya. And yes, before ye' ask, this is the best my bar has to offer."

Talk about rejected. Peering over at the table where the boys sit snickering to themselves, I think of how this looks. This is so *not* good. I probably shouldn't start a bar fight, seeing we have other matters that are a bit more important, but this impotent man child has. Pissed. Me. Off.

Taking a deep breath, brushing my hair behind my ear, away from my face, I pull down my shirt, showing just a smidgen more of my nicely sized tits. At the least, that'll give the old men a story for later.

Standing to my full height, I walk nicely towards the end of the bar where my whiskey went. "Now that wasn't a nice way to talk to your elder. I know you may feel you have an advantage as it's *your* bar, but I can assure you the tables are *always* in my favor. I'll give you one more shot at this. Could I please have a drink poured before I break the bottle over your arrogant head." With just a hint of sarcasm, I lean forward across the taps, revealing more of my assets, and give myself a better range to beat his ass.

“I would be more inclined to help ye' if yer’ weren’t in me back, come to the front of the bar. Like *regular* folk.” As he turns towards me with his arms crossed over his expansive chest—might I add a nice chest—I slowly draw my eyes up to match his glare. His steel blue eyes have switched to a bright amber, freezing me in place. Shaking myself, I walk very carefully so as not to catch my heel in the water mat. I step out from around the edge of the bar.

The cat calls and giggles from my brother and Arif laughing out loud is almost unbearable. *Shut your mouths, both of you, if you wish it to be used for breathing in the near future.*

Sorry, Ni, this is too hard to resist. Holding up his hands in defeat, both he and Arif silently turn back to their drinks and food as I return my attention to the godlike body in front of me.

Ignoring their derisive noises, I smile sweetly to the pup holding my liquor hostage. “Sorry about that, sire. Of course, a sweet damsel like myself should always defer to her master. Now, have I been a good enough girl to deserve that drink?”

“No.”

Are you for real?

“What do you mean, no. No! What kind of bartender are you? I would like a drink. I've asked nicely quite a few times now, and I'd like that drink. I suggest I get it before I force you to give it to me.” I'm pissed off totally by his arrogance, audacity, and hostage taking of my drink. Today is not the day to pull rank on me.

“Today, I’ve been kicked out of a perfectly good limo, stranded and left to walk in heels, no less to a barn. Then, of course, my favorite part, I end up at the bar where the bartender feels I am rude and unworthy of his liquid bliss.” Leaping up onto the chair in one swift move, I reach across and hold his crisp white collared shirt in my hands. I’m pulling his neck to the bar with one hand as I grab the whiskey in the other.

Uncorking it with my teeth, I pour a shot into the glass. Upending it in one gulp, I set the glass back on the bar with a slam, walking away with the bottle in hand.

“Thank you for your acquiescence. Was that so hard?”

“No, but it was terribly enjoyable,” he says, laughing mercilessly at my expense, just as I reach the cubical.

Speaking to me internally. *I’m hard just thinkin’ on it, darlin’.*

My brother, Arif, Antonius, as well as most of the patrons, are killing themselves laughing.

I hate being singled out. If most of them knew what I’m capable of, they would hightail it to the moor, leaving me to stew in peace with the lovely bottle I just procured.

I’m steaming mad, hungry, and upset that I let him get the better of me. Turning, I walk away from the table and out into the sunshine. At least out here I can't hear the hysterics.

Off to the side under a massive Wych Elm is a little park bench in a sparse grassy area. Sitting, I turn away from the pub and look out over the spectacular view of the Causeway.

Why the fuck did I let him get to me? Over a whiskey? I know why. It wasn't over the whiskey, it was over him. The bartender. He's good looking and he knows it.

And rude! I hate rude.

Unplugging the amber once more, I lift it to my lips and chug it back in gigantic gulps. The burn fuels my hate.

From behind me, I hear the door to the pub open as the sexier than all hell bartender walks out with my lunch in hand and another whiskey glass. I can see this going wrong.

Chapter THIRTY-ONE

A Scotch in the Hand is Better than two on the Bar

Niamh

"Truce?" he asks, still grinning.

Like bringing out my lunch is going to cool me enough to forgive his brashness.

"Why did you do that? It wasn't necessary. I just wanted a drink and you were awfully rude." He lets out a sigh, puts my meal on the bench and offers to pour me a drink, like some type of peace offering.

"Sorry, but it was too hard to resist. I don't get a great deal of *our* kind here anymore."

"There was a bar full of Dark. I'm sure you have *loads* of fun with our kind all the time," I say crassly.

"Not *our* kind, Love."

Huh?

"What are you?"

"Does it matter?"

"And you'd fuckin' wonder why with the fabulous hospitality you exude I was reaching into your bar for a drink?"

"Sorry, it was just fer' fun. How about we try this again. Civilly. My name is Cohen. And you are?"

Reaching for the glass nervously, expecting a crowd to gather to watch the show as he puts me in my place once more, I take a leap of faith. "Niamh."

Looking at his face, I realize the offer is sincere. "I'm not normally that impatient. Okay, that's a lie. I'm impatient, but I'm sure you're not the fucking prick I took you for. I'll go out on a limb and apologize first. I shouldn't have gone behind your bar, it was—"

"Wrong," he finishes.

"Yeah, it was wrong. I don't do well with—"

"Disappointment, rejection, and all out refusals."

"Now we're going a bit far on the truth and apology, but yeah. I was wrong. Now, I don't want to point fingers, but isn't it your job to pour drinks when someone asks for it?"

"Ya', but like I said, yer' not someone we get in the area much anymore. And, to be totally honest with ya', darlin', you are one beautiful Goddess. Might I ask—"

"Let's just say I'm not your typical Dark."

He raises his hands in defeat. "Fine, I can handle that as an answer after everything we've had as a relationship thus far. I apologize too. I should notta held back yer' drink. It was not fair." Holding out the tawny liquid to me, fingering my hand around the glass, we touch briefly.

"Fuck, that hurt!" I say as pain shoots up my hand. It was as if I'd been hit with a bolt of lightning. "Shit, what did you do? Did you hook the fucking drink up to a car battery before handing it to me or what!” The glass falls to the ground, smashing to pieces.

“Me? What d’ ye’ do? That wasn't one sided ye' know, Love. Next time, I won't bring out yer' meal. Ye' can come in to get it ye’self.” Looking as upset as I feel, he rises from the bench in sweeping strides, back to the bar.

“Fuckin’ immortal. Wanna her own drink she canna come get it.”

My hand tingles from the spark. Itching and shaking off the feeling, I glower at the door. Fuck.

Maybe it was a fluke? Tentatively touching the surface with my fingertip, then surround the glass piece with my whole hand, there’s no shock this time.

"Are you okay?" Shoan asks as I turn from my meal.

“Ah, yeah. Yeah, no problem. I can't believe I let that guy get the better of me. Was I really that funny?” I ask, knowing the answer.

“Yep. Warrior Princess. It was nice to see you letting off a bit of steam. It’s been awhile. Normally it's me or Arif that tosses the first punch. I particularly loved the shirt grab for the whiskey move though. Very comical.”

“Are you guys done with lunch?” I ask. Shoan nods and I continue. “Fine. I'll scarf down this pie so we can get going.”

As I dig into the pie, Shoan asks, “When I came out, you were talking about your hand. Did you hurt it grabbing the bartender?” Taking my hand to inspect it, he turns it over, front to back, checking for damage. Shoan still acts the big brother part, forgetting I’m a big bad girl who can look out for herself.

“No. When that guy gave me my drink he shocked me. Just another trick to piss me off, I guess. Maybe they don't get a great deal of entertainment."

"Okay then. Well, let's get going. I paid the bill already so we can head out." Shoan settles on the bench, while Arif and Antonius join us on the dilapidated wooden bleacher. "I asked after you left for your little episode where the oldest graveyard in the area is. I was told what direction and it sounds close. We'll go there, then taxi out to the fight."

I speak with my mouth full. "Shoan, they've been dead for close to nine centuries. The graves won't be recognizable anymore. Hell, all that marked them was a lone stone with the etch of Romulus. I doubt it's even there."

"I have to go. I promised myself I would see them. Whether they're dead or alive, when I got home, it was a promise I intended to keep." Shoan looks sullen again as he walks away, gathering up our gently discarded bags where Arif and Antonius wait. Chickens. Too afraid to deal with me? Fine. I'll handle that later.

"Don't expect any hysterics from me. I wept for them centuries ago. It would feel fake after all this time." Wiping the smear of mustard off my cheek, I rise off the bench to follow my brother and our friends to see those long dead.

Just as the taxi pulls up, I scarf down the last few bites of my pork pie and fries while the boys shuffle into the nondescript black four door sedan.

"Where to?" The driver asks once we're all seated in the car. I'm in back between Arif and Antonius, while Shoan takes the front seat. The seats are ripped, stained, and I think there might have been something furry scuttle under my feet.

"We're off to the graveyard at Coleraine first, then on to Beltane if you wouldn't mind." Shoan says quietly to the driver as he buckles up his belt. With a quick nod from the driver, the vehicle is slammed into gear and screeches down the road, just missing a blue Mini.

Shoan, couldn't find Mario Andretti to drive us? Arif comments.

Not to be picky, but if we're to save the world, I would at least hope we can arrive alive first, then die trying, I concur mentally.

"My Goddess. I don't mean to alarm you. Please accept my apologies. I will slow down." The driver states with downcast eyes as we comes to a roundabout on the road ahead.

"Did you just call her Goddess? Don't increase the size of her ego. She's bad enough as it is. Fuck, why not bow and kiss her feet." Antonius lets out a barrel laugh. Looking at the driver, I catch his glance through the rearview mirror.

Shoan smirks and glances over his shoulder at me while the driver careens down the B17 towards our next destination.

Antonius has no idea.

I'll leave him in the dark just a bit longer.

Let's hope we make it there in one piece so I can enlighten him. I can't wait for the entertaining parts to start. Now that I'm full, I'm ready to take the mickey out of someone, and not just *anyone*. I want to peel the skin off at least one of those vampire brothers.

This is going to be fun.

Chapter THIRTY-TWO

Be Aware of Small Packages

Garron

Fuck, do I hope this goes well. I don't want to be on the losing side of this fight. My mother may think she has the upper hand with the two women contained, but I don't feel the same confidence that she does.

After we landed in Shannon and hired cars, I'd say the trip has been pretty uneventful, except when Sully just about crushed the luggage trying to get it into the undersized boot.

The landscape looks the same as it had since meeting Cassie just about twelve years ago. It's still the same old ruined homes left bare, with no new buildings in their place. Sheep still wander the roads, and rain falls off and on, drenching you to the bone.

Like the land is unhappy to have our kind back. It *knows* we're here to create more of our kind. The mother Goddess has gone quiet like in the eye of a storm; like the calm in a hurricane, just before all hell breaks loose.

Thiea has been quiet since we landed too, which kind of freaks me out, what with her new way of speaking. George was placed in the car with us, so I was holding myself back from speaking to her further about the newfound talent. I know my brothers can be gruesome, vindictive, and harsh, but I think they're as much afraid of the outcome as I am. I'm still not sure this is the best idea. Sure, I want to become immortal again, but to curse the world with half-breeds once more? Those nasty living dead are the pestilence of our kind; I'm not sure I want to be a part of it.

We've been driving for just shy of four hours. Thiea and her mother both decided they needed to pee and eat, or *they were going to cause a stink,* as they called it, so we stopped at a small tavern for a bite. Well, the girls and I ate, the rest had a bite out back, all except for mother. She's still reeling from the lovely feast of Shoan, so while the others took off to find meals, we sat in soundless purgatory in a very noisy bar. Thiea and Anna were silent, which was a bit unnerving. Feeling like a kid with a crush, I'm awkward and unsure of what to say to start a conversation, so I try meaningless words to fill the air.

"How's your lunch, Thiea?"

"Fine, I guess. What can you really say about a battered piece of fish with fries? At least it's not cold." She's speaking to me, that's a plus.

"How about yours, Anna. Edible?" I ask.

"Enjoyable seeing your *dear Mother* wouldn't let us eat even peanuts on the plane. How much longer till we reach where we're going?" Anna asks, cutting her steak pie into pieces.

"We should almost be there. About ten minutes away, not much more." I turn to Thiea and place my hand on hers, looking into her eyes. "I know this is hard to fathom. Mother won't even bat an eye if she can condemn one of you to some type of half-life, so I'd do as she asks. Whether you want to hear it or not, I am sorry for involving you in this. I didn't have a choice any more than Anna does. We both do as we are told or watch harm come to the ones we care for."

"Yeah, but, difference is *my mom* is doing it to save me. Yours is doing this to cause harm to thousands of countless others because she wants hell on earth. It's not just to see you be a full vampire again and you know it. That is in no way the same thing. I'll be glad to see Shoan condemn you." With a vengeful look in her eyes, she turns from me and back to her lunch.

Great. I may be an asshole, and I may have involved her in this, but I still don't see myself as the same evil as my mother. She has me by the balls, more than Thiea knows.

I lean down on the table to speak quietly and with conviction. "Shoan was close to death when we left him, Thiea. It will take him days to recover his strength. I know he has to get here to cancel the curse, but I don't think he will be powerful enough to do anything else."

Placing her fork on the table, gently, and in such a way to show she's controlling her temper, she says, "Listen to me. Shoan will get here. He will kill you and your whore of a mother, as well as your asshole brothers. I will stand by and watch you be measured because to me, this is your fault. Your family caused this. Shoan was doing what he was created for, and because your *mother* didn't want to die for being a horrible being, she caused a chain reaction that brought us here. So excuse me if I feel that your reasons aren't the same as mine." Crossing her arms across her chest, she turns away from me to stare out the window beside our table. "My appetite is gone."

I can't even assume to argue the points she made; this is our fault. Flat out. The truth hurts, but it is truth nonetheless. Calling over the waitress, I pay her, then we make our way to the door, just as Sully enters.

He seems so much more hulking, standing in the doorway with the light streaming in behind his form. “It’s time to go. I hope you ate well. I know we did.” Licking his lips he smirks at me, removing the final scant traces of the person he enjoyed. He may be my favorite brother, but he can still be an arrogant prick.

“Yeah, we're ready. Let’s get on with it,” Thiea says, shoving herself past Sullivan, pushing him into the side of the door frame. The look on Sully’s face is that of disgust and awe as he stumbles to catch his balance from her thrusting motion. I myself am a little taken aback as well. Sully is never taken off guard, or off balance.

Anna makes her way past us with a giant smile flitting across her face. “The bigger they are, the harder they fall, I guess.”

I turn to Sully with a perplexed look. “What the fuck? Are you standing in a hole?”

Turning, he stares at the door frame, dented and cracked where he shoved into it. “No, she pushed me. I mean she *pushed* me. How the Goddess did that happen?” Sully is wild, with a look of uncertainty.

“She’s at least a hundred pounds less than you. She shouldn't be able to do that. Even a full immortal would be hard-pressed to do that.”

“Agreed,” Sully says as we make our way to the rental car.

Making a mental note to keep an eye on her as we drive off for the last leg of our trip, I feel there are some surprises in our future. Yes, there are.

Mother is wrong; we’re fucked.

Chapter THIRTY-THREE

At the End is the Beginning

Niamh

Okay, so I didn't think it would make a difference seeing the graves of our parents. I knew all it would do is make Shoan wistful and apologetic. *Sorry for not being there. Sorry for not being the son they needed, for not being their true son. For being who his...*

Everything came to the surface and it was pathetic to watch. He broke down on the site, crying like a fucking baby. Not at all the brother I know. The strong, dangerous, powerful, not sorry for shit asshole that I love and care for was missing.

Goddess, if this is the way that he's supposed to be, then how are we going to defeat Morrigan and the half-breeds she's going to create? This is going to be a shit storm from hell. We need him to be strong and deadly.

Sitting in the back seat, behind Shoan in the taxi, I decide it's time to get him back on track the only way I know how. Hitting him in the back of the head as hard as I can, he falls forward, then turns with a look of pure malevolence.

"What the fuck was that for!" he shouts.

"For the lazy ass way you're reacting right now! That's enough of this bullshit. You need to get ready to kick ass. No more worrying about shit you can't repair. Thiea needs you! We need you to be the asshole you *can* be. You have to prepare for whatever Morrigan is going to throw at us. We need *you* to tell us what to expect from Morrigan as you've been there and we haven't." I hope I made it through that thick skull of his, and by the look on his face, that downgrades from wanting to kill me to that of remorse, I'd say I have.

"My bad. Sorry. I just feel like I keep letting everyone down. First you, then Antonius, and now Thiea. I left her in the hands of that monster." Shoan pauses, looks at me, then to the others. "I've been a jackass. You're right, we need to be prepared for Morrigan. I better tell you what happened originally then we can work from there."

"Are you sure this is a good story for a taxi? Last time we were kicked out of a limo for doing something strange. Now you want to have strange conversations in front of this man? Is that wise guys?" Antonius pipes up.

"Don't worry yourself, sir. I ain't about to say nothin'. I swear to you, Goddess. Plus, yer friend here told me about the woman yer looking for. I know that whore. She's all yers."

"Huh. Well then, don't hold back." I for one would love the whole story for once. "All I remember from then is that you went out for a walk to clear your head after an argument with our father. You didn't come back, then I remember Giza running around, gathering a parcel of your things. Shirts, some food, and that was it. You were gone."

"Back then, you didn't know what I was. Your adopted parents did. They always did. When they found me on the beach, they didn't know what I was. They just knew I was different and I was in need. They brought me into their home, fed me, clothed me, and loved me for years before you were even thought of. I don't even really know how old I am. I know I was living with them for close to twenty years before you came along.

“They were the kindest people I’ve ever known. They had no reason to even help me. Hell, I was ugly on the inside and out. I was so upset not knowing my history and my mind was a blank from before I met them. I tried to hide from you my true form, but there were times you knew I was different.”

"Actually, up until about a week ago, I still thought you were a cursed Daywalker," I mutter while he talks.

"I get that. With everything bound, I could see how you would assume that. Anyway. Back then, we lived with the humans, protecting them without their knowledge. Kind of like secret service agents. Our parents didn't want me going to this particular party. They didn't think it was worth my life or our lifestyle being made public, so they asked me to stay out of it and let nature take its course. I argued with them. If I don't comply with my nature, it’s painful. That's the argument you saw."

While we wind the roads closer to the city up ahead, I let him continue without my interruption.

"When I saw the first one, it was Charlie, a local vampire from our area. He was always very clear of his intentions but also cautious, never taking what he shouldn’t, never killing. He was always a very strong opponent, and he fought valiantly. Afterwards, I understood why. He was protecting a smaller child that was drinking from a little boy in the corner.

“You know it’s forbidden to turn children, but this one wasn’t. It was a half-breed, part human. I was disgusted that he was allowing it to feed; protecting it. I immediately attacked Charlie and measured him. After he was gone, I moved on to the young half child. She was just a little girl, no older than five, with large golden curls and blue eyes that were rolling back into her head in elation. I pulled the little girl off before the child she fed from perished, but she lunged for my arm.

“As she finally calmed down, I found out she was from Potsherd, just north of our home. She told me that she’d been sleeping one night when she had an awful dream of a demon in her house. Awaking, she found her family all dead on the floor with a tall woman standing near the fire in the middle of the room. With an outstretched hand, she told the child that everything would be all right, and that no harm would come to her. She felt secure, and in her innocence, she followed Morrigan before everything went black. When she came to she was thirsty, and her head hurt like someone was constantly screaming. That's when the woman told her to feed, that it would make it feel better.

“She had no recollection of when this happened, but she knew the woman's name; Morrigan. Dispatching the child, of which she was grateful, I then went in search of Morrigan. That’s where everything went bad. Me hanging over a manure ditch, being cursed, and subsequently banished."

"So what occurred when Morrigan and her band of uglies caught you? The cursing part?" Arif asks.

"I was tied to a chair. Giza was helping unbidden, she spoke an invocation worked with herbs. I remember it vividly; how they smelt, and how it felt as George cut my arm, placing my blood in a goblet before I had to drink it down." Shoan grows quiet as he thinks back on all of this, but I'm pissed.

"Why didn't you fight? Why'd you drink it? Why didn't you just judge them and leave the room empty? I don't understand what stopped you?" I'm angry for answers that make no sense.

"You were there. They held you. I either cooperated or they killed you. I couldn't let them harm you."

"I don't remember any of this. How can I not know that I was there when you were cursed and condemned?"

"You were asleep. Harrison had gone to our home, threatened father with harming you, so he went along with what they were doing to me. I couldn't see any harm come to those who had raised me, and that's why you only remember the packing and the argument after I was gone. I always loved you. I thought you the most beautiful little girl I had ever seen, and I couldn't see you harmed." With sadness, Shoan looks at me like he's seeing the little girl from all those years ago.

How can you be mad at that, for Goddess' sake?

"Fine, so that's the story. You were tortured into giving into her. Giza was giving in to save her family, and here we are, repeating history. Let's not let her get away with it this time. She'll assume you have your powers back, but Antonius and I—"

"Yeah, lets touch on that. What are you exactly?" Ant asks me.

"Let's just say there's more than meets the eye, darlin'. I don't give away all my trade secrets." I wink at Ant and toss an orange smiley face grenade towards his head.

"I don't think Morrigan realizes that the curse has started to work against her," Arif interjects our convo and adds his own take on this. "My daughter will be a power to be reckoned with. Morrigan thinks she's a were, just like Anna, but she has no idea that she is Farie and vampire as well. I think she will surprise all of us in the long run."

"So where are we going when we reach town? Second question, why did you need to visit the grave so bad? Remember I know you don't do anything without a reason." Shoan ignores my question as the taxi corners a roundabout. Taking us to the far side of town, up ahead are fields upon fields of wheat and corn stalks stretching for miles. There's nothing here but a rundown cattle shed with over-grown trees, creeping vines, weeds, and rambling livestock.

"Yer' address is up ahead here. I wish ye' luck. Kick her arse. We need more like you and less the likes of them rabble around," the taxi driver says as he pulls to the side of the road. Shoan pays the man, we get out and grab our bags. As we await Shoan for the final stretch of this hell-guided tour of Ireland, I laugh aloud.

"Funny much?" Ant asks, wondering why I'm giggling like a fool.

"A bit. I can't want to cut a bitch." Tweeking my eyebrows up, I let my eyes glow slightly while I twirl a throwing star.

"Ready?" Shoan asks. Each of us nod as the taxi pulls away.

We walk towards the outbuilding, none of us needing to speak or comment. We know it will be hard and deadly from here on in.

Just another walk in the park, I guess.

I'd already checked with the boys and Terese, knowing they would be within range if we needed their help, but they're afraid to be within range of Shoan when the time comes, where he can condemn again. All of us are afraid, but we'll stand by him, knowing we have a better dip in the scales for good.

"Niamh, I want you to wait inside. It's not bright in there and you can be in one of the corners. No one will be wiser until they light some lamps or bring in lanterns. After that, bring the rain. I want the full power of the Goddess here. No holding shit back today. Arif, I can't tell you what to do, what with your daughter and Anna inside, but I would ask that you stick to the back of the building. When they bring the girls, you can contact them to let them know we're already there, surrounding the building with help. I want you to devote yourself to making sure that Harrison and Garron are clear of the girls. They will most likely be guarding them.

"Antonius, they think you're a shifter. Let's use that to our advantage. Don't shy away. Hang out front with me to await them. I want you to be concentrating on Sully and George, use their stupidity against them. Divide them. I only need to be close enough to touch Morrigan to condemn her, but she has to get the curse lifted first."

"Fine, that sounds all right to me." Smacking his hands together, there's a shine in his eyes. "This will be so much fun." Bellowing, he slaps Shoan on the shoulder.

Arif nods, grabbing Shoan's arm in their usual manner of hand-shake, then walks off to the back of the shed. I, of course, being careful, set my Louis bag behind a large boulder for safe keeping.

"Be safe in there. No theatrics. I am not losing you or anyone else here today," I tell my brother as I walk away to stand inside the animal shack.

Turning around, I see Antonius and Shoan sauntering through weeds to sit down on a clear patch of grass in the sun. If this wasn't a war we are heading into, I would say we're all at peace and content in each other's company. As it is a war, I'll be damned if I lose any one of these people.

Lighting up my power I make a vow; I will fight to the death for them all.

Chapter THIRTY-FOUR

All Good will be Rendered

Morrigan

Since landing in this Godforsaken land, I have had to deal with incompetence from my sons, attitude from the weres, horrible driving skills from Harrison, and poor directions on the GPS. With a lack in ancient language skills, I was only able to read half the spells and notations in the book. Finding the spell that was originally used to curse the Chimeric, I searched out the spell for creating more of our kind. Having used it before, I knew what to look for. As for the counter action necessary to reverse the restraints on my kind, I was at a loss.

I have no idea what language it is written in. The ancient Sumerian, Celtic Gael and Greek I follow, but do you think I could read this last page? The letters don't even coordinate into a language I remember, and I've learned a great deal of languages over the centuries.

My love, you have been pouring over that book for over four hours, and are still no closer. Wait until we get there. Remember, that's why you brought her. To read it. You'll burn through your last meal quicker, Harrison tells me as he makes a U-turn again, because the GPS said so.

The only worry I have right now is Garron. I want him right. He's been a shell, a corpse, and I don't want that to happen to any more of us ever again. I want that Chimeric killed and the disgusting weres will see it all. But before that, I want my son whole so he can join the fight, I say with a look of distaste on my face. My son may be alive but he is a lie; no longer a true child of mine since becoming a trappa.

Darling, I understand how you feel about Garron. He's a wet sack of shit, and his distasteful wife, her humanity is harsh. Now about this directional system. I am totally fucking lost. Do you know where we're going?

Ask for directions over at the roadside stand, I say, pointing out a small market stand. Pulling the car over to the edge of the road to ask the young girl attending the fruit stand, she points us in the direction of a roundabout ahead, and indicates to take the road to the left. He thanks her, then directs her to the rear of the building quite calmly. They disappear from view for a moment or two, then Harrison reappears from behind the stand, wiping the sides of his mouth with a look of pure excitement and joy.

Stepping back into the car, I ask him how it was. He smiles, buckles his seatbelt, and we continue down the path indicated. Within minutes, the building that I could recognize anywhere appears on the horizon. A small outbuilding with nothing of note, but it is so ingrained in my memory that it's hard to not envision it any other way. To my amazement, Shoan and his friend, the one that came to his rescue at the temple, are awaiting us outside.

"Well this makes it more interesting. Harrison, would you mind pulling up here so that the boys can bring Anna and Thiea to us? I would hate to lose our guests before we have a chance to deal with the Chimeric properly." Harrison nods. Taking out his phone, he calls the other car.

"Done. Now let's meet our fate on our terms. George is going to pull up ahead of us, so that when we get out of the cars, the girls will be in front of us." Shutting off the engine, he reaches over to kiss me and I allow it. Not that I have been the most affectionate person to him, but it was nice to see him feel the need before we go to battle.

Stepping out of the car, book in hand, I fall in step behind Sullivan, who has Thiea by the arm. She's struggling, which is to be expected, but it's the way she is. She's actually giving Sully a run for his money.

"What the hell was in that lunch! Fuck. Sully, control her," Garron yells at him, while Thiea has almost wiggled out of his grip.

"Garron, stop yelling like a barmaid and help your brother handle Anna. Maybe controlling Thiea isn't the way," I holler over to stop all this tomfoolery. "How are we to win if we can't control the two simplest women?"

Shoan has watched this whole incident take place, and as he and his friend laugh aloud at the predicament, I become more enraged with the display. As Sully and Garron are still having an arduous time with Thiea, I hand Harrison the book and stomp over to where she and the boys are. Grabbing her by the back of her head with a handful of her hair, she squeals out in pain, but stops struggling for the moment.

"Now, are we done? Don't worry at some point in this day you and your mother will be together, so help me Goddess! Get along, or I will make sure that not only you and your mother die by my hands, but your friends will meet the same end. Are we clear?" She nods her agreement with gritted teeth.

If only she were a vampire, I think I could like her spunk and vigor. With Thiea finally under control, we start across the road towards Shoan and his friend where they await us. Shoan looks pretty well, which surprises me. I didn't expect him on the mend yet. Hell, I didn't think he would be on his feet for at least a week. It is worrisome how he's healed faster than I imagined, but this gives us the opportunity to start and finish this earlier than I thought.

"Hello. Welcome to Ireland. I see you've brought our friends, unharmed, I hope? I would hate to have to torture you before condemning your ass to purgatory." Shoan tells me with such a fervor, that I think he really believes he can win this little soirée. The look on his face puzzles me though. He's gleeful, smug, and almost prepared for a fight.

"Which one of you ugly brutes is the one that hung me from the temple? I would like to have a word with you before we go in," Shoan's friend says to the boys.

"Aye, that would be me. You fared all right it seems. Would you mind a rematch?" George, with Sully in tow, moves away from the girls to engage the friend. Stepping around to the front of building is Arif. I guess a rematch was inevitable. It shouldn't take long and I can work the magic without my sons or those two useless immortals anyway.

"Harrison, will you deal with the other piece of flesh that just rounded the barn, he shouldn't be too much trouble for the likes of you." Taking the book back from Harrison, pulling ever so perfectly on Thiea, she's guided tightly by the hair.

"Let's get on with this. Shall we?" As I indicate for Shoan to lead us, I drag Thiea quite unwittingly towards the dilapidated building, while Anna follows closely, like a mother protecting her cub. Weres, such ungodly beasts.

"Ladies first." Shoan holds back the door for Anna and Thiea. I still have a hold of Thiea by the scruff of her head, as they both walk in the shed ahead.

"Don't worry your pretty head, Morrigan. It'll be over with shortly." With a scowl of pure hatred, Shoan falls in step behind us, into the dim barn. It's dark and musty smelling. Not much different than the last time, as I still hold all the cards. Only now, Shoan is not tied to a chair in the middle of the room. Oh, how I love to revisit that time in my mind.

"It's truly amazing how history keeps repeating itself, eh, Shoan." Out of the corner of my eye, I see another person appear; a woman.

"Who are you?" I ask.

"I am Niamh Mac Cathmhaoil, and that is my brother. You and I met a very long time ago, at that time you didn't know me very well. Now would be a good time for you and I to meet, but I'd suggest you release Thiea before we get reacquainted. I'm about to go all nasty on your ass."

"Why would I be afraid of a shifter? You're a hopeless mess. And by that reasoning, why should I?" I'm smug enough to understand that I hold all the cards here, not them. "*He* isn't going to do anything. You see, I haven't released him yet. He can't do shit to me, and the only one who can do anything about releasing it is being held by me, right?" As I finish saying the words, Thiea turns in my hands to face me, peeling her hair out of my grip. "How?"

"You really aren't that bright, Morrigan." She steps closer to Anna. "My mother is a direct descendant of Giza, and yes, she was bitten by a were, while I was still in her womb. So technically, you have most of the story about me right, but there's a bit more to it. My father is a very old, very strong vampire, and I've been kind of in protective custody, but not anymore. I decided to let the wild child lose." Reaching into her pocket, she takes out a tiny amber necklace and twirls it around. I don't get the relevance, but I'm sure it will come to light. Do I care? No. I still have the book and the curse controlling Shoan.

"When you had me read from the book, you didn't have me just read the release of Shoan, you drank from me, and in essence, released me too. It allowed me to gain all of my powers, both Farie, vampire, and were. So I must thank you for giving me such a gift, and for returning me to my mate."

Standing aghast, not knowing what to do next, I do what I know best—up the odds into my favor.

Chapter THIRTY-FIVE

Mother Nature Takes Back

Thiea

Taking the book from Morrigan was effortless, but she moves way faster than I anticipated.

"This isn't over. Not by a long shot." With a knife to the throat of Niamh, I bet she thinks the weakest link has been found. Wrong choice.

With a blade to her carotid, Niamh laughs, at first schoolgirl silly, like first boy crush. Then it turns maniacal and downright scary. It reverberates off the walls, bouncing in the most sinister way. "Good luck, Morrigan. I'd run now," I tell her but it's lost in the noise.

"Shoan, what is with your sister? Is she mad in the head?"

"Yes, but that's what makes her fantastic."

Moving away to stand beside Shoan on the other side of the room, the door to the shed closes with Harrison, George, and Sullivan walking in with cuts and bruises aplenty. Obviously, they lost.

Close behind them walks in Chad, Pat, and another guy I don't know, without a single scratch on them. Garron is nowhere in sight. I bet my shoe store he ran.

Shoan indicates wordlessly to his friends to toss the boys over by Morrigan, where she's still dealing with Niamh's explosive laughter.

"Make her shut up. It's really quite annoying."

Spinning just her head, not her body, Niamh allows the blade to cut her skin while she smiles in the face of Morrigan, who's is in utter shock.

Pulling the blade away, Niamh's eyes glow a deadly red shade. "Is it my turn to play? I brought my own toys, and they're dying to make new friends." From the shadows, forms gather from the smoke, taking on the shape of hideous dogs with snarling maws. Paws the size of shoe boxes and scaly bodies that almost seem armored. "You might want to reconsider your position, Morrigan."

There's an unpredictable fear in her eyes that tells me, danger or submission. I'm expecting the danger, but again she astounds me by handing over the book, easily, and without further maiming or ridicule.

The two hounds saunter over, almost bored with the display, and slip close to Niamh as only a pet would do, curling into her hand, asking for scratches. "Good girls. Sit now and wait your turn," She tells them, and even my mouth is slightly ajar.

"Now what do we do? Everything hinges on you, Shoan," Anna states, snapping me from my focus on the smoke created beasts. Wrapping her arms around my father in a loving embrace, she pecks him on the cheek. I can tell the conversation they're having right now is internal, as their attention is not wholly here.

"Shoan, I say we do as we came to do." Turning to Morrigan,

Arif grins wide, tucking my mother closer, as close as he can. “I told you I would watch you become condemned by Shoan to purgatory, and the course has not changed. Any last words?"

Morrigan is far from defeated and broken, and I’d bet she has a trick or two still up her sleeve. Looking to her sons, George and Sullivan, they stand there, deflated and puny. Harrison, who seemed the pillar of strength and arrogance only a few short moments ago, stands quiet in the corner, awaiting his fate as he stares into the face of two evil poodles.

"None, I suppose."

With a smile, Shoan turns to his friend, the one I haven’t met yet. "Which two would you like, Antonius? You can have first dibs."

Oh.

That’s Antonius. The one with the grave marker for his wife and son. So he’s still alive? Good to know. Smiling, Shoan takes my internal diatribe as comical, even witty, I guess.

"Ah, well I won't take the real fun away, *brother*. I just want the asshole that hung me in the temple and his brother. You can have the woman and her mate. After all, they are the ones that started this whole rigamarole." Smacking his hands together, rubbing them, he looks at Harrison and Morrigan with an indication for them to move away from George and Sullivan.

Closing his eyes, his body starts to shimmer, glowing with an internal light. He seems like a video out of focus; scrambled and blurry. As quickly as I blink, he rematerializes, but, differently. His face transforms into a crocodile, and I swear his arms grew thicker with hair than before. His eyes are still human, a beautiful blue shining through.

Watching Shoan, I see changes in him as well. Where his soft caressing eyes were, there is now a set of slitted eyelids, like a reptile, and instead of the golden hue, they're a soft green, like the ocean at dusk. His arms that were once so strong have grown bulkier, like giant lion forearms, complete with paws. The proud strong chest that I loved to stroke and claw at seems to have grown in girth too. I guess he saw the awestruck look on my face because he lifts his shirt to show me the steely grey body beneath. It's like a Sherman Tank; tough and hardened.

"Morrigan, I must thank you. Without your selfish ways, I wouldn't have been strong enough on my own to deal with you and your family. I understand that now. You gave me something I cannot repay, nor will I. Antonius, if you could concentrate on one being first we can begin. If they are destined to die, you will feel what to do."

Looking directly at Shoan is difficult. His face is bright and his soul is on fire. Alight. It's so powerful and awe inspiring.

I would have thought you'd think this hideous? How do you see it as beauty? Shoan asks me.

How can I not? Look at you, you're a pillar of strength. And I thought you were sexy before? Just wait till we're alone so I can show you how sexy I think you are. You beast! I say teasingly. That earns me another toothy smirk.

I turn back to the festivities as Antonius directs all his attention on Sullivan. His eyes are intense. I'd be fearful if I were Sully.

"Shoan, I don't see any light. There's only darkness there."

"What about the other brother?" Shoan motions towards George.

With a nod, Antonius closes his eyes once more. This time, he's longer than before, reopening his baby blues. Shaking his head negatively once again, it's as I suspected.

Shoan pats his friend on the shoulder. "Can you imagine where your wife and child are in the Elysian Fields?" he asks quietly. Without a sound, Antonius nods his head, pulling in a soul deep breath. "Concentrate on Tartarus, picturing the Nether we visited. Once you picture that, you need to approach and touch both of them near their heart."

Wordlessly, Antonius moves to George first.

"Mother, I'll see you in the afterlife," George tells Morrigan without even a single tear in his eye. With disdain, he stands proudly, facing Antonius. "I'm ready. Do your worst."

He touches his fingers firmly to the spot Shoan indicated. Within moments of touching George's chest, a brilliant rainbow of light exudes from his body. It streams out of his eyes, ears, and mouth. Removing his hand from where George stood, his body falls to the ground, separating like leaves on the wind, blowing around the room, leaving the scent of damp wood.

What a beautiful death.

He turns to Sullivan. "You're next, big boy. Anything to say?" Antonius asks with a heady glance. The larger, more dangerous of the two brothers doesn't wish to accept his fate. Fighting to leave the space, he attempts to zip past those blocking the door and miniscule window that gives the tiny barn light.

"I'm not going down without a fight. Fuck you, Shoan," he spits, leaving a wetness on Shoan's shirt. Grabbing him by the arms and pulling them tight behind his back, he holds Sullivan, trapped. Watching the approaching Antonius, the simple fight evades him.

"Mother, I was happy. Shoan, you piece of shit. I'm glad we stopped you for so long. Be prepared for a war that you'll lose. We're not the only ones approaching this endgame." Standing straight backed in defiance, Sullivan stares down at the godlike being. Antonius places his hand on his chest, just like he had with George. The light that beams from him is not a rainbow this time. It's like a yellow reflection through a heavy malt whiskey. I swear there's a smile on his face as Antonius removes his hand. The smell in the room is heavy, like a musk. Almost as if you'd had a heavy woolen coat in the rain. His body too falls to the ground, though instead as wisps of fur.

Watching the fluff roll by, I have the oddest sensation, like being stung by a bee, or a few bees actually. Scratching it, my arm throbs and tingles. Hoping it will go away, I work from the top down to my fingers that are quickly becoming numb. The last thing I want to do is alarm anyone. Standing off a bit, back from Anna and Arif, I try to shake off the feeling and concentrate back on the matter at hand.

I don't know him well, but Antonius seems content; almost gleeful after performing this conviction as judge and jury. Looking to Shoan, I understand that he has tried for centuries to finish this. This must seem surreal and upsetting that he isn't the one performing the dispatchment. Morrigan has tried to abate this tide. She knew it was inevitable and her avoidance has made this a sweet revenge for him. I can feel it and hear Shoan's thoughts as they stir, echoing his satisfaction.

Avoiding the strange sensation in my arm, I try my best to watch for Morrigan to do something purely evil. So far she's been quiet, silent, and biding her time, like she has a secret that the rest don't know. Looking at Harrison with a sideways glance, I can tell they're conversing together, blocking out those who can hear as they scheme and plot.

"Your turn first, Harrison. I'm leaving the best and worst for last, as it were." Standing only steps away from the door, Shoan puts himself directly in the path of Morrigan and Harrison's retreat if they try to bolt.

"*Is tu' mo ghra,"* Harrison says, glassy eyed.

What did he say? I ask Shoan.

He told her she is his heart. His love.

It sounds so beautiful, and under different circumstances, I'd love someone to say that to me. I never want to hear that ever again after this.

Without trying to, Harrison has said the one thing that made Morrigan choke back a tear. Wow, who would have thought that her children dying before her wouldn't phase her, but Harrison does?

"I will hope to see you soon."

Taking her hand in his, kissing it gently on the back, I see a softer side of him.

Maybe she can feel love and compassion?

Shoan's smile is anticipatory. If I understand this, he's waited so long for this that he is entitled to a bit of glee. "This will be over soon. I'll be kind, making it quick." With the same fervor as Antonius, Shoan sighs, concentrating on Harrison's soul. I assume he would reach out his hand to do the same as Antonius had.

Morrigan speaks up then, just before the finality of everything. "Harrison, I—"

That's when a gutwrenching scream rents the air, making everyone in the shed stop what they're doing.

Not me, though. No. I'm the one screaming.

Chapter THIRTY-SIX

Split Personalities

Shoan

"Oh my Goddess! Thiea!" I scream as Anna and I both run to catch her before she falls to the floor. It's like a car accident. You know what's coming, you see the casualties all before the end. Everything is in slow motion. I can't seem to move fast enough.

Pushing past Morrigan, vaulting over Ant, I get to her just in time to catch her head before she lands on a sickle that's pointed up. Brushing the hair out of her face as she screams over and over again, clutching her stomach, rubbing her arms, and tearing at her skin like it's on fire, I have no idea what to do to help her.

Thiea, talk to me! What's happening? I'm so afraid I yell at her mentally. "Did anyone see what happened to her? What's going on? Someone, please help!"

Everyone is just as shocked as I am as they stare down at the prone body in my hands. Thiea is clearly in excruciating pain. Her body feels cool and clammy as she sweats excessively. Her heart races away, faster than I think her human body can handle.

"It hurts! Make it stop!" she yells.

"I—I can't. I don't know what's wrong. What's happening, Thi? Where does it hurt?" Everyone by this time has ignored Harrison and Morrigan, everyone but my sister and Ant.

I glare at Morrigan as I hold Thiea close. "Do you know what's happening? Tell me," I say tightly, deadly. "It might save one of you."

Morrigan turns to Harrison, and without a thought for him, she answers. "I know, but you must swear on the Goddess you will not harm me."

"I can't promise you forever, but I will give you today. Tell me before I change my mind and figure it out for myself," I threaten through gritted teeth.

"Easy, Shoan. You wouldn't have figured this out, and I accept your day. Thiea's body is fighting her nature. This is why we never mate with *dogs*. Her body wants to phase with the moon outside, and her blood calls to kill that same beast. She's tearing in two. The blood is fighting itself." As Morrigan tells me this, Thiea's body rattles and shakes. She screams a blood curdling sound, curling upon herself tight before stretching out fully like a shot arrow.

I can't believe I'm trusting her, but what choice do I have? "What can I do? What do we do?"

"Ah, that was not part of the bargain," Morrigan smirks coolly. Anna squats on the floor, pouring over the book, looking for anything that could help. I had a dream that the war was over and we were at peace just days ago. Now it seems my happiness is torn asunder once more. Why must I be tortured? Why are the people I love pained because of my faults?

Moving for the door, Morrigan takes a step towards the threshold, where Niamh crosses her path.

"I made a vow and it will be kept. Harrison won't leave this shed, but she will. For now," I tell Niamh seriously.

Looking at me incredulously, she turns to scowl at Morrigan., "No fucking way!"

"Ni, we have bigger problems right now. Let her leave—"

"No! No fucking way!" Pulling her strength, glowing and stretching out, I know how this will go if I don't get her to back down.

"Niamh, back down. I *will* find her. She doesn't have the book, we do." *This isn't over.*

Fine, Shoan. For now, I'll back off. Don't expect I won't hunt her ass down before we leave this island. "Don't worry, Morrigan. Me and you still have a date, old lady. You've maybe missed out on all my party tricks for the moment, but I have tons of evil shit tucked up these sleeves. There's a fate in your stars for sure." Ni steps aside, twirling a bright grenade and flashing her power slightly.

Moving to let her exit into the moonlight, I see the fight still brewing in her eyes. It took a great deal of control for Niamh to back down, but I know that it's necessary. If we don't have our oaths, we'd never hold to anything. I can't live like that.

"Goodbye, *mo ghru'*." Morrigan turns to Harrison, who is in the stiff grip of Ant, and as she exits, you see the unspoken love pass across his face. He loved her and she left him to his fate.

"There has to be something about the curse…the bloodline mixing or something? Find it. Please!" I plead, caressing Thiea's forehead to remove the hair that has now plastered itself to her pasty skin. She's ceased in her screaming audibly, but incredibly, I hear it clearly in my mind.

"Shoan, I can't find anything of use. Everything is mixed in this damned book…it's jumbled. I—I just don't know what will help." She flips page after page, clearly as bothered and as scared as I am. Reciting clips of passages here and there, changing the order of them, trying to find a cure, I watch as tears stream down her cheeks in heavy rivulets. She's distraught, grasping at straws, and probably making things worse, but anything is better than nothing.

"Come on, sweetheart, I trust you can do it, Anna. You will find something to help." Arif moves beside her, holding his daughter's hand, saying comforting words to them both. Nothing can seem to abate the torrent that Thiea is waging inside herself.

"I got it! Hold her still. Ni, find me heather and wolfsbane. Now, quickly!" Anna, grabs the sickle from the corner, a dented milking can, and a rock from the floor.

Bending low by her ear, I whisper, "Niamh is going to get something, sweetheart. Hold on. Just hold on. I can't go on without you. Do you hear me? You can't leave me, not now." Niamh returns, holding the herbs, glowing and smelling like a soft summer day.

I've just found my soul mate after all these years, and to lose her in Ireland would be a sick fucking joke. Calming my mind, phasing back to my human form, I talk to her softly. *Remember you have to learn how to cook. I have to teach you to play the guitar. Plus, who else will keep me in check if you're not here?* I smile tightly, trying to talk more for myself than for her as my body returns to its natural state.

"Anna? Have you got it yet?"

Anna sets the herbs down on the sickle. Careful not to touch the wolfsbane, she pounds the two together with the rock. The smell in the room is potent. It smells like a dog rolling in wet fields of the moors. "Shoan, take this and rub it on your neck," Anna says, holding the sickle out to me. "I can't touch it. It's too strong for me, but you need to rub it all over your neck."

Holding Thiea up on my lap, I reach across to smother my hand in the paste. Scrubbing it into my neck as much as possible, I leave nothing unmarred. "Now what?" I ask.

"She has to bite you. Not drain you, but bite you. She has to take in your blood with the mix. It will—"

"I don't care what it does, I'll do anything. She's fading, and I just want her safe, even at my expense." Wiping my hand on the bare floor, I drag her body up closer to me. *Thiea, sweetheart. You have to bite me. It will stop the pain.* Lifting her off my lap, rocking through her spasms, her heartbeat becomes increasingly erratic.

No, I can't. I won't.

I can see the strain her body is taking. It's dangerous. "Please, for me. You have to live for me. I can't live without you. Take my heart, my blood, my soul; it's yours. It will always be yours."

Reaching the sickle, I take the wide wooden handle in hand and swing it wildly around. The sharpest point cuts me. It's dull, but it does the trick. Leaving a small opening, the blood trickles down, mingling into the noxious pulp. Lifting Thiea's head closer, so that she's close enough to smell, touch, and lick it, she turns limp in my arms.

"Thiea! Thiea, please. Honey, please!"

*I promise to take you shopping. You can buy anything you want. Please just...*then just as if imagined, I hear a soft sound. A tiny moan and a feather light touch brushes my neck. Feeling a tiny pinch on my skin, it's erotic, and simply fantastic. Immediately my cock strains in my jeans against the confines of the material, rubbing to escape.

Licking my lips, I grasp the back of her head. I feel on edge. All it would take is a hair trigger and I'd come in my pants.

Releasing her hold on my neck, the feeling dissipates. *My heart, huh? That's what you said? And I believe I heard something about shopping?* Without lifting her head from my shoulder, she slowly drags her tongue across the open wound.

Name the time and the place, and it's your black card to pillage. I let out the breath I didn't realize I was still holding. Tucking my throbbing cock down deep within my jeans, I cover it slightly with my shirt.

Extremely relieved, I ask her, "How are you feeling?"

"Fantastic, actually. My arm isn't itchy anymore." Lifting off my lap with assistance from Anna, she brushes off the dust.

"Quite the scare you gave us. Next time, how about you leave on the necklace?" Anna tells her, taking her in hand and hugging her tight.

"You took it off? When?" I really hadn't noticed, what with everything else happening. I didn't catch it was missing.

"I took it off on the plane ride from Greece to Paris. I felt fine. Nothing weird really, other than I could make things happen against someone's will. Actually, I guess that is weird. I thought for sure I would grow fur or wings, and when everything seemed okay, I didn't worry. So I kept it off."

"Well, if it wasn't for the book, Morrigan, and the Goddess, you would have died," Arif states, then motions to Niamh, who looks very uncomfortable with the attention.

"Ah, I wasn't about to let Shoan lose her. It's not right. Plus, who will I spar with if Shoan has a broken heart? There's no fun playing with broken toys."

Turning to Harrison, I feel sorry for him. Morrigan was not an easy being to love, yet he somehow did it over the centuries. Even after she betrayed him time and time again, he loved her unconditionally.

"Ant, can you take care of Harrison. I don't have the heart for it." I can't bring myself to judge him if my judgement would be clouded with my own feelings. He deserves everything he gets, but I'd probably release him like her, then we'd be back at square one.

Chapter THIRTY-SEVEN

Forgiveness for All?

Thiea

I don't want to live in this life without affection or without love. I refuse to be denied that after finding it in such an unorthodox means. I know I have said that over and over to myself, but it still rings as true today as it did when I was a young girl, hoping for a Prince on a White Steed. The only difference between that dream and now, I'd always assumed he'd ride up with his banner blazing in the sun to sweep me away from the evil stepmother that I never had. The reality is so much better. My prince made me drunk and swept me into a war of epic proportions that I had no chance of avoiding.

Living my life as a human, I was lucky if I punched a pillow without damaging my hand. Now I feel like I could take on an army without a scratch. I'm definitely not about to take shit from anyone anymore.

As we traversed to our war, I seemed to gain new strength by the hour. I never noticed how heady it would be to have. Standing in the barn, I felt all consumed by the strength that has been gaining exponentially.

After Antonius dispatched Harrison to the Nether, we all started to relax and calmly deal with the fact that I just had a full-blown, out-of-body experience. Not to mention, I nibbled on Shoan like a buffet at the Mandarin.

“Where’s Garron?” I ask them.

He quietly answers me. *Lying outside in a puddle of his own tears I think.*

I’ll be right back.

It’s not you I worry about anymore, Little Love. You’ve morphed to an immortal. It would take me to remove you from this plane for good. I smile at the idea that I’m different. That I’m strong.

I’m who I was meant to be all along.

Stepping out, I shout into the outskirts, hoping that someone else doesn't hear and wonder what I’m doing. "Garron? Come out, I won't harm you. I promise."

Over by the boulder, where Shoan and Antonius had been standing as we arrived, I see him curled up in a ball at the base, lying on what looks like luggage. It’s a Louis bag. If he’s crying on it, I doubt Niamh will be the forgiving type if he stains it.

"Garron, what are you doing?"

"I couldn't fight and I couldn’t help.” He slams his hands against his chest. “I’m so fucking weak. What kind of father will I be if I can't stand up to others of our kind? I can't teach them anything that will help them survive. Harrison is right, I am a pile of human mush." Choking back air and tears, he’s wallowing in self-pity.

"Harrison? You're worried about what Harrison thinks? Don’t worry, he isn’t thinking *anything* anymore. Garron, you were strong enough to get me here. Pretty conniving if you ask me. But at the same time, I have to thank you. Without you, I wouldn't have found out about all of this." Flourishing my hands down my body, I bend down to sit on the ground beside him, realizing just what he gave me. Yes, deceit and lies, but also love, strength, family, and a confusing fucking ride.

Worth every fucking minute.

"Garron, your wife and sons don't know anything about your involvement in this, right?" He nods, wiping snot on the bag. Oh yeah, that's going to go so bad if she catches him. "So you have a clean slate. Cassie loves the man, not the immortal, and your sons will grow to be strong. You can teach them how to live as good vampires without malevolence in their minds or hearts. You don't want to witness what I just saw firsthand. You don't want your boys to be judged, do you?"

Rising off of the bag, he leans hard against the rock.

"Why are you caring for me? Even after all that we've done to you, to Shoan and his family, for Goddess' sake? You owe me nothing. You could leave here and tell Cassie everything." He starts to laugh as he's wipes the eye snot and slobber away from his face. "To be honest, she'll probably think we had an affair."

"You're right, she probably will. So why are you out here crying?"

"Harrison told them that I was a worthless piece of garbage. I'm not sure, but maybe he was trying to save me."

"I don't know if he had enough soul to care about your fate, but I suggest you leave. Now. Good-byes would not be in order unless you want it to be *your* last."

He stands to his full height. "Thank you, Thiea. You won't regret this. I promise."

Smirking, he walks away down the road towards town, where I hope to never see him again.

Standing there with my arms crossed, watching as he walks away, I see Niamh, arms crossed with a mad as a hornet look.

"Hi, yeah." I say sweetly, hoping to avoid her wrath.

"What was that?"

"A favor. One I hope doesn't cause me to feel remorse in the future." Walking closer to where she's standing in hip-high grasses, I see she has a prize at her feet.

"What's that?" I ask her coyly.

"A favor. A party favor."

Oh. Okay. "And what pray tell do we intend to do with said party favor?"

"We're going to string it up and use it as a pináta. I've already kicked it around for a couple rounds. Feel like taking a swing, or should I give it to Shoan for the final burst?" Niamh lifts the sad excuse off the ground by the scruff of her neck, until Morrigan stands weakly on her own.

"Oh, how I wish I could enjoy it, but it's not my party," I quip sarcastically.

"Fine. Your loss." Niamh laughs and pushes Morrigan back towards the shed we vacated a short while ago with glee in her eyes.

Walking back into the building, I see things have changed drastically. Shoan's friend that had the head of a crocodile is back to normal. Harrison is no longer in the room, and there's an odd scent in the air of fresh cut pine.

"Lucy, I'm home," Niamh calls into the space as I move to the side, exposing her *party favor*.

"I said she was—"

"To be let free by you, and not condemned *by you* for one day. You said nothing about the catch and release renetted." She looks down to her watch. "Oh, and it's the next day now, Shoan. I think you are entitled to a swing at her after a millennium of waiting."

"I gave her my word, Ni."

"Fine, then *I'm* dispatching this one. She's still in my realm and I'm entitled to recompense for the years of anguish I've endured." As Niamh's eyes glow a bright yellow, her skin becomes transparent as she increases exponentially in height.

The tiny, once five foot nothing woman has extended out to over six feet of pure raging muscle. Strung across her shoulders sideways are a pair of AK-47's, a rocket launcher, two rows of brightly colored grenades that look deadly, and I'm not even taking into account the changes to her features. Her hair has warped out to two massive braids, one on either side of her head, woven with leather straps. Tattoos break out all over her skin, and her face hardens through the cheekbones and lips. She's scary as fuck.

"Oh, shit. This isn't good. Thiea, I think you should leave," Anna tells me as her and my father start to back out of the building, along with the remaining members of the Berserker team that had joined us when she kicked Morrigan through the door.

"Back down, Goddess," Is the last thing I hear Shoan say as Chad pulls me out into the night, away from the line of fire.

"Someone want to explain how and what is going on?" This shit just keeps getting better and better.

Chad is first to explain it. "Well, you know how we taunt and call her Goddess all the time? It's not really a taunt because she is.

We're her warriors." He turns to his friends. "The falcon," he points to Patrick. "Myself, the wolf." To Marcus, "The bear." Then to Terese. "The wild cat. Niamh is Freyja. Mother of the Norse Gods, Goddess of War, Queen over all fertility. She's head bitch, and if you try to take her on you will lose. Trust me, when she's this way, there's no stopping her wrath."

"I call bullshit." Starting back towards the shed, I'm pulled back by heavy hands.

"Sweetheart, you may be new to this life, but take what we say at face value. My little girl, Niamh, is not one to trifle with when the Goddess takes her over. Trust us and stay back for now. Shoan will be the only one to appease her," Arif tells me as he holds me in his embrace.

"Oh, well that explains so much more then," Antonius laughs, pulling up a spot on the boulder out front as we back away from the tiny encased enclosure, awaiting the outcome.

"Anyone have popcorn?" Ant asks, grinning. "I have a feeling this is going to be a good show."

Chapter THIRTY-EIGHT

Heavy Handed Gods and Mortals

Shoan

Oh, we are so screwed now.

"Ni, not now. This isn't the time," I say from my position outside the door. There isn't much room with her at her full power. Niamh becomes so much more.

"Bullshit," she says. Her booming voice carries across the tiny shack. "No better time than the present, Chimeric. It is your duty."

Morrigan understands her predicament. She's curled up on the ground, immobile, avoiding Niamh's destructive gaze. I've seen stronger men fade in the face of her true form. I'm different. I was created to deal with Gods, Goddesses, and deities of all religions; I can handle her virile power.

Everyone else backed out as soon as the Goddess exploded out in all her glory. Niamh keeps it in check, and even though she likes to toss about the powers she controls, she never abuses it. This is a first. Never has she ever, and I mean ever, tried to use her power to sway me to do her bidding. And seeing the Goddess is in control, this is something I can't fight as I normally would. I have to agree with her or face my own demise.

"Fine, I'll do as you bid."

The Goddess smiles devilishly with fire blazing in her soul. She's a force to reckon with, but at this point, I can't reach her.

Morrigan understands what strength she's up against, and knows what must be done.

As the light in her eyes diminishes from the defiant to defeated, I tell her, "I'll make it quick, Morrigan."

Nodding and rising slowly off the ground to stand on shaky legs, she's prepared finally to accept her judgement.

Thinking about what gives me my power, I pull the flames to the forefront, causing a glow like lightning bugs in a jar. It's warm and inviting. I don't need to look within her to see the depths of her malice. I've known it was limitless for centuries. Touching my hand to her chest, the light travels through into her easily. There is a small smile on the face of Morrigan as it ignites within her as I pull back. Falling to pieces like smoke and dust on the autumn breeze, it smells sick, like burning wet wood.

"Was that so difficult, Chimeric?" The Goddess asks, pleased that her bidding was fulfilled.

I acknowledge it as such, bowing. It's not often we see Ni pull the power trip and become as she is in her natural form, making us bend to her will is something I enjoyed nonetheless. I'm a bit perturbed that I was made to break my promise to Morrigan, but I guess it doesn't matter. She's broken more vows over the years.

The Goddess, feeling acquiesced, abates her power, letting it leave her. Diminishing her size and potency until the petite, adorably pixie-like sister I know and love is within the space.

"Sorry," she says. I know she doesn't mean it as *sorry you had to do that*, or *sorry I kind of lost my cool*, she means it as *sorry I made you.* I know her intentions were just, and made with my peace of mind in her actions. As always, I'll forgive her and myself for the act.

Looking down at the tiny piles of dust that linger on the floor, this is all that remains of the four horsemen of my apocalypse. Giving them nothing more than a thought, Niamh kicks the stacks, sending the dust motes flying into the air. With a quick blow, the dust swirls and leaves the tight barn to blend back into nature itself.

"So, girlfriend is kind of badass, huh?" Smacking my shoulder, she pulls me from my musings. I grin.

"She could take you, I think." Pulling her arm, I wrap it around behind her back, tangling her up in a small move. She lets me, that's clear, but I love it. It feels good to win sometimes against her.

"Dreams. Only in her dreams." Turning, we walk back towards our family and the dark starry night. I feel a weight lift.

"Dreams do come true. I found mine, maybe—" Covering my mouth with her hand, Ni shakes her finger at me.

"No. Not. Not a fucking word, brother." I laugh at the simple moment of peace, and hope that this won't be the first or only one to come.

"Why? You are such a poor loser, sister." *I think a little mating could do you good.*

No. Now fuck off and kiss your prize. That I can't fight her on.

Looking at everyone that waits outside for us, I feel at ease. Anna and Arif are tight within each other's arms. Terese and Patrick are as usual—she in her human form and he as the falcon. Marcus paces the grounds as Chad stands with fear clearly written across his features. He watches every move Niamh makes.

Stepping forward, Chad pulls her into his chest and sighs deeply. She may not believe, or want to live with a soul mate, but Chad has been hers whether she understands it as that or not for as long as I can remember.

The face that takes my breath away is the one I least expected in my life, Thiea. I think that a bed-only vacation may be in order. It's a vacation I wish to start as soon as possible. After all that we've been through in the past few days, Thiea has taken everything in stride like a champ. She deserves some tongue lashings for her patience.

That can be arranged, you know. She speaks into my head softly. *I know this great travel agent that can get us our dream vacation for under five thousand bucks. You up for it?* Walking towards me, she giggles internally all the way. *I could show you what a dirty girl like me can accomplish if you just give me five minutes of your time, sir.* She shows me in her mind what she has in store.

Feeling my cock stand at attention, I'm waiting for the cuffing to the back of the head from my sister, or the groan from Arif and Anna. I't doesn't come.

Everyone can hear us, Thiea.

No. No they can't. I have mad skills. No one hears what we're saying at all. Looking around, I have four pairs of eyes directed on me, all smiling, but fairly oblivious to our internal sexcapade.

"So, what's next for you then, Antonius?" Niamh asks while she punches him in the shoulder. "Not like you can really go back to farming after looking death in the eye. Plus, we could use you after all." Shrugging his shoulders, he laughs.

Waving his hand, he starts off down to the road. "I'm gonna call the cabbie back here. He may be a horrible driver, but he's safer than this group. If anyone needs me, I'll be asleep on the curb," he laughs happily.

I'm really glad to see him that way.

"So, daughter. What's your plan?" Arif asks Thiea as he tightly tucks Anna into his embrace.

"Well, I think that my store can live without me for a few more weeks. As *someone* told me, they were going to give me a guided tour of Athens and I still haven't had that. Plus, I think a firsthand tour of someone's homeland would be wicked too. What do ya say, Mr. Mac Cathm, Catheder. Fuck it. Campbell?"

"Way to butcher a beautiful name, love. And Campbell will do just fine," I say, pulling her tight to my chest. *I think I could be persuaded to travel a bit, Athena. Maybe we won't be back in Canada for a few years.*

I'm fine with that, Mr. Campbell.

Kerri Ann

Contemporary Romance Author

With an avaricious appetite for stories, Kerri Ann can be found quite often with her nose in a book or writing it. On many occasion it has been said that she's in her own world, living in the stories of those she reads about, giving them a life they deserve.

She can easily be found under a tree in the shade, or reclining at Starbucks scribbling notes about new stories and new characters, while keeping the coffee chain in business.

Whether late at night, at a music festival, or sitting on a ski lift, when the thoughts arise Kerri will add them to those in progress. So be wary, you could be next.

This is her first self published book and she hopes you enjoy reading it as much as she enjoyed writing it.

Goodreads Link https://goo.gl/lnLsoX

Facebook Link https://goo.gl/9GS9uF

Twitter Link https://goo.gl/pqQWg1

77978315R00176

Made in the USA
Columbia, SC
07 October 2017